Forks & Knives

A Marriage at the Crossroads of Addiction and Codependency

A NOVEL BY
MIMI WAHLFELDT

Black Rose Writing | Texas

ISBN: 978-1-68513-465-5
LIBRARY OF CONGRESS CONTROL NUMBER: 2024933263
PUBLISHED BY BLACK ROSE WRITING
www.blackrosewriting.com

Printed in the United States of America
Suggested Retail Price (SRP) $21.95

Forks & Knives is printed in Gentium Book Basic

*As a planet-friendly publisher, Black Rose Writing does its best to eliminate unnecessary waste to reduce paper usage and energy costs, while never compromising the reading experience. As a result, the final word count vs. page count may not meet common expectations.

Forks & Knives

My mind wanders and wonders about alternate endings. "What ifs" cloud my thinking. It's "The Road Not Taken" all over again. I lose sleep imagining how our lives might have been different had we chosen another path at any given fork in the road. There are so many . . . and oh, like knives, how some of them cut deep.

Contents

Prologue: December 1992

His words grabbed me, of course, but the way he said them is what I remember most. They seemed rehearsed. Although *I'd* never heard this speech, I suspected he'd practiced it aloud before, if only to himself, to convince me, I suppose. But then, I didn't need convincing, because these were the words I had longed to hear, although I didn't know it until they were loose in the air: "I'm sick and tired of being sick and tired," he said. I wanted to believe he meant it, but that would also mean admitting I was finally hearing the saddest, most heartbreaking thing a wife could hear: My husband had been lying to me for years, and I had blinded myself to it and believed every word.

Sick and tired of being sick and tired . . . the verbal acquiescence of hitting bottom in the world of recovery. People who've reached the point of no return often utter the phrase when they finally choose to end the suffering they've been living with in their closeted addiction. They are psychologically sick of being physically sick, and they're exhausted from the intensity of deceit required to cover up their dependency. They've had enough.

At that time, I'd never met anyone who'd reached that point and turned his life around. Since then, I've heard my share of sad-but-powerful testimonies. When it works, the results are profound. Men and women who get there are amazing; they make incredible changes to live healthier lives. They *live* after gaining the unique perspective that true Sobriety allows. It's a second chance most of us never get, or never see the opportunity for, or never take when we do.

I use the word Sobriety, with a capital -S, because it's inherently different to me from the small -s sobriety that only means "off the booze." Most alcoholics can refrain from drinking when they try—or if they have to. This dry period can even last years. But there are few real changes in the person with small -s sobriety. Capital -S Sobriety takes real courage. It takes guts to look at yourself brazenly and see your flaws head-on. It takes uncommon humility to admit mistakes you've made, then face the people you've hurt and make amends to them. It takes being truly honest, owning your actions (even when those actions were made under the influence), and working to better the parts of you in need of improvement. It takes ... hell, I can't really tell you what it takes because I was blessed not to be cursed with that particular disease. My illness was loving a man who had it and not knowing where he ended and I began.

So, when I heard his words that day, my heart soared and sank in the span of a single moment: *He's finally admitting the depth of his problem!* And *Oh God, he's finally admitting the depth of his problem!*

Part of me was relieved. Maybe I wasn't crazy after all. Maybe all those times I suspected a drinking problem weren't just sour grapes—no pun intended. Maybe I wasn't imagining the acidic sweat as it filtered through his clothes, his breath, his hair. I'd always taken him at his word that the chemical odors wafting off him when he got home were from working at a paint manufacturing plant. Maybe I wasn't wrong to question him, doubt him, accuse him. I hadn't known *what* to do with him. I loved him, and when he said he hadn't been drinking, though everything in me knew otherwise, I chose to believe him.

People rarely understand how a reasonable person can deceive herself so easily. I explain it like this: It's as if your father has told you the sky is red from the first time he explained clouds and the weather. He's your *father*. Of course, you trust and believe him. You live your life, every day for years and years, calling that particular color red. The sky is red; therefore, your favorite sweater is red, and the napkins on the kitchen counter, your mother's eyes, the ocean.

Then, someone else who *really* cares about you says, "I hate to tell you, but the sky is actually *blue*. That color is blue, not red." Suddenly, you can't trust your eyes, your own judgment, your very instincts. Because not only did you trust someone who was so untrustworthy, you also aren't sure you can trust your own senses ever again.

Yes, part of me was relieved to learn I'd been right; his revelation justified that my perceptions weren't as off as I'd believed. But another part of me sensed I was supposed to be more than just relieved. I was supposed to *do* something, *say* something, *show* my shock and outrage. Wasn't I supposed to jump to my feet and cause a scene? Wasn't I supposed to cry? Bad dialogue from *The Young and The Restless* sang in my ears: "How dare you keep this kind of thing from me all this time? I'm your *wife!* What kind of fool do you think I am?" Over-the-top sobs, accompanied by piped-in Muzak climaxing in the background . . .

The truth was, I did feel foolish—and embarrassed, shocked, angry. But since I was also speechless, the myriad of emotions swimming through my brain went unvoiced a while longer.

We sat side by side in the intake room of the substance abuse wing at our local hospital. The nurse jotted notes in her file with an ennui reserved for medical professionals who deal with crises every day. Eric answered her questions with an ease and honesty I'd never heard from him before:

Mostly vodka, but sometimes schnapps—the peppermint kind to hide the alcohol—it smells like breath mints.

I just keep some money out of my paycheck every week; I only take $40 so Kat never knows.

I heard his words and felt the look of disbelief on my face. *How did I get here? Have I really been this naïve?* Torn between two visceral responses, I could either crawl under the desk to hide or throw my chair at the man—this stranger!—beside me. I did neither. Just sat there.

Then, "through sickness and in health" taunted me, daring me to deny it. He was admitting to a *disease* after all. I had to stand by him, didn't I? What kind of monster would abandon her husband after he'd poured his soul (and his bottles) out and admitted to being out-of-control, helpless, and in-need?

Although I felt validated on some level, something else nagged at me. Now that there was a *name* for our problem, I had a new role in *solving* the problem. This job title weighed me down: Supportive Wife. Admitting the full depth of his "difficulty"—and giving it a label—meant no more pretending there *was* no difficulty. Because even though I'd suspected, I'd deferred to his protestations. I'd played a part in pushing this painful reality a little further from our collective grasp.

Denial serves a real purpose for those of us living with an elephant in the house. It's understandable—no, it's vital—to ignore the enormous creature eating your food, shitting on your carpet, and making lots of noise. You do it for as long as you can because it's too embarrassing to *look* at it while you clean up after it. You don't want to see it. It's degrading to realize you opened the door to your home and let the animal in. You feel the fool for finding a place in your bleeding heart to love the damn thing. It becomes easier and easier over the years to close your eyes. Like a child covering her face with her hands: If she can't see you, then maybe you won't see her either. It's four-year-old logic, but you grab hold of it to avoid seeing the uncomfortable truth.

But once the elephant is acknowledged, when your husband is finally labeled an Alcoholic (capital -A), you can't ignore the mess he created—or is—anymore. Now, there's something expected of you, too: Wake up! Suddenly *you're* the one with a problem if you ignore the problem once it's been unearthed. So you open your eyes. Slowly. The light hurts. You've been shielding those baby blues for so long. But this is your life, your husband. You deal with it.

Yet, with all those conflicting emotions souring my stomach, I just looked at him. Numb. Eric sat there next to me, my husband of three and a half years, confessing like a guilt-ridden mobster in church for the first time in a decade. One at a time, he revealed secrets I never dreamed he'd been keeping. *Who was this guy? I hadn't washed his underwear for years without knowing these things, had I?*

I thought I knew who he was; I thought I knew who *I* was. Yet, at twenty-eight years old, with my college degree proudly displayed at my parents' house two thousand miles away, I had become every sad cliché about "women who love too much" or "smart women who make dumb choices." If my life wasn't what I thought it was, then what was it?

All I knew for certain was, two months pregnant with our first baby, I suddenly felt trapped. And very, very unprepared.

PART I

A memory: Oozing apprehension, Kat looked up at the stalwart animal. She'd never been so close to a horse before. Despite growing up next to an apple orchard in Upstate New York, her childhood revolved around theater, music, and baseball games, not fishing, camping, or horseback riding. Eric bounced on his heels beside her, eager to help Kat into the saddle.

This was their third date outside of the rehearsals where they'd met, and those didn't count; that was work, though fun work. Eric was excited to show her all the outdoor Colorado activities he loved. Kat was skeptical. She wasn't sure she would enjoy the vulnerability of being out in the mountains, not to mention the prospect of running into a snake.

"You're gonna love it," Eric said, his eyes wide and his smile dazzling. "I'll be right behind you on the trail, and these guides know their stuff." His confidence was contagious. Kat decided right then to be braver than she felt.

As soon as she was safely settled on the back of a golden-brown horse named Sunshine, she breathed more evenly. The view was amazing; she hadn't noticed it before through her nervous energy. From the height of the saddle, she looked out beyond the nearby trees, all the way to the back range of the Rocky Mountains, snowcapped throughout the year.

She held onto the reins as the guide had instructed her. Patting Sunshine, smoothing her soft mane, Kat leaned forward and murmured her plea: "Please keep me safe, okay? And don't let me embarrass myself. I'm on a date."

As she waited for the trail ride to begin, Eric sauntered up next to her on his majestic white horse. The story of Cinderella flashed in her head. Not that she needed to be rescued, but . . . the way he looked at her. It felt nice.

Revelation
December 1992

* Fork 1 *

Chapter One: Reaction

Eric was admitted to the rehab hospital that night, but they let us go home for an hour to pack some clothes for his two-week stay. As we drove home in silence, I knew that everything in our lives had changed during one conversation with a nurse carrying a clipboard. I didn't know what to say to him. "Nice of you to be stealing money from our nest egg, hiding bottles around our house, and getting shit-faced while I went off to work every day, thinking you were doing the same. And thanks for telling a total stranger, not me, that all my suspicions about your drinking were true."

No, there was nothing to say, so we went through the motions, quietly.

After I drove him back to the hospital, I spent my first night since our wedding alone. I sat at our kitchen table with a cup of scalding tea, staring into space, listening to silence envelope our house.

My mind wandered in circles as I relived key moments in our marriage. I saw for the first time the reality that existed right below the surface. Which of the thousands of sentences he'd spoken to me over the years had been lies? Which days had he come home drunk, taken a lengthy shower, put on cologne, and brushed his teeth an extra-long time so I wouldn't smell the truth? How many nights had he rolled away from me in bed, mumbling something about a stomachache when he was really suffering from self-induced nausea, alcohol mixed with Scope?

Hospital policy didn't allow patients phone calls during the first week, and although I'd thought that a little harsh, prison-like, I was now glad for the respite. I needed a few days.

At 10:00 p.m., I left a voice message for my boss. I knew she wouldn't get it until the next morning, but I told her I'd be taking the day off. Fridays were normally slow at our magazine's office, but two weeks before Christmas, you'd think the entire staff was shopping en masse at Macy's. They wouldn't miss me.

Around midnight, I snuggled into bed. The darkness felt like an empty movie theater as I made myself think about things I'd spent the last few years avoiding or rationalizing. The slide show of my marriage played across the blank walls of my imagination, and I recalculated my new true north.

•   •   •   •   •

The next morning, I went for a walk. I usually spent my neighborhood strolls noticing other people's landscaping. Eric and I always talked about making our yard look more "finished," but neither of us had those skills or vision, so it remained undone.

As the sun took its place above me, I noticed the people around me instead of the shrubs. Mr. McGuire across the street was bringing in his garbage bin, even though our pickup was two days before. I didn't know him well, but he looked lost. Even from across the street, I could see the faraway look of loneliness in his old eyes.

I saw two preteens playing basketball in a driveway up ahead. Outdoor basketball in December. That's Colorado weather. The boys were teasing each other with playful pushing. The sound of the ball as it dribbled and then smacked the backboard took me back to high school gym class, though I'd never been good at sports. *I wonder why they're not at school . . .*

Finally, a young couple was out with their baby. Dad pushed the stroller and Mom walked a fluffy brown mutt on a leash, allowing a long lead. Of course, my thoughts turned inward, and I whispered to my tummy, "It's okay, baby. We'll have our own sweet times like that, too."

I wondered what Eric was doing right then. Was he in a group session? Individual counseling? Reading a homework assignment? The nurse had explained the daily schedule to me, but I couldn't recall those details now.

As I continued my walk, I thought more about "in sickness and in health." Those words were part of our wedding vows, and I had meant them. I married this man, fully intending to live with him "'til death do us part." But we had spoken other words that day, too. Words like, *I give to you my trust, and I will be worthy of yours; I promise to walk beside you, as your partner, facing life's challenges together.* What happened to *those* words? Why was "in sickness and in health" more important than the others? You don't get to pick and choose which promise is worth keeping just because one suits your purpose more than another on a given day. Eric had been selective about his vows; why was I expected to keep the rest of them alive?

During the next two days, I wandered around our house like an eighty-seven-year-old widow, slow and deliberate. I touched picture frames carefully and ran my fingers over Eric's jacket; it still hung over the dining room chair where he'd left it. My hands worked hard to evoke some nostalgia. I wanted to feel sentimental and connected to him, but nothing felt familiar. I was out of place in my own house.

We'd had a typical courtship, though the word sounds antiquated today. His mother had introduced us; maybe that should have been a warning. But at the time, I thought it was sweet and harmless.

I was new to Boulder, having moved cross-country to attend graduate school at the University of Colorado. When I first got to town, my supervising professor told me that the program I'd applied to was experiencing budget cuts; my teaching assistantship was postponed for a year. I got a job teaching preschool, putting my previous camp leader and babysitting skills to use. To fill my off-work time, I got involved in a community theater group. Having grown up doing plays in my hometown, it had always been the way I made friends.

At the first production meeting for a relatively unknown show called *The Art of Dining*, the director asked if I'd do props. This would be a challenge because half of the set was a functioning kitchen where food was prepared live onstage. The idea intrigued me, and I was up for the task. That night, I met Helen Torrington, a woman in her early fifties, who'd been involved with the theater company on and off for ten years. She had three grown children, she shared, and ever-so-carefully intimated that her younger son, Eric, was single . . . was I? She was fishing, and I was the trout.

I'd been "hit on" by mothers before, but she was a real pro, promoting her son's selling points like a secondhand car dealer. She went on and on about Eric's glowing qualities. By the time she took a breath, I asked with a coquettish lilt in my voice, "If he's so wonderful, why isn't he already taken?" She smiled amiably (though I'm not sure genuinely) and said, "He's waiting for the right woman." Good answer, but I was still skeptical.

By the next production meeting, I'd forgotten about my little dating-game-conversation with Helen, but she walked into the theater that night with a solid-looking blond guy trailing behind her. He was dutifully schlepping several boxes and bags down the aisle toward the stage. Enter, The Son.

Helen was so bold in her matchmaking attempt; I swallowed a laugh and hurried backstage to witness the scene as it unfolded. I watched closely to see if the young man *knew* he was being pimped out or if he was simply helping his mom because he was a good guy. In the meantime, I observed that Helen's son was quite handsome: tall, nicely built, and sporting a sparse mustache—a bit old-fashioned, but it added to his quirky charm.

After unloading his cargo, Eric (I assumed) stood self-consciously with his hands shoved deep in the pockets of his Levi's. He clearly didn't know what to do next, and although he looked helpless, he also seemed content to stand there waiting for further instruction. I wandered back on stage to inspect the props Helen had brought, and I stole a closer look at her second-born child.

After his first visit to the theater, Eric started hanging around once or twice a week, even though he had no real reason to be there. He wasn't officially working on the show, but he kept showing up.

Because the play took place in a restaurant, much of the food served onstage had to be prepared backstage ahead of time. My tasks included chopping veggies, stirring sauces into various bowls, and mixing beverage concoctions (soda and juice) so they looked like real beer or wine. This way, the food was ready for placement into baking dishes that actually cooked in the onstage working oven, and the drinks were primed for pouring into appropriate glasses.

Eric had barely said more than a handful of sentences to me over the first few weeks. I wasn't sure if he was shy or uninterested. Time to find out.

"Hey, I could use a hand over here," I said to him one night. If he'd declined to help, that would have been the end of it, but he hesitated for only a second before wandering in my direction.

"I can get those carrots ready," he offered. "You have a peeler?"

"Thanks. It's around here somewhere." I searched randomly through a nearby box. I handed him something metal and he laughed. It was the first time I'd seen him smile. It caught my attention. "What's so funny?" I asked, realizing he was laughing *at* me.

"That's a grater, not a peeler."

"Oh! Jeez. Okay, secret's out: I'm not a good cook. Obviously."

"No worries. I know my way around a kitchen. I'll make sure you don't get hurt." My turn to laugh then. He was chivalry wrapped in a chef's hat, minus the chef's hat.

Since the actors ate meals on stage, part of my job as prop mistress was cleaning dishes between acts. Without a dishwasher backstage, off to the bathroom sink I went. Yuck! One night, before I could start whining to myself that I should have gotten involved when the theater company did *Our Town* instead of this kitchen-based show, there was Eric, scraping off plates and rinsing glasses. I never asked later if he jumped in just to help me or to make me notice him, but the result worked both ways.

Eric's help backstage wasn't only useful, it also allowed us time to get to know each other better. Although my chatty nature dominated most of those conversations, he offered up enough about himself for me to know I liked what I heard.

"I can't imagine being an only child," he said one night as he scrubbed a difficult pan with a soapy sponge. "There were three of us using one bathroom before school. I brushed my teeth in the kitchen sink more times than I can remember."

"That's so different from my childhood. My alarm got me up well before my parents, so I was the only one awake in my house before school. Mom was just getting up as I was leaving for the bus. I never liked those quiet mornings."

Eric handed me a towel to dry the now-clean pan as he pulled it from the sink, and I flashed to a possible future domestic scene in our fantasy married life. Really? All I needed was a guy who could cook and do dishes, and I was ready to walk down the aisle? I must have been shaking my head to clear the silly daydream because Eric bumped his right shoulder against my left one and said, "Earth to Kat. Hellooo?"

I felt my face heat up as I redirected the conversation, "So, tell me more about your job."

"My dad co-founded a paint manufacturing company with his brother before I was born. We make coatings for outdoor use. You know those dark green metal posts along the highways? That's probably our paint."

"Cool. I've never thought about those before."

"Yeah, most people don't, but it's important to have the right chemicals on board to ensure they don't rust. Anyway . . . my dad died two years ago—"

"Oh, I'm sorry!"

"Thanks. It's been a transition for sure, both at work and in our family. He was our rock, ya know?" Eric grabbed a new pan from the box that sat on the toilet seat. He ran it under the hot water.

"I can't imagine. My dad is so important in my life . . ." A lump caught in my throat.

"I'm glad you're close to your dad. I was with mine, too, but only to a point. Maybe it's different between fathers and sons? I mean, I loved him, of course, and I miss him, but I think it's harder for dads to show their sons affection. Do you think so?"

"I know that's stereotypically true, but I don't know. I guess I've never looked around to see if people I know fit that myth or not. Did you feel a lack of closeness with your dad?"

It was a deep conversation to have shoulder to shoulder over a sink in a three-foot-square bathroom. But it pulled us toward each other in a way that chatting over dinner at a fancy restaurant might not have.

"Yes and no. I knew he loved me, but he wasn't the kind of father who played catch with his son. He looked over my homework from time to time, but it seemed more like his duty than a genuine concern for my ability to learn geography."

"So, a fatherly tie, but from a slight distance?" I summed up what I read between his lines.

"Yeah, a clove hitch, rather than a double-constrictor knot." Eric chuckled.

"You know I have no idea what that means, right?"

"So, you don't cook, and you don't fish? What good are you?" He winked and I blushed.

"I have a few talents up my sleeve," I said, looking at his reflection in the mirror. The blue of his eyes matched my own.

"I look forward to learning them," he responded to my reflection, the heat between us palpable for the first time.

I turned to look directly at the shy young man who had found his voice. Back to business. "So, what do you *do* at the paint company?"

I carried an armful of clean dishes out of the bathroom, setting them on a folding table in the dark corner of backstage left. Eric followed, doing the same.

"After my dad died, my uncle bought out my father's half of the business. I'd been working at the plant since high school, so I knew how to make the paint, but I wanted a new challenge. I didn't want to be wearing jeans to work when I was forty."

"That makes sense. A good goal."

"I trained with a sales agent my dad had hired when I was a kid. Jerry had to be pushing seventy by that time. He was thrilled that I wanted to learn his side of the business because he was more than ready to retire. And that's what happened. I shadowed him for six months or so. He taught me a ton. When I was ready to take over, we threw Jerry a huge retirement party. The last I heard, he and his wife were traveling, trying to visit every state in the U.S."

"Has it been helpful to sell the paint after you made it for so long?"

"Definitely. I can help customers troubleshoot problems they're having with any coating we've made. But I do still help in the shop sometimes, if someone's on vacation or something. It's nice to be able to do both. A good variety."

During those nights prepping food and doing dishes, I learned a lot about Eric's family and his interests. Our discussions were long and varied. We talked about politics and religion, why he hadn't gone to college, our hobbies (his: gemology, mushroom hunting, dabbling in cooking; mine: writing, singing, theater—obviously). We both liked to read, but different genres, and we'd each tried, but weren't good at, tennis. And if seeking the best hamburger in town counted as a pastime, we shared that interest.

I'm sure I led the conversation most of the time, but he made a consistent effort to work through his shyness a little at a time. Once he got talking, he seemed comfortable. He was so different from East Coast guys I'd known, and he was growing on me. Like Colorado itself, Eric was a different pace of life.

By the time closing night of the show was looming, I was thinking proactively: *If we don't "get together" before the production closes, we probably won't see each other again after the cast party.* But I realized Eric might need a nudge. As we sat side by side on the director's couch after the last performance, with cast and crew members celebrating all around us, I unleashed my inner New Yorker. With the subtlety of a freight train—in what would end up being a turning point in our lives—I looked over at Eric with flirty eyes and said, "Are you gonna kiss me or what?"

We managed to navigate the rest of our dating years with a bit more romantic equity, but in truth, we'd probably still be sitting on that couch in a platonic dance of nervous energy if I hadn't taken the lead. Maybe I shouldn't have. Maybe I was too assertive. Maybe he'd never wanted to get married or own a house. Was that Helen's goal for him, but not his own? Perhaps growing up happened too fast for him, and he wasn't prepared for the pressure.

But I hadn't pointed a gun at him. He signed up to play house with me, and from what I could tell, he'd been happy—until maybe he wasn't.

•   •   •   •   •

After two days of mulling and moping, I woke on Sunday to a typical Colorado December morning. The sun was bright, offsetting the crisp thirty-eight degrees. While shuffling to the bathroom, I remembered the two-hour family workshop I was invited to at the hospital that night: *How Family Members Can Support the Recovering Alcoholic at Home.* It would be the first time I'd seen Eric since the surreal night he was admitted. I was nervous about facing him with all the doubts and questions I had. Would he notice if I hesitated before kissing him? I was ashamed my trust had been so easily abused, and I was anxious, thinking I'd probably aided in his drinking without even knowing it. How responsible was *I*?

As I sat in our living room, decaf coffee in one hand, a throw pillow clutched to my chest in the other, I tried to talk myself into going to the meeting. I knew I should go, and I knew why everyone expected me to attend, but my mind kept arguing back. I looked around at all our things. I remembered George Carlin's routine about a house only being important as a place to keep your *stuff.* You accumulate more and more *stuff* as you get older, so you need a bigger house to put all your *stuff* in. Something along those lines; obviously, he said it better. I had thought this was our Home, but now it just felt like a place we kept our stuff.

How many of those things were important now? Did any of it mean anything to me after what I'd learned? I knew I was being melodramatic, but it seemed like we'd built our life together on a history of lies. I tried to reconcile the shy young man I'd fallen in love with and the husband I'd learned had been hiding bottles in our garage. Were they the same people or was one an illusion? If so, which one? Could I trust him? Could I trust myself?

Everything I looked at held a memory, and I couldn't help but wonder about each one: Had Eric been drinking the day he gave me the cute statue of the little boy holding a bunny? The vase on the counter held the spare change we'd been saving for a vacation to Ireland, but we never seemed to accumulate much; had he been dipping into it between paychecks? And when we bought our beige recliner, we giggled in the store about making love on it as soon as it was delivered—and we did. But how many hungover mornings had he slept, passed out on that very chair, while I was at work? Suddenly, I didn't want any of it.

It took me less than two hours to put the few things I *did* care about in the back of my Subaru wagon: photo albums, a little jewelry, the beautiful letter my mom had written to me when I turned twenty-one, my Dan Fogelberg tape and CD collection, and the journal I'd started the day I found out we were expecting. Amazing that my life condensed into one box and a suitcase of clothes.

I told myself it wasn't forever. Just a little time and distance from him and the immediate disorder I felt growing around me. Inside our house, I felt disoriented. In opposition, inside my body, I had a more immediate concern, and he or she was growing bigger every day. I needed to be strong and focused, to think beyond myself. How could I bring my baby into such a confused house? Not the version of marriage I'd signed up for, and I didn't know how to change it.

I softened my anger enough to acknowledge maybe this was the end of the lies. He was, after all, in a hospital of his own accord, saying he wanted a more honest life, acknowledging his desire to be a sober father to his child. While I hoped he would conquer the vodka in the end, I'd never been more sure of anything as I shut the door to our house: He would have to get to that point alone.

•   •   •   •   •

The landscape along I-70 heading east dragged on in horizontal, monotonous contrast to the glorious Rocky Mountains I was leaving behind. I didn't know there were so many shades of brown. The lack of visual interest had taken its toll on me by the time I reached Hays, two hours past the Colorado-Kansas border. I'd wanted to get as far as Topeka, but I couldn't stand looking at all the flatness anymore. The local time was 6:30 p.m. when I found a Comfort Inn on 41st Street. Daylight Savings Time had already shrouded the hotel in darkness. I checked into a nonsmoking room on the first floor and wondered how comprehensive the free continental breakfast would be in the morning.

I remembered little about the five-hour drive, except there was a long, annoying stretch of highway that only got one AM radio station in clearly, an all-talk news show. It had bored me so much I turned the radio off and drove in silence for over an hour. It reminded me of the countless times Eric said he'd install the CD player he gave me for my birthday two years ago, but somehow never got around to.

What I was doing didn't really hit me until I was lying on an ugly green bedspread, staring at a "Welcome to Kansas" tri-fold brochure on the nightstand next to me. I'd stopped for a quick lunch during the day, but my mind was so focused on driving, it didn't register where I was. Not completely.

My head was throbbing, and suddenly, my face was wet. I hadn't realized I was crying. I lay there, slobbering all over the pillow, shaking with chills as if I had a fever. I wanted to be under the covers, but I didn't think I could get up. Grabbing a few Kleenex from my purse next to the lamp, I snuffled into the wad of tissues, a chorus repeating in my head: *How did I not know? How did I not know?*

Immobile and prostrate, I wasn't sure how long I lay there. A couple of kids ran past my room, rousing me from my lost thoughts and paralysis. I heard a boy shout, "Betcha I'm first off the diving board!" The giggles of two or three other kids followed him down the hall to the indoor pool.

With reluctance, I pulled my legs over the side of the bed and planted my feet on the floor. Semi-vertical was a start.

In the bathroom, I splashed cold water on my face; it shocked me into the here and now. When I looked into the mirror above the sink, I almost didn't recognize myself. It had been years since I'd cried like that. I had a flashback to my teen years, adolescent fights with my mother over responsibility and freedom. My eyes, light blue, seemed to turn iridescent green, as if the discourse between my mother and me actually altered something chemical inside, changing the color of my irises. They looked that way now, staring back at me with an accusation I didn't understand, a thing apart from myself. *Was I doing the right thing?*

When I returned to bed, I gathered the courage to make three necessary phone calls: to my boss, to Eric, and to my folks, telling them I'd be sleeping in my old room by mid-week. The first call was easy. I'd grabbed Jo's home phone number before I left the house. When I found out I was pregnant, I told my manager I'd be leaving in May: "I've accepted the CEO position at a new baby development company." She'd laughed at my self-promotion to full-time parenthood. I was thinking about her warm smile and tight embrace as her phone rang. It would cause them a little disruption to start the replacing-me-process now, but it wouldn't be a real inconvenience. I wasn't the type of person to leave a job without warning, but then again, I wasn't feeling much like myself.

After I apologized and told her I'd enjoyed working with her—a truth I felt fortunate to share—Jo wished me luck. She asked where she could send my last paycheck; I gave her my parents' address. Even if I were only there a few weeks, the money would be helpful.

The call to Eric at the hospital was more challenging. I encountered a nurse who explained, in a voice that vacillated between C-sharp and E-flat, "New patients aren't allowed to receive personal phone calls." She went on to recite more rules and regulations from their handbook (from memory, no doubt).

I kept my voice calm and said, "I appreciate your need for strict guidelines, ma'am, and I'm confident these rules are set in place for your patients' well-being. However, I'm calling to tell my husband I've left the state for an undetermined amount of time, and unless you want him to go home next week and find an empty house with no note explaining where I am and why I'm gone, I suggest you let me tell him myself on the phone." I paused for dramatic effect and added, "This, too, will be for his well-being."

She paused and said, "Just a moment, please." I heard the familiar click as she put me on hold. I couldn't be the first spouse to make this call; the nurse knew when to bend the rules.

"Hello?" said the voice I'd known intimately for so long.

"Hey."

"Did you bribe the nurse?" he said with a slight chuckle. "I was told I couldn't use the phone at all this week."

"Uh, no. She was being nice. I told her I needed to talk to you."

"Are you okay?" he asked when he heard the serious tone of my voice. I fought not to yell into his ear, "No, of course I'm not okay.

And what's more, I'm in fucking Kansas!" Instead, I took a deep breath.

"I won't be coming to the meeting tonight." He started to say something but waited a beat, ready to hear what else I might say.

"I'm going to my parents' for a while, Eric. I need some time to myself." He exhaled dramatically and made a "hmmm" sound.

The moment stretched out, lasting a beat too long. I knew we were both thinking many different things and trying to decide on the best approach. I spoke again before he could come up with something.

"Look, I know this isn't what you want to hear from me right now. Maybe you think I'm taking the easy way out while you're in a tough situation, but that's not my motive."

"Well, it did cross my mind. I'm not on vacation here, you know," he said with just a hint of self-righteousness that made me angry enough to say:

"No, but you *have* been on vacation for quite some time, from what I learned the other night, so now you're feeling sorry for yourself. Reality has intruded, and you have to do some work to make things right again." I regretted the scorning right away, but the sentiment was true. Why tiptoe around his feelings now when he had disregarded mine without concern?

"That's not fair," he said like a child losing a game of *Candyland*, but then he added nothing else to argue my point. I steadied my voice and backed away from arguing fairness for the time being.

"I'm in Hays tonight; I'll be in Poughkeepsie by Wednesday. When you get home, why don't you call me there and let me know your plans." I knew I sounded businesslike, but it was either that or yell or cry or swear, and I didn't want to get emotional. It seemed like my feelings weren't something to be shared with him; he'd lost his right to know those personal, private parts of me right now.

"Okay," he said. I could hear his resignation. Later, I imagined him twisting this conversation to paint me as selfish and abandoning him in his time of need. Somehow, he would make this my fault. But not yet.

"Kat?"

"Yeah?"

"I'm sorry," he said.

"So am I," I said, holding back another wave of tears until I hung up.

•   •   •   •   •

I used to hate my name. Katharine. Though named after my mother's favorite actress, I never developed the grace and charm of Katharine Hepburn. So somewhere in junior high school, I gathered up my gumption (*very* Hepburn-like, although I didn't make the connection then), and started going by Kat. It seemed cool and different. That felt more like the me I wanted to be. Since being thirteen is all about trying on different personality hats to see which one fits best, I ran with it. My mother adjusted, eventually.

I always thought it strange she gave me such a "girly" name. She was quite devoted to the Women's Movement in the 1960s. When I came along smack-dab in the middle of the decade, I would have thought she'd pick a feminist name for her civil-rights-inspired daughter. Something like Charlie or Rikki or Sam, a derivative or abbreviation of a male name, but empowered with female strength and ingenuity. But no, Katharine it was, and Kat I became. Maybe that same determination would help me again as I worked to make the uncomfortable things in my life more comfortable.

After crossing the Missouri River, I stopped at a truck stop just west of Columbia to get gas, use the restroom, and grab a snack. I still had three hours to go before reaching the small city of Vandalia, Illinois, where I planned to spend the night.

Waiting in line to pay for my essentials—bottled water, an apple, and a Snickers bar—my eyes wandered to a woman in the line next to mine. Around my age, she balanced a baby on her left hip. I imagined the little girl to be eight or nine months old; she had those ultra-chubby thighs that hadn't experienced walking yet. While the mom struggled to get her wallet out of the diaper bag hanging behind her right shoulder, frustration shadowed her face. She looked exhausted, as if her features hadn't been exercised in far too long.

The little girl started to whine. Mom tried to pay for her Diet Coke and apple juice and return to her car before the persistent, nasal "MaaaaaMaaaaaaa" turned into a full-fledged howl. The clock was ticking, and the woman was losing.

I don't know what made me look, but I checked her left hand for a ring. None. Then, the child kicked the diaper bag so hard it flew off her mom's shoulder and half the contents soared out, scattering in several directions. My reflexes were fast. I stepped out of my line and swooped to the floor, searching for a pacifier I'd seen tumble under a nearby display rack. I also picked up the tiny denim jacket and car keys strewn a few feet apart from each other next to the cashier's counter. As I handed these items back to the woman, I realized she couldn't reach around and put them back inside the diaper bag without putting her baby down. And where was she supposed to plop her? On the sticky, dirty tile floor?

It was only a fraction of a second, but her sideways look revealed embarrassment. I placed the dislodged bag back on the woman's shoulder, put the objects I'd found into it, and zipped it back up. I heard a soft "thank you" in what I thought was a Southern accent, and I issued a "not a problem" back.

My interaction momentarily distracted the baby. She peeked over her mom's shoulder to flash a smile that made my heart race. Her apple cheeks rounded, and she blinked her heavy eyelids, sending her lashes into a frenzy of motion. They made me think of a hummingbird's wings.

The entire exchange lasted about a minute, but I spent the next two hours reflecting on all the emotions that duo stirred in me. Was this a glimpse of my future? A single mom, frazzled and struggling, reluctant to rely on helpful strangers? How would I handle the stigma and the stress of caring for a baby by myself? What would Eric's role be?

As I drove across Missouri, I kept seeing the little girl's eyes: trusting and happy, oblivious to the difficulties she presented just by being. Secure in her mother's arms, that baby . . . that sweet, frustrating, needy, perfectly normal child . . . so innocent and dependent on me—

I mean, her mother.

Chapter Two: Options

The house I grew up in was a split-level ranch, common in the late '70s and early '80s. My parents and I never liked the layout much, but over the years, we created a million wonderful memories within its walls: I had my first kiss in the dining room when I was sixteen, at a cast party we hosted for our community theater group. My grandmother once made inedible meatballs there. They were supposed to be sweet-and-sour, but she'd forgotten the sour, so they ended up candied meat! We threw them in the backyard for the squirrels to eat. And I'd spent weeks of my life brushing the soft coat of our beautiful golden retriever, Sunday, now long gone, on that brown carpet.

Every corner of the house held a ghost, but most of them were warm and welcoming.

After tight parental hugs and reunion tears, I dragged my suitcase into my old bedroom. In typical empty nesters' fashion, it was exactly as I'd left it when I moved out. I felt both strong and weak as I considered my situation: Was I brave for making this trip, doing a difficult thing in my baby's best interest? Or was I copping out, running away?

Despite three-plus days of driving, I hadn't come up with an honest answer, so I left the room and went to the kitchen for some cookies.

We sat at the kitchen table for over an hour, and I answered question after question about what had brought me to their doorstep. Although my parents and I were close emotionally, the two thousand miles between us created a natural physical barrier, keeping them just removed enough to be shocked by the details of my marriage. Of course, they had no idea how bad things were; hell, I had only just found out.

"Are you sure you shouldn't have stayed home and worked on this *with* Eric? It feels . . . odd. You're here and he's there," my dad said. His honesty pushed against the sore spot in my chest where my heart lived.

"No, Dad. Actually, I'm not sure. I'm not sure at all," I said, trying to keep the urge to defend myself in check. "I know you want me to live the happily-ever-after life Eric promised us, but right now? I'm not confident we'll get there."

"I'm not saying marriage should be roses and rainbows every day, sweetheart, and certainly there will be hurdles. But you face them. I'm worried if you're not physically together, you won't be able to work on the emotional stuff together." His fatherly advice was steeped in concern, and it accompanied the wisdom his sixty-seven years and two marriages had earned him.

"I know that intellectually. And yes, I agreed to 'for better or for worse' when we got married. But I also expected him not to lie to me and take money out of our joint savings without telling me. I assumed he would be my partner, not a child I needed to watch over. I'm having a baby now. *This* little person will need me to take care of him or her. Shouldn't the baby receive most of my caregiving attention?"

"Eric loves you, Kat. You know that, right?" It wasn't a response to my question, but my dad looked at me with a combination of hope and apprehension. My happiness was his goal. If my marriage ship was sinking, his solution to save me was throwing out lifejackets, anything I could grab onto.

"Yes. I do know it. I also know, and so do you: Love isn't always enough." Regret crossed his face as he remembered his first wife's betrayal.

I heard the thin layer of affront sitting on top of my words, and I knew I should watch my tone. Dad wasn't the enemy here. He'd always liked Eric, and he must be feeling his own frustrations, if not betrayal, now.

He looked down at his hands and fingered his wedding band. I read his mind and offered a softer remark. "Dad, you taught me that love is a verb, an action, and marriage is a commitment, a decision. I'm trying to figure out how love and commitment have been working, or not, between Eric and me. If committing to me and our marriage was too much for Eric, what if he never fully commits to our baby?"

He took a breath deep enough for me to see, and he nodded, pausing to consider his response. During the brief silence, my mother stepped in to play mediator. She was familiar with the role; she played it whenever my dad and I didn't agree.

"You know, Kitty Kat, I love you more than anything in this world, and I think I know you better than anyone else. I raised you by always speaking the truth." Mom's preface prepared me to listen closely to something I may not want to hear. "This bit of honesty might sting: You talk about taking care of Eric like a child who needs raising, but honey, that's part of what attracted you to him. And him to you. You're a competent woman who gets things done. Eric has always been a laid-back, Colorado kid, but I don't mean 'kid' in a childish way." I listened with intent as she continued.

"You fell in love with his sense of whimsy and wonder, the way he always arrived ten minutes late because he wasn't tied to his watch. You thought it was sweet when he puttered around the kitchen without a recipe to make dinner. His idea of traveling was heading to a fishing pond in the next town over. He wasn't as studious or ambitious as you, and he still lives two miles away from his mom, not across the country like you do. All those things help a person navigate into adulthood."

This dose of reality was bitter to swallow, but I waited to hear where she was going.

She reached across the table to hold my hand. "As for you, you seemed to enjoy guiding him into grown-up life, remember? You showed him how to balance his checkbook a few months after you met. You're the one putting money away like the good saver we raised you to be, and you were the one who initiated buying the house."

"All of those things are true, Mom, but Eric never said he *didn't* want those things. Do you think I pushed him?" I wasn't feeling angry at her bluntness; rather, I was worried. She knew better than anyone how my take-charge ability could steamroll people around me—even if that wasn't my intention.

"I'm not sure, but I *am* saying you have a particular nature and so does Eric. Your natures have blended and balanced each other nicely for several years."

Yes, Eric loved me and needed me, and I loved him and needed him to need me. Ours was a codependent match made in dysfunctional heaven. When our "sicknesses" aligned, we were both happy. But something had changed.

Somewhere along the way, maybe Eric had stopped wanting me to take care of him but didn't know how to tell me. Or maybe he still liked how I managed our lives, but his drinking was something he owned which I couldn't control? And maybe I was changing, too?

"I hear what you're saying," I agreed. "But what if I don't want to be responsible for him anymore? What if I need him to be the man I know he can be if he tries a little harder? I shouldn't have to direct him for the rest of our lives, should I? Especially not now. And what does any of this have to do with his excessive and sneaky drinking?"

My parents looked at each other and spoke a whole silent conversation in a language only they understood. It took ten seconds.

"You talk about the commitment of marriage," Mom said. "Of course, we agree. You committed yourself to Eric, and he made the same pledge. I'm sure you feel sucker punched right now. But your dad has a point about working on what's wrong in your marriage together."

"I know. I probably panicked when I came here. It was a gut reaction. I felt hurt and scared, then angry and unsure of myself. I just wanted to get away from it all, you know?

"But as I was driving here, one thing became clear: I need some time alone to think. I'm not saying I'm ready to throw in the towel," I said, making my closing argument like a seasoned attorney in court. "But I need some space from Eric. I don't think that's unreasonable, is it?"

"No," my parents said in unison, then they both chuckled. It allowed us all a moment's relief from the conversation's intensity. Mom continued with, "We're on your side, honey. You know that. Always."

"No matter what you decide in the end," Dad added. "You know how much we love you, Kat. We'll support you however we can."

Mom stood and crossed to me. "I'm so sorry—and if I'm honest, angry—that you're going through this. Especially now, with the baby." She put her hands on my cheeks and turned my face to look up at hers. "You're welcome to stay here as long as you need. But it's not a vacation. You have big things to think about. I don't envy you." She leaned down and kissed my forehead, a place reserved for her maternal pecks.

"I know, Mom. Thank you both for everything. I never doubted I could just get in my car and drive here. I knew you'd say all the comforting, wise things you've said tonight, and I'm grateful."

An hour later, I lay in the twin bed that had been my sanctuary during the social and emotional drama I survived called high school. So much teen angst; so much of it stupid compared to the adult problems consuming me now. My parents had seen me through those ups and downs then, and I knew they'd travel this bumpier road with me now.

I was blessed to be the sole recipient of their parental spotlight; the weight of their love sat on my shoulders like football pads, protecting me. However, it also made my movement through life cumbersome. Since they were constant companions in my mind, I always carried them with me. Their voices whispered unasked-for advice, but I (usually) welcomed the guidance. I knew they wanted the best for me, so I relied on their combined wisdom to steer me.

But this time, their words stood on both sides of their advice. On one hand, they were saying I should give Eric the benefit of my love and focus on my commitment to him; after all, I knew who he was when I married him. On the other hand, they were saying they would support any decision I made, including one that might break the bond my husband and I had forged.

The confusion fueled my insecurity . . . or maybe my insecurity made room for the confusion? Either way, I wobbled. Hesitation clouded my thinking and ignited my indecision. I felt annoyed that I couldn't sort my feelings and know what I needed.

But at the end of that first day in New York, after two thousand miles of solo driving and then heavy conversation, exhaustion seeped into my bones and brain. No one was surprised when I missed breakfast and woke up at noon the next day, sporting deep creases on my cheeks.

•　　•　　•　　•　　•

My parents' marriage was a bit unconventional compared to their peers, both having walked down the aisle before. Maybe Fate had something to do with their meeting since his name is Jack and hers is Jillian; the jokes never ended. That befitted the sense of playfulness they created together. Perhaps the long and often-painful road to finding each other allowed my parents to relax into the laughter, openness, and fun I grew up in.

Mom never had children with her first husband, George, whom she married the autumn after her high school graduation. He died at twenty-three of complications during surgery to repair a ruptured appendix; they'd only been married three years. She stayed single for several years after, paving a path of self-sufficiency few women were able to experience in the early 1960s. But Mom enjoyed working for the insurance agency, and she got involved with various social causes. At the local theater group, Community Players, she surrounded herself with a diverse assortment of friends who filled in the patchwork of her life until she met my dad.

Jack had also lost his first spouse, but not to disease or death. Rather, to the allure of another man. He and Fran lived in Germany at the time, where the Army had stationed him after WWII. They were raising their daughter together, but Jack's increasing responsibilities required him to work assignments away from his family more often than ideal.

In 1959, when my half-sister, Laura, was only twelve, her mother took off with a lowly corporal (Dad's description) several years her junior. Fran left in the middle of the night to avoid confrontation and tears. In the good-bye letter she left Laura, she wrote, "One day you'll understand that I, too, have a life to live, and this one is not right for me. I do love you, and I know this choice will hurt you, but that's not my intention. Please forgive me. I pray you will find happiness. That's all I'm seeking, as well."

Shortly after being thrust into single parenthood, Jack put in for a transfer back to the States. He received his request to be stationed at Fort Monmouth Army Base in New Jersey, close to his sister Mary, so she could help him raise his soon-to-be teenaged daughter. His extensive background with the Signal Corps while overseas made him an ideal trainer for fellow officers at the renowned base. Jack helped the men prepare for their next leadership assignments in a post-Korean-conflict world.

For Veterans Day when I was in eighth grade, we had to interview someone who'd served in a branch of the military. I interviewed my dad, a retired lieutenant colonel, about his twenty years in the Army, specifically about his experiences during two wars. The takeaway I remembered most was the fact that he considered himself a pacifist. This seemed at odds with a man dedicated to protecting our country within the framework of a military organization. But only at first blush.

"The atrocities I saw during combat—" My dad paused as if seeing bloodied bodies right there in our living room. "Well, it scarred me. I was barely eighteen years old when I went to the Pacific. The war was in full swing then, in 1943."

"What were your responsibilities there?" I asked. I sat on the edge of the couch with my notebook open and a pen at attention like the troops he served alongside. I was thirteen, but I tried to act mature enough to hear the details he'd always protected me from.

"My very first job was putting bodies—or body parts—in plastic bags to be shipped back to the States." His face paled as he shook his head. I knew he was leaving out specific gory details, and I was grateful. "I still can't believe it, even now. It's been thirty-five years, but it still seems like a terrible movie I lived through."

What could I say to that? Nothing. I sat silently and waited for him to continue.

"I guess that's why I always try to teach you there's no such thing as a minor job. Any task you are expected to do should be done right, with your full effort and care."

"You say that a lot."

"Yes. It would've been easy for me to skirt that horrendous responsibility, but I couldn't. I kept thinking about the families at home who needed to bury their sons, their brothers, their husbands. It was about the soldiers' dignity and my respect for them. I couldn't focus on how distasteful the job was to me."

"How did being in the war shape you?" It was a required question my teacher expected us to ask. I couldn't have come up with it myself.

"It solidified my belief in the value of communication," he said without hesitation. "People need to find ways to *talk* to each other, no matter their differences. Killing has no place in a civilized society."

As an adult, I realized how that value directed his career and his life. This, in part, was why he admired John F. Kennedy so much. Kennedy spoke of the power of words and how people should focus on what they have in common with others rather than what separates them. He seemed the right man to lead our country through the Cold War and to help the world navigate a nuclear age.

And so, on June 11, 1962, Jack drove to New Haven, Connecticut, to hear JFK give the commencement address at Yale University. He didn't get to shake the President's hand that day as he'd hoped, but he did meet his future wife.

Kennedy's messages to the country captivated my mother. He spoke to her heart about civil rights, and she loved how he encouraged everyday people to commit to doing their part, to doing good. She wouldn't miss an opportunity to hear him speak live when it was a mere ninety-minute drive to get there. In her excitement to get a good spot in the crowd, she was crossing the New York-Connecticut border before she realized she'd forgotten to ask any of her friends to go with her.

So it came to pass that my parents met at Yale University, even though neither of them attended the school or lived in Connecticut. Somehow, they ended up standing next to each other after the speech was over, sharing their enthusiasm with audience members near them. By the time they realized others had disbursed, they were alone and still talking. An instant connection. The twelve years between them, irrelevant. The rest, as they say . . .

For the next year and a half, Jack made the two-hour drive to Poughkeepsie every other weekend to woo my mom. Laura was scratching her way through her teen years: When she wasn't actively rebelling, she was sullen and withdrawing from home and hearth. She made it easy for her dad to "move on" when she started staying out all night, skipping school, and dabbling with drugs. Navigating adolescence must have been difficult without a mother, but Laura pulled away from her father before he had a chance to bridge the gap between them. Instead, she turned to the comfort of a boyfriend who encouraged her to "take it easy" and "hang out." A month after she turned seventeen, Laura became a mother herself.

By the time I'd come along, my half-sister's life had stabilized. She and her husband and son called California home. I only met her a few times during my entire childhood; our eighteen-year age difference made us more like distant cousins than siblings. But family is family, and I was always happy her story turned out better than it could have, considering her initiation into what motherhood looked like.

Maybe it was because they were a little more experienced, and jaded, than most parents by the time I was born, but Jack and Jillian raised me in a laissez-faire, para-equal way. This fused the three of us in friendship as much as in blood. Being involved in the civil rights issues of the day, my folks were freethinking and open-mouthed about their beliefs. We were a liberal family that my friends always envied. I had "the cool parents," and our door was open to anyone who needed a meal, a bed for the night, or intelligent conversation with a hint of humor.

But more than anything, at the core of who we were as a family, was the fact that I was the center of their lives. They loved me unconditionally. Maybe that spoiled me and my expectations for love and marriage. Could any mortal man ever love me as valiantly as they did?

•   •   •   •   •

"Whatcha doing today, honey?" Mom asked. I set my decaf coffee on a coaster by the couch I was lazing on, suddenly feeling self-conscious. I'd been hanging around the house for well over a week, fluctuating between bursts of energy and sulking. I wrote a lot in my journal, watched tearjerker chick flicks, stayed up late with my parents solving the world's problems, and took daily walks. My folks never pushed me about going home. They either thought I'd know when I was ready or maybe they actually enjoyed having me around?

That week, the festive energy of Christmas glowed and twinkled outside, but the holiday wasn't a big deal in my family. Mom was born Jewish, though she didn't practice beyond Rosh Hashana and Yom Kippur in September, and Dad had abandoned his faith in any God on the battlefields during the war. Our Christmas Day tradition was seeing a matinee and then heading out for Chinese food.

On the evening of the 25th, Eric called. It was a brief conversation filled with more pauses than words. The two-week treatment program had discharged their charges a day early, on the twenty-third, so people could be with family for the holiday. Eric let me know in a pseudo-whiny voice that he was "all alone" for Christmas, though he'd spent Christmas Eve with his mom and brother.

In the living room, Mom looked at me with eyebrows arched, waiting.

"Well, maybe I'll take a drive," I blurted out, deciding on the spot.

An hour later, I found myself on familiar roads, driving through disconnected pieces of my past. Although school was out for winter break, a group of kids huddled in front of my old high school, their breath making steam conversation bubbles above their heads. Maybe some of that was cigarette smoke? Or pot? Several of the girls wore t-shirts despite the forty-three degrees the meteorologist had correctly predicted. More important to be showing off their curves than preventing winter colds.

The car drove itself next to the parking lot of a movie theater I patronized a hundred times in my teen years. I remembered singing along at the midnight showings of *The Rocky Horror Picture Show*. How exciting it was to be allowed to stay out until 2:00 a.m.! And how titillating the movie was. My attraction to a man in drag had confused me . . . what did that mean?

Pathetic in every sense of the word, I was traveling down memory lane, but it was comforting. Since my memories had less to do with specific places and more to do with people, there weren't many destinations to hit after that. I drove around without purpose, thinking.

I'd spent most of my time as a kid in choir and acting in plays. I wondered how many of my old friends were still in town; then I wondered if I'd even recognize them if they were. Had they changed as much as I had, or had I mostly changed on the inside? Or had I changed at all?

Moving to Colorado after college, I'd envisioned a passionate and successful life, born out of the brave adventure of being on my own in a state where I knew no one. I would always be a New York girl at heart, but the Wild West was sure to bring out the grab-life-by-the-balls in me, right? Hmmm . . . maybe not. I guess more than anything, I'd mellowed. My faster-than-you-could-listen-to speaking voice had slowed down some, and I wasn't always in a hurry to get somewhere only to sit and wait.

But had I really lived my life with the gusto I'd set out to? Had I done curious and spontaneous things? Not yet. I hadn't even gone to grad school, and that was the entire reason I moved to Boulder to begin with. Life had gotten in the way. Eric had been a fun and worthwhile distraction, and I loved my job. Graduate school had taken a back seat.

Driving by the house my best friend used to live in, I saw the rosebush we'd planted together in the summer of '81—still thriving though bare of flowers in December. I reminisced about how the biggest problems I had back then were dealing with blemished skin and cramming for *WordPower* exams in AP English.

I stopped at Zoe's Bakery a mile from my parents' house to pick up a Dutch apple pie. When I was in high school, there were rumors that the little old lady who owned the place was a hundred years old. I was surprised when she came out from the back room (slowly) to take my order herself. She was still very much alive, and clearly, still very aged.

Her trademark dessert was legendary in our town, and my mouth watered at the thought of a slice after dinner. Still lost in the twirling of my thoughts, a low voice snagged me out of my reverie.

"Kat? Katharine Morrow? Is that you?"

No one had called me by that name in a long while, so even before I turned around, I anticipated having a hard time placing the face. But the face I saw was the last one I would have expected, and I knew it right away. I could feel the heat blooming red on my face like the blushing eighteen-year-old I was the last time I saw him. Andrew Bellante. Drew.

My heart did a flip, and my brain did a quick self-assessment to remember what I was wearing. I stumbled through an "Oh, my God! Drew! I can't believe it."

"Wow!" he said, brazenly looking me up and down. "You look amazing." Drew was always one to speak his mind with little censorship. Our history of familiarity, though ten summers had passed since then, made him even more straightforward.

"I do not, you liar, but it's nice of you to say anyway," I said, letting him off the hook.

He pulled me into a hug before I knew what was happening and planted a friendly kiss on my cheek. "What are you doing here? I thought you moved out west somewhere."

"I did. Colorado. I'm visiting my folks for a few weeks."

Before the conversation went any further, I tucked my left hand into the pocket of my jeans. I swear I felt a prickle under my wedding band, as if it were hurt by my denial of its existence.

"That's great!" Drew said. "I'd love to see you while you're in town. I'm working with my dad, building upscale houses for lawyers and local politicians and such. You can't believe how much money some people spend on ridiculous extras no one could seriously need. But hey, they wanna pay for it, we're here to help 'em spend it, right?" He laughed and shook his head, clearly an inside joke he and his father shared often.

Despite the chill in the air, Drew wore a thin sweater, the sleeves pushed up to his elbows. I looked at his forearms. Just enough hair to be masculine, but not enough to cover his light brown skin. I remembered how whale white I used to feel next to him: my cold Russian and Irish heritage paling in the glow of his prominent Italian genes. His next question forced my eyes back to his. "What have you been doing for work since college?"

"I'm an assistant editor at a weekly business magazine. Mostly proofreading and doing design layout. I also get to help interview new employees and train them on our company procedures and stuff. I like it a lot, but I don't know if it's my forever job, you know?" My verbal resume did not include the fact that I had just quit that job.

Old Lady Zoe had finished packaging my pie in an ornate box. *Why so pretty? Is she expecting people to keep the box after the pie is gone?* As I handed her my credit card, Drew ordered a German chocolate cake and continued our dialogue without missing a beat.

"Yeah. I don't think many people have one long career in the same field anymore. I love working with my dad, but do I want to be working construction when I'm forty? Probably not." I found myself watching his mouth as he spoke, and I panicked for a second when he paused. Had I missed a question while lost in less-than-platonic thoughts? But he went on. "I've thought about going back to school, but I'm not sure for what, so I keep putting it off until I know what I'd do with that piece of paper. Anyway," he shook his head, dismissing his ramblings, "What's Colorado like?"

"It's beautiful. Everything you've ever heard about it is true: three hundred days of sunshine a year, mild winters, except in the high country, but that's where they want the snow with all the ski resorts. The back range of the Rocky Mountains are covered with snow all year. And it's DRY! God, I hate the humidity here; it's never even *close* to being humid there," I smiled, recalling sweat-less summer afternoons sunbathing by the pool at my mother-in-law's.

My turn to ramble. "And the people are great. Life's a little slower there, and people really seem to enjoy whatever they're doing, especially if it's outdoors." I sounded like a paid advertisement, so I stopped. Drew seemed taken in.

"I guess with all that going for it, there's no chance you'll ever find yourself back here for more than a few weeks, huh?"

"Probably not. But I love coming back to visit, especially in the fall. We don't get the same colors when the leaves change."

Drew reached for his wallet, handed Zoe a $10 bill and told her to keep the rest. Before she could respond, he turned his attention back to me. He pulled out a business card and continued: "Here. Call me, okay? I can't believe I have to cut this short, but I'm meeting my brother and his family for dinner. I promised my nephew I'd be there at five o'clock to watch *Rugrats* with him. Have you seen it? Silly show, but I kinda like it." I'd forgotten how much his sentences could run on and on together, like a millipede inching along, elongating itself and then scrunching up, only to stretch out long again.

I took the card he extended as he glanced at his watch.

"I have just enough time to break only one or two speed limits and get over there," he shrugged at his admitted guilt and smiled at the same time. "I'm really sorry, Kat. *Please* call me. I want to catch up and hear more."

"Okay," I mumbled, feeling embarrassed about something I hadn't done yet but knew I wanted to do. "It was good to see you," I said as he turned to go. Jingle bells hung from the top of the door, and they made a cheerful sound as he walked away. That seemed wrong, though, because I missed him already . . . and I knew that was wrong, too.

I looked down at his card. I fought the urge to smell it. Did he still wear Halston for men? It always seemed like such a manly scent when he was nineteen, but it fit him. I loved smelling it when I kissed him on the neck.

We'd been each other's first significant relationships: first lover for me and first love for him. Or so he'd said. Maybe that was part of the adolescent swirl of getting laid, but I had bought it. Then I'd spent my early twenties trying to find a man who made my skin tingle the way Drew did.

•   •   •   •   •

At 11:43 p.m., the phone next to the bed startled me out of a deep slumber. I grabbed it before a second ring so my parents wouldn't be disturbed. I knew it would be Eric, and I knew why he was calling so late: He'd forgotten about the time zone difference. He could never figure it out, always arguing with me that East Coast time was two hours *earlier* than Colorado time. I got an atlas out once to show him the facts.

"Hi Eric," I said before confirmation, all traces of sleep instantly gone from my voice.

"How did you know it was me?"

"Because it's quarter to midnight here. You forgot about the time difference."

"Oh, shit. I did it wrong again, didn't I? Sorry. Did I wake you?" he asked, totally oblivious to a world that didn't call its equator by his given name.

"It's okay," I lied. Protecting his feelings had become as natural to me as blinking. "How are you?"

"I'm all right." He paused, probably unsure how to proceed. "The house is quiet without you."

I ignored his attempt to soften me up. I still wanted to be mad, though I realized we needed to be able to talk. I was more than half a continent away, after all; there was no chance of reconnecting in any significant way. I tried to relax.

"How are the classes and everything?" I asked, referring to the twice-a-week outpatient classes he was expected to attend.

"They're pretty good. I know most of the people from the hospital, and the counselor I liked best leads the Thursday night sessions, so that's good."

"Hmmm." Trying to sound neutral wasn't working. I heard myself and I sounded cold. Maybe that wasn't fair. I forced myself to move forward. "Did you get a sponsor?"

"No, not yet, but I'm looking for one. I've only been to four AA meetings so far. They say it takes time to find someone you click with. But I'm looking." I listened for sincerity in his voice. Was he really trying or just saying what he thought he was supposed to?

"That's good."

"Kat?"

"Yeah?"

"When are you coming home?"

"I don't know. I really don't. I need some time, Eric." *Please, don't ask me anything else.*

"Okay," he said. "I guess I've got my plate pretty full here, so . . ."

I wasn't sure what the end of that sentence was supposed to be: "So . . . sure, take your time figuring things out while I work on my own issues," or "so . . . I won't really notice if you're here or not," or "so . . . I guess you truly are a selfish bitch and don't care about me and my problems."

For a minute I was transported to a happier time, when pauses in our conversations held warmth and comfort, the ease new lovers have when they're content just to be with each other. We didn't need words at the beginning. Or was that just a Hallmark notion we bought as willingly as we did their cards? Maybe that myth helped people ignore they had nothing in common, and therefore nothing of significance to say to each other? Romantics find it easier to believe love fills the spaces between syllables.

I cleared my throat. "Are you back at work?"

"Yeah. Mr. Kaufman has been great. Says his brother went through this . . . uh . . . recovery thing, too. He's been real nice about the time I took off, and I don't think he told anyone at work why I was gone. Tim Gavin, you know, from accounting? He asked how I was feeling yesterday. I think he meant physically, so I guess he believes I was gone for some kinda medical thing."

"Well, in a sense you were. I think it's fine if that's what people think, don't you?"

"Yeah, I guess. I don't want them asking me blunt questions about being on the wagon and stuff, so . . . yeah, I guess it's good." He shifted the conversation: "How are you feeling? Any morning sickness or anything?"

"No, just a little gaggy when I smell certain things, like meat cooking and popcorn, of all things. You know I love popcorn. Weird, huh?" I chuckled, remembering having to run to the bathroom the previous night while my mom made a meatloaf. I didn't get sick, but I looked like an actress in a bad sitcom. My parents had teased me about it all night.

This must have stirred the reason for his call because the next thing Eric said was, "I should be with you now, Kat. I want to be there when things like that happen."

"Eric, don't. I—"

"Why? Why shouldn't I say that? I miss my wife. Is it such a terrible thing to say?"

I hated when he referred to me as a possession, in the third person, but that's not what I was protesting. "No, it's not a terrible thing to say. It's just . . . I can't do this yet. I can't think about us right now."

"How can you *not* think about us? You're pregnant with our child. How much more *us* could there be? Are you thinking about me at all or are you trying to forget me?" I knew he wasn't trying to take on a tone, but he was. His voice seemed a few notes higher than usual as emotion squeezed between his words.

"Please stop. This isn't about you right now, or us. It's about me and how much you hurt me. I have a right to be hurt, and I have a right to be mad. Most of all, I have a right to be confused. I need some distance from our life there. Please. If you love me, give me this time. Let me work through my feelings."

I wasn't even close to tears. I was calm. I sounded confident, but not antagonistic. It seemed to settle Eric a bit. His next question was almost a whisper.

"But . . . what if you decide not to come back?" And there it was. The question I had been struggling with for weeks. The question for which I still had no answer.

"Eric," I spoke his name with a tenderness I used to feel without effort. "One day at a time. Isn't that what you're doing now?"

"Yeah."

"Then let me have that, too. I don't know about tomorrow yet or next month or next year. I don't want to think about more than waking up tomorrow morning and deciding between scrambled eggs and pancakes. That's all. One day at a time for you, and one day at a time for me. That's fair, right?"

"Okay," he conceded. "I'm not happy about it, but okay. Can I still call you?"

"Of course. I want to know what you're doing—and how you're doing."

A long pause. I tried to think of a way to hang up without guilt or coldness.

"Have you been thinking of names?" he asked, creating another sudden turn in our dialogue.

"Sure. You?"

"Yeah. But maybe now's not the time, huh?"

"Probably not. Soon, though."

"Okay. Sorry to call so late. I'll try to remember to *add* the two hours next time. Bye." Then he hung up before I could say goodnight.

He didn't sound angry or annoyed, maybe resigned, as if trying on this new role pinched him around the waist like jeans a size too small. I hadn't been calling the shots in our relationship since we moved in together. Even though I probably looked like the leader in our marriage from the outside, much of my behavior was in *reaction* to his. He acted; I responded.

Setting the pace of our partnership was a new feeling for me, too. But unlike feeling confined and uncomfortable, my new role felt like a flowing summer dress: I was swimming in its freedom, and I could move miles without getting twisted in its material.

•　　•　　•　　•　　•

"So, you never got over me, right? That's why you haven't gotten married." I said this with just enough tease to expose the right amount of my ego. He burst out laughing, as I tucked a swath of hair behind my right ear—a nervous habit that reminded me of my teen years.

"No. *That's* why I never got married: No one's made me laugh like you do," Drew said, peeking at me over the rim of his wineglass.

We were having dinner a few nights before New Year's Eve. There were only a few other tables occupied, most couples waiting for the actual holiday to indulge in an expensive dinner.

"Aaaah, so it *does* have to do with me in some way, see?" It felt good to laugh and even to be laughed at. And the flirting wasn't so bad, either.

"You know, it's been ten years, but I swear you look just the same. Your chestnut hair still has that tinge of auburn in it. You don't color it, do you?"

I laughed. "No, I don't. No gray hairs yet, but thanks for the compliment."

I'd finally decided to wear my wedding ring, after an hour of internal debate. As I was getting ready for this meeting (shouldn't call it a date), blow-drying my hair, the diamond caught my eye in the mirror. Its sparkle poked at me like a pitchfork, daring me to disregard it. It won. Despite my intrigue at seeing my old flame again, I was still a married woman, and I wasn't the kind to lie about it.

As I spread soft butter on a piece of warm bread, the conversation turned serious. Drew asked the $64,000 question: "Why are you in New York without your husband?"

"God, it's too bad I'm not drinking tonight because I could use a gin and tonic right about now," I said, reaching for my ice water. "Okay, here goes." I took a deep breath, but nothing came out. I refocused my thoughts . . . still nothing. "Hmmm," I offered, "I guess this is going to be harder than I thought."

"What is it, Kat? Are you all right?" Drew put down his wine and reached for my hand across the table. The lights in the restaurant were dim, encouraging romance, but all I could think was *Thank God he can't see my cheeks turning red.* His fingers closed around my hand, and I felt a tingling between my legs. I squirmed and changed positions. As I shifted, my hand pulled away from his. He misinterpreted my withdrawal.

"God, I'm sorry, Kat. I—I didn't mean. Jeez. You just looked, I dunno, choked up or something, and I thought . . . damn. I'm sorry."

The way he stumbled through his concern and embarrassment was adorable.

"No," I said. "It's my fault. I want to tell you, but I haven't said any of this out loud yet to anyone besides my parents, and the words wouldn't come together. Let me try again."

I took another breath and looked away from him this time. "I recently found out my husband is an alcoholic. I mean, I'd suspected for a while, but he kept lying to me about it, and I believed him. I found out for sure about three weeks ago when he checked himself into the recovery unit at our hospital."

I braved looking at him. His brows furrowed as he absorbed my words, waiting for more.

"I . . . I couldn't handle it and I left. Not for good. Well, I don't think it's for good. I don't know. I can't sort it all out yet. I'm a mess of mixed emotions, and I needed some distance from it—from him. So, I got in my car and kept driving. Real adult, right? First sign of trouble in my marriage, and I'm back on Mommy and Daddy's doorstep."

"That's understandable. I can't imagine what I'd do in the same situation."

"Well, I'm still not sure I've done the right thing, but it's what I needed to do for now, if that makes any sense at all?" I looked down and studied my fork with an interest it didn't deserve.

"I think so. Look, Kat, if you're worrying about this, here, us having dinner—"

"No. That's not part of it."

"Because we're just two old friends catching up, right? You didn't set out to find me ... did you?" His eyebrows rounded up over his melted-chocolate brown eyes with a silly hopefulness that defied his attempt at maturity.

I giggled like he'd expected me to, and said, "No, of course I didn't. Running into you was the last thing I planned. But is it wrong for me to say I'm glad it happened?"

"*Hell* no," he said, flashing me his best imitation of a Tom Cruise smile. "I'm glad it happened, too. But I really am sorry you're going through this. What are you going to do?"

This time, my spoon grabbed my attention. I picked it up to have something in my hands. "I'm embarrassed to say I don't know. My folks said I could stay here as long as I need while I think things through. I don't want to tell you all the gory details, but he hurt me," I said. The rawness of Eric's offences stung. "I trusted him with every part of me, and he lied right to my face. I don't even know for how long. What if our whole life together has been one big lie? I feel so stupid that I didn't see it."

"People get fooled sometimes when they love deeply. But how else *should* you love?"

"Aren't the people you love—the ones who are supposed to love you back—aren't they supposed to be honest with you? Don't they care they're making a fool of you by lying and letting you believe in them?" I was getting too philosophical—and too personal. For the first time, I felt like I was betraying Eric.

"You know, I've never been married, so I can't really answer that. The couple times I've been in love, I tried to be as honest as I could, but we're human, Kat. People fuck up sometimes. The other part of love is forgiving, isn't it?"

I couldn't believe what I was hearing. I hadn't thought about my situation that way at all. Drew was right. I was entitled to feel hurt and angry, but in the end, I was going to have to move past those feelings if I loved Eric. Forgiving him would be my first hurdle; forgiving myself would be the second.

"Wow. What do I owe you, Doc?" I asked, smiling at the realization that talking about everything out loud had helped.

"What kind of insurance do you have?" he joked back. "I'm glad I could help a little."

Drew picked up the silver napkin ring next to his plate. His turn to distract himself before speaking. "But don't go thinking I'm this great guy. I'm mad as hell this husband of yours has hurt you. And maybe a little jealous, too—though I have no right to be—but that's my deal." My cheeks heated again. I put my hands to each side of my mouth and smiled, shaking my head. "But most of all, I want you to be happy. Only you can make that happen. That's as much as I've learned so far in this life."

"That's a lot," I said. "I'm still learning that."

·　　·　　·　　·　　·

When memories of youth collide with present intellect and circumstance, a person can feel misplaced. Like a scene from *The Twilight Zone*, where a character walks down a familiar road but ends up in an unknown place.

I was sleeping in the same room I'd spent my adolescence in, but woke each day with the woman's body I had grown into in the decade since. The twenty-eight-year-old Kat pushed against the teenage version of me as I scanned my closet for "the right outfit."

Applying makeup the next afternoon for my second meeting with Drew, I looked at myself with an objective eye. I wasn't simply examining the features and the image before me; I was scrutinizing the *person* I was behind the mascara and eyeliner.

What the hell am I doing? Was I the kind of person who could cheat on her husband? Is that what I intended as I fixed myself up for what could only be called a date? Eric had hurt me, shaken me to the core. Was I using that as an excuse to act out now, to seek revenge for his selfish actions? Or did I truly feel something genuine for Drew? Had seeing him kicked up the dust around my complacent heart (and libido)? If so, was it *he* I yearned for or any man's attention? All these realizations were possible, and most of them were not flattering.

The truth was, I'd felt unattractive for a long time. Eric hadn't been interested in intimacy much over the past year. I didn't understand back then how his drinking had replaced me: The best part of his day was spending time with his liquid mistress, and much of his energy went to hiding the affair. This was all below the surface, of course. I sensed it, but couldn't see what was happening. All I knew was, we were out of sync.

I could draw a picture from memory of the way the streetlight cast shadows on our bedroom walls at midnight. Countless nights I'd lain in bed, wide awake while he snored a soundtrack to his own oblivion. My thoughts often centered on my body: My butt's too big. My hair isn't bouncy enough. Tummy isn't flat. Breasts aren't firm enough. As if any one of these things, if transformed, would arouse my husband's interest again.

He said he loved me, and when we did make love, he was "present," but I didn't feel his affection or attraction to me outside those moments of entanglement. Mostly, I felt interchangeable, as if any woman in my place, in that bed, would receive the same consideration. It wasn't me, Kat, who satisfied him; it was the act. He said he loved me, but I didn't feel loved, and my self-esteem sank.

In front of the mirror, more in tune with my body than ever before, I let my robe fall open. Looking at myself without prejudice was hard—a task many women find impossible. But what I saw was . . . well, lovely. My skin was smooth, my body soft: the swell of my abdomen, not yet revealing the baby inside; the roundness of my breasts and how the skin *gives* to allow their movement, their pride; and the swooping concave arcs under my ribs bowing inward toward my belly and then out again to encompass my hips. There are so many curves, a lover would want to run his hands along them, wouldn't he? And the supple flesh that yields when squeezed . . . is that what we call fat? Why do we do that to ourselves?

A knock at the door broke me from my sensuous trance. "Yes?" I pulled the robe back around me and tied it closed.

"Andrew's here, honey."

"Okay, Mom." I'd lost track of time. "I'll be out in a few minutes. Do you mind sitting with him?"

"Happy to. It's been a long time. I'll get caught up on his family."

"Thank you!"

I hadn't considered how odd it might seem to my parents that I was "going out with" Drew—for the second time now. So far, they'd said nothing to indicate they didn't approve, but I wondered . . .

As I pulled on my jeans and sweater, I admitted I was going on a date. I would allow myself to enjoy the glow of an admirer's attention. Nothing had to *happen*, of course; I was a grown woman with restraint and values. But I could let myself feel sexy and desirable in a safe way, with a friend I trusted. I was entitled to feel like more than someone's obligation.

I fluffed my hair one more time and applied some lip gloss. As I glanced at my reflection one last time in the mirror, I saw a confidence looking back that I hadn't seen in far too long. And the woman smiled.

•   •   •   •   •

The ceilings were the best part. Everywhere I looked there were nooks and shelves and flashes of light coming in from places unseen.

The angles were dramatic, yet practical, and I could envision baskets and plants or unique objets d'art gracing the alcoves. With good taste and a fat wallet, a person could make this room scream *I am comfortable!*

As Drew toured me through his latest almost-finished project, I tried to picture living within its walls. The house was 4,200 square feet: five bedrooms, two living areas, a loft/office, four bathrooms, and a gorgeous wrap-around porch I would have paid a fortune for, even without the house attached to it. The colors were earthy; various shades of browns and beiges covered the floors and walls. Although the windows were uncovered, they begged for swooping patches of green fabric that would make its inhabitants think of woodsy forests. I knew someday a leather couch would sit facing the stone fireplace in the corner, and I envied the future owners the luxury of the peaceful evenings that would unfold there.

The house was beautiful and beautifully made, though I teased Drew about the garage entrance not coming directly into the kitchen. I explained that the person carrying heavy bags of groceries would have to navigate a beautifully tiled, but too-long passageway, around a corner and past the mudroom, before unloading *her* arms. Hint, Hint. Designed by a man for form but not function. Drew said I should become an architect and then we could go into business together, designing and building perfect houses for today's working families. "If you can devise toilet paper holders that automatically refill, then we'll talk," I said with a tease.

"Speaking of making life easier for people!" He said this as he grabbed my hand. "I've got to show you the closet in the main bedroom." He pulled me behind him like a little kid leading his parents through his kindergarten classroom on Back-to-School night.

We draped our coats on the kitchen counter and headed up the winding staircase.

Sure enough, the closet was phenomenal. Larger than the bedroom I grew up in, it held floor-to-ceiling cedar shelving, most of which was electric. With the push of a button, shelves from up high magically moved down, while the lower ones disappeared behind them and out of reach. Dresses and suits would eventually hang from the large oval rack in the center of the room, like the conveyor systems used in professional dry cleaners' stores. There was no way one couple could own as many pairs of shoes as the closet could hold.

Another lavish amenity beyond my comprehension: The well-to-do couple who would someday live in this house of convenience would be able to do their laundry right in the privacy of their own suite! A full-size washer and dryer stood at attention on one side of the closet, waiting to be useful, with a sink and built-in ironing table next to them. I couldn't imagine doing laundry without having to lug a hamper up and down stairs.

I must have looked astounded, because Drew came up beside me and waved his hand in front of my face. "Hellooooo?" he said, trying to get my eyes to blink.

"Wow," was all I could muster. "This is amazing, Drew. You and your dad have done a remarkable job here. Are all your houses like this?"

"First, I wish they were my houses. I only built it; I didn't design it. Don't give me too much credit. But this is one of the best."

I walked around the perimeter of the closet that was a room, touching the shelves and inhaling their earthy smell. "Still," I said, "your craftsmanship shows in every aspect. It's something to be proud of."

And then he was there. I *felt* him behind me before my ears confirmed it and before I saw his profile as I turned my head in his direction.

He didn't touch me; he just stood there close. I knew he was trying to smell my hair. He whispered, "I wish I could build you a house like this." I knew I should say something to stop what was coming. I knew I was supposed to protest. He had no right to want to do that for me; I was another man's wife. But I liked it too much. I liked the idea of a man wanting to take care of me, to give me something unique, made of his own hands, a structure to protect me from wind and snow and summer's heat. A home: a place to raise a family on a foundation of love, as well as solid hardwood floors. In one fantasy statement, Drew had summed up what was missing in my marriage.

I didn't say a word. I let his fingers rest on my shoulders. I closed my eyes, waiting for whatever contact would come next. He raised his hands up and lifted my hair off my shoulders; a shiver ripped through me. In one easy movement, he stepped closer putting his lips on the back of my neck. I leaned my head back and turned sideways so my throat would be the next recipient of his kiss. Then, I turned to face him so my mouth would know the same thrill.

Like the first time he kissed me eleven years before, my knees buckled, but it didn't matter. He wrapped his arms around my waist, holding me up, and I relaxed into his strength. His whole body kissed me, not just his lips. He pushed against my thigh. His right leg wrangled its way around the back of my left ankle, completing what must have looked like a vertical pretzel, our bodies entwined.

He kissed me until I could barely breathe. I was floating, hanging suspended between realities: one in my head and one that was my real life. Then, I heard a single word from somewhere far away seeping into the furry fringes of my awareness: "Oh, baby. I've missed you," he said, but all I heard was "baby."

"Aaah-oow!" The sound that escaped me was a cross between a cry and an "ouch," as if a pound of sugar had landed on my toe, hurting like hell and catching me off guard. I pushed him away with a force that shocked us both, but I held onto his elbows. We stood two feet apart, staring at each other for a long, awkward moment. His handsome face was a question mark, and I knew my features were showing a disgust and horror coming from deep within me. I had to swallow hard to keep from throwing up.

"What's wrong? What happened?" he asked, moving a fraction closer.

"I . . . uh. God . . ."

"What? *What?!* You're pale as a sheet. Come on, sit down." He moved me out of the closet, which was the right thing to do, as I was sure there was no more air in there.

"Drew . . . I can't. But . . ." It was useless. My words made no sense without air behind them.

When we got into the bedroom, he lowered me to the floor. I felt insanely stupid, but since I wasn't certain I was safe from passing out, I let him help me to the sand-colored carpet. It was so soft; I imagined ten pads underneath. The color made me think of the beach, so I closed my eyes to listened for the ocean.

Drew said nothing. He sat beside me and held my hand. I concentrated on breathing and making the tingles stop along my scalp.

When I was sure I could talk without fainting (or worse), a new terror seized me: How could I look him in the eye and tell him what a horrible person I was? My eyes blurred with tears. He must have thought I'd cracked, but he was more patient than a priest supervising his hundredth communion.

Finally, I faced him. I turned so we were looking at each other, sitting cross-legged in the middle of the sprawling suite. "I'm so sorry. For what happened in there," I said, nodding my head toward the closet, "and for this crazy dizzy spell or whatever the hell it is."

"You sure did look sick. Am I that bad a kisser?"

"God, of course not. I loved it. That's the problem."

"What do you mean? What's going on?"

"Being with you these past few days has been amazing. I feel like I've been transported back in time and allowed to relive the passion and purity of my teens, but with the wisdom I've acquired over the years."

"I know what you mean," he said, smiling, but guarded.

"But it's also been confusing. I like being with you, and I'm definitely attracted to you. I think you know that."

"Well, *that's* certainly mutual." We shared a smile. "But I feel a 'but' coming," he said.

I nodded and squeezed his hands. "But I'm still married. I know it's easy to forget that when he's two thousand miles away, and you can't even picture him. It's not your job to remember him; it's mine. And honestly, I've been doing a shitty job of it. I haven't *wanted* to think of him. I've been happy just thinking of myself—something I rarely do."

He sat still, like a defendant waiting for the jury's verdict. "There's something else. God, I'm so embarrassed. I'm pregnant, Drew. I'm sorry I didn't tell you before. I wasn't sure what was happening between us, or if I'd see you again after that first time in the bakery. Then, I couldn't find a way to fit it into conversation. I know that's a terrible excuse, but . . .

"When we started kissing, I had a physical reaction, as if someone punched me in the stomach. It was like my body was saying, *Uh, what the hell do you think you're doing? You're pregnant, you idiot. You can't sleep with another man.* That's why I pushed you away. If I hadn't had that reaction, I would have gone too far. I know it."

I couldn't ramble anymore. I sounded ridiculous, so I waited for his rebuke.

After a proper pause, he asked, "Are you excited about having a baby?" Not the response I was expecting.

"Yes. I mean, my life is all messed up right now, and I don't know what I'm doing half the time. My marriage is in the toilet, and I'm on the verge of having an affair with my high school sweetheart, but yes, I'm happy about the baby," I said in a tumble of honesty.

He smiled and moved to sit next to me. He put his arm around me, and I rested my head on his shoulder. We were moving into "friend" mode, leaving "passionate lover" behind us for now.

"That's all that matters. I'm bummed about the timing, of course, but that's my problem. Right now, you have to figure out what's best for you and your baby. It's why you left Colorado, isn't it?"

I nodded. "Everywhere I looked in our house, there were memories I started to question. I'm not sure I can raise a child with this man. I don't know how to trust him anymore."

Drew stayed quiet, urging me to say more.

"I can't decide what shoes to wear these days; how am I supposed to decide about the future of my marriage? Also, how am I supposed to be near you—and keep you at arm's length —while I make that decision? Sorry, that sounded like I'd be keeping you as a pet; I didn't mean it that way," I said, shaking my head. Shame made it impossible to say the right thing.

"Stop being so hard on yourself. You're going through a tricky time, and from what I remember when my sister-in-law was pregnant, you're the victim of wild hormones taking over your body, as well. It wasn't pretty." He nudged me and tossed me his famous sideways grin.

"All of that may be true, but *you're* the cause of some of those hormonal surges, too. Between you and my body, I don't stand a chance!"

"Guilty as charged, and happy about it," he teased. "But we're not kids anymore, Kat. I'm not trying to get in your pants. Well, I mean, that *is* a goal, too, but what I'm saying is . . . what?"

My laugh stopped him. His honesty—and the sexiness of it—made me giddy, despite the seriousness of the conversation. "Go on. I'm curious where this is going."

"What I mean is, yes, I'm interested in what a relationship with you would be like now. Part of it would be rediscovering that kind of intimacy, but I'm an adult now. I can wait. Maybe there'll be a time for us to explore that down the road, but this isn't it. I care about you more than just for now. Does that make sense?"

"It makes perfect sense. Very mature sense. Is it weird you're the best friend I have right now, and I haven't seen you in over a decade? I could use that kind of honest guidance, but I'm afraid to be this close to you right now. I'm vulnerable."

"Well, then, as your friend, I'm going to make this easier for you." He stood and leaned down to pull me up with both hands. Once I was vertical, he reached toward me and held my face between his hands. "I am not going to be the reason your marriage ends. If that's what happens, it has to be because of what's already going on between you guys. I also don't want to be a convenient distraction for you. God," he said, looking up at the coffered ceiling, "that's hard to say, because I'd *love* to be a convenient distraction for you!" We both laughed, and then he leaned close to me. His lips bypassed mine, and the kiss landed on my left cheek instead.

"I feel a 'but' coming," I said, parroting him from before.

"But, I'm going to bring you home now, and I won't call you for a while. I can't be the kind of friend you have coffee with and bitch about your husband to. You can't tell me intimate things about him and expect me to be objective, because my only response would be, 'Dump his ass and move in with me.'" He grinned like a greedy frat boy.

I smiled and said, "Fair enough. I know you're right. I have to get through this on my own."

"You know where to find me. I'm not going anywhere. I love New York." And with the confidence of a man following his conscience, he winked at me and led me out of the gorgeous bedroom suite he'd built for a happy couple that was not us.

•   •   •   •   •

The drive back to my parents' house wasn't uncomfortable, just quiet. There wasn't much more to say after we'd made our peace with the situation. Drew turned the radio up a shade too loud so we couldn't have talked easily if we'd wanted to. Instead, I hummed to the familiar tunes on the "oldies" station, dismayed they were songs I'd listened to on my mom's record albums when I was a kid.

When we pulled into the driveway, Drew said, "I hate to ask this, but can I come in and use the bathroom?"

"Sure. You even have your choice of two," I said, just to say something.

When I reached the top of the stairs, I was lucky to be holding the railing because seeing Eric sitting on my mother's prized white velvet couch caused me to stumble on the last step. The pause in my stride also made Drew bump into me from behind. I couldn't help but think *my past is literally colliding with my present.*

Awkward took center stage, and although my mouth was dry as dirt, I somehow got through an initial, "Oh, my God, Eric. What are you doing here?" and "This is my friend Andrew; we went to high school together. Ran into him at the bakery a few days ago."

The two men regarded each other with suspicious eyes, but Eric stood and the guys shook hands to be correct and polite. Then nothing. No one knew what else to say or do, and we stood there like three sides of a triangle that didn't quite connect at the intersections. I hadn't rushed over to kiss Eric when I saw him, and like a naughty child who knew a lecture was coming "after the guests left," I looked down at the carpet.

My mother broke the stalemate by inviting everyone to sit down. Drew excused himself to use the bathroom. Mom silently escaped into the kitchen to start dinner. She probably knew a "scene" was about to unfold, so she left Eric and me space. I imagined she would also fill my dad in on what was happening in his living room.

I plopped on the blue straight-back chair, leaving Eric no possibility of sitting next to me. But he didn't sit at all. Before Drew was even all the way down the hall, Eric started.

"What the hell is going on here? Were you out on some kind of *date*?" He spat the word out like it was a piece of fatty meat he'd been chewing on too long. He paced the floor, making me think of the expectant father he was, but in this context, it was not a joyous thing.

"I told you, I ran into Drew a few days ago. He's an old friend. We were just catching up." But no matter how accurate my explanation was, I was holding back part of the truth. I didn't want the conversation to go on that way because I knew I'd sound defensive. I pushed the dialogue in a new direction, a trick Eric himself had perfected—one I now tried on for size.

"Eric, why did you come here?" I wished Drew could sneak out a back door; I was dreading his coming through the living room again.

"Why do you think? I came here to bring you home with me," he said as if speaking about a wayward animal that had run away and gotten lost.

"But I told you I wasn't ready to go home yet. I need more time to sort things out."

"Yeah, and more time to consider jumping into bed with an old boyfriend—if you haven't already." His words conveyed a superiority he didn't have any right to.

"Eric, stop it," I said and stood to stand my ground. "We won't get anywhere if this conversation dissolves into those kinds of accusations."

"How am I supposed to react to this, Kat? I spent all day on two airplanes and another two hours on an airport shuttle to get here. I'm tired, and now I'm pissed off. I didn't expect you to be out on the town when I finally arrived."

"Well, *I* didn't expect *you* at all," I snapped.

"I thought it might be a nice surprise," he said slowly. He sat down on the couch, containing himself physically, as if that would help him contain his anger verbally.

"All you thought about was yourself. You wanted to play the rescuing husband. You wanted to make this—no, to *keep* this—all about you. If you waltz in here and *save* me," I made quotes with my fingers in the air, "then you get to look like the hero in this twisted soap opera. But I don't want to be rescued. I want to come home on my own when I'm ready. If I'm ever ready."

"So, what, now you're *never* coming home? Is that what you're saying?" he asked, overlooking everything else I'd said and only focusing on the part he had no control over.

"I don't know anything yet. If, when, why, or how. I don't know." I sat back down and leaned forward, elbows on my knees, to address him straight on. "This is not your decision to make alone, and you can't force me to pretend this mess isn't a mess. I'm not okay with going back to our pretty little world of denial. I know too much now, Eric. You can't expect me to forget I don't."

"But I'm doing everything I can to make things right," he said with a hint of self-pity, wondering why his attempts weren't working to win me over.

"And that's great. That's what *has* to happen. But you can't rush me. I told you on the phone: You're taking this one day at a time, and so will I. We're each dealing with different stuff, and I'm not sure we can do this together." He looked at me with a combination of sadness and acceptance, though it couldn't have been what he wanted to hear.

"You can't understand how this is affecting me," I continued, "because you're looking at it only from your perspective. Maybe the same is true the other way around, too? All I know is, I'm not ready to move into the next chapter without first understanding the last one."

I knew I was talking circles around him, but this was the first time we'd had to talk since That Day. As the words tumbled out, it felt good to confront him. Maybe I needed this step to help me *get* ready to go home?

Eric and I both stood when Drew came back in the room. I wanted to walk him to the door, to step outside and kiss him, have him hold me close one more time, but that wasn't possible. He took care of it for me.

"Kat, it was really good to see you again after all this time." He walked toward me with the self-assurance of a man who's done nothing wrong and kissed me on the cheek, as any old friend would do, male or female. Then, he held out his hand to shake Eric's again, saying to both of us, "I hope everything works out for the two of you and your baby."

As he turned to walk away, he winked at me, then went down the stairs. Eric and I stayed in our spots, waiting for the front door to close, as if that were our cue to move.

Eric sat first, and I followed, thinking how gracious Drew had been. Letting Eric know he knew about the baby was the perfect thing to say. It was subtle, yet important. Eric knew I wouldn't tell an old boyfriend I was pregnant and then try to have an affair. Maybe some women could do that, but he knew me well enough to know I couldn't.

I said a silent "thank you" to Drew in my mind. As I heard his car pull out of the driveway—making his literal and symbolic departure from my life—I knew I'd never see him again.

But what about Fate? I must have run into my first love again for a reason, especially at this divide in my life. Maybe glimpsing a possible escape from my heartache was enough to make me realize I wasn't ready to abandon everything I'd spent years building with Eric. It would be easy to find assurance in the arms of another man, but I had unfinished business at home.

I turned to my husband, who was leaning back against the plump cushion behind him, resting his head and wrestling with the turn of events he hadn't predicted. I decided right then I was not the kind of person who would choose the easy way out. If my marriage failed in the long run, it wouldn't be because I didn't try everything in my power to make it work. Having an affair would not be evidence of that. Enough fantasizing. My real life was waiting, and the man I needed to join forces with was reeling from a sucker punch.

"Feeling a little blindsided?" I asked in a more friendly tone.

"That obvious?"

"Yeah. Welcome to my world. I was blindsided a few weeks ago; I know how it feels."

He leaned forward to face me. "I'm so sorry, Kat. I'm sorry that I lied to you, and I'm sorry you found out the truth the way you did. I know you can't believe this right now, but I never meant to hurt you." He looked down at his hands before adding, "You were right before when you said I was only thinking of myself. Not just now, but when I was drinking, too. I wasn't able to think about how hiding things would affect you."

His self-awareness and admission of his mistakes surprised me. I didn't know if I should respond or wait, but he took a breath and went on.

"I hate that you think you can't trust me, but I know I brought it on myself. I also know you have a right to be angry at me and need time to get over it. I'm sorry I tried to push you. I'm just scared you won't give me a second chance, and I need one. I need to prove to you I won't fuck up anymore." We stared at each other across the living room.

He kept talking. "I love you, and I want this baby so much. He deserves more than a drunk for a father. That's why I went to the hospital. I wanted to change, and I knew I needed help. But more than anything, I need you to believe in me again."

These were magic words. They entered my head and my heart and started melting the cold crystals of confusion that had formed inside me over the last few weeks. He was fixing everything with easy sentences, nouns and verbs placed in proper order to bring stability to the shaky walls surrounding me. But could I believe him? Could I trust those fragile words? They could always be misplaced, replaced, transformed again. They were not as formidable as the steel I'd started erecting around my spine.

"Eric, you're saying everything I want to hear, but that scares me, too. I want to believe you, more than you know. I want to come home and work together to make our family strong for our baby. He or she deserves no less from us. But I'm terrified of being hurt like this again. What if it doesn't go as you say? What if you start hiding things from me again? I feel like such a fool that I didn't know what was going on right in front of me."

"That's not true," he said.

"What?"

"You knew. You knew in your gut something was wrong. You confronted me several times. *I* was the one who didn't acknowledge what was happening, and since I couldn't see it, I couldn't admit you were right. It's not so much that I lied to you; I was lying to myself, so your suspicions didn't make sense to me. I had no choice but to deny them."

Wow. Maybe he *had* been learning stuff at the hospital and at meetings. I certainly hadn't looked at it that way before. "But I still feel stupid—or at fault in some way. Why were you drinking like that? Are you unhappy or angry with me? Why did you need to escape?"

He got up and moved to the part of the couch closest to my chair, but he didn't touch me, and I was grateful. I wasn't ready. Not yet.

"I'm still trying to figure that out. That's why the meetings are helpful. Every time I go there, I learn something new about myself or this disease. And I do believe it's a disease. I'm allergic to alcohol, and yet I crave it. Even though I know the damage it does to me. It's a terrible sickness—doing something you know will harm you and not being able to stop yourself from doing it."

"That doesn't answer my question," I stated, letting him know I needed a better answer.

"No. It doesn't. What I *think* I'm learning in this program is that there is no answer—at least not only one. No, I'm not angry at you. And no, I'm definitely not unhappy with you." He flashed me his sweetest self-effacing grin and added, "Sorry about the double negative. I *am* very happy with you.

"I've learned alcoholics drink because they're alcoholics. That's it. The problem is, we start *creating* reasons to justify drinking. That makes it easier to excuse our weakness. You know, *My boss is a jerk, so I need a drink,* or *I wish I could afford a bigger house for my growing family, but I can't, so I might as well drown my sorrows.* Or whatever. It doesn't mean those are the *reasons* a person drinks; those are just the reasons he gives."

I couldn't believe what I was hearing. Eric sounded like a professor. He must have been ready to hear those messages and to try to make sense of his life. For the first time since I left Colorado, I was proud of him.

"Look, I'm impressed with what you're saying; it sounds like you're taking this seriously and working hard. I'm asking you to be a little more patient with me. Talking like this has helped. I'd like to keep doing it, if you will."

"Yeah. It helps me, too. One thing I need to focus on is communicating with you more. I get in trouble when I stay inside my own thinking. I need you to give me perspective."

"But I've always been here for you to talk to. You just haven't," I said, wounded that he hadn't noticed.

"I know. I didn't mean it that way. When you come home, *when*," he emphasized this for effect, "I hope you'll give me another chance with that. Remind me how I need to keep you in the loop. I know we need to be a team—in this and everything—especially with the baby coming."

"Okay, Eric." I stood and looked down the hall. "I'm tired now. I think I'll lie down before dinner. I bet you're tired, too; it's been an emotional day and you've been traveling. I saw your suitcase by the kitchen. I assume you've asked my folks if you can stay here?"

"They said I could."

"That's fine. I'm staying in my old room," I said, as I turned to face him. "You can have the guest room in back." I waited for him to protest, but he nodded his agreement.

"It's good to see you." He moved closer. Although I worried he would try to kiss me, I stayed put. "It's good to be in the same house with you. Hell, the same state!" His smile relaxed me a bit, and I let him take my hands in his. "I know you're scared and unsure, but everything's going to work out. We're going to be okay. I know it. You'll know it soon, too."

He squeezed my hands before letting them go.

That night, for the first time since I was forced to break free from the blanket of my denial, I had a dream I remembered when I woke. Eric and I were walking around the lake by our house, as we often did when we were dating. This time, I was pushing a stroller, but we weren't walking together. I felt overwhelmed by loneliness, the six feet between us represented an emotional chasm I couldn't bridge.

The majestic Rocky Mountains stood solid in front of us, and I wondered how we would ever climb them. *Maybe we can't,* I thought before opening my eyes, *but we have to try.*

But what if I hadn't run away?

Revelation
December 1992

* Fork 2 *

Chapter One: Growth

Eric was admitted to the rehab hospital that night, but they let us go home for an hour to pack some clothes for his two-week stay. As we drove home in silence, I knew that everything in our lives had changed during one conversation with a nurse carrying a clipboard. I didn't know what to say to him. "Nice of you to be stealing money from our nest egg, hiding bottles around our house, and getting shit-faced while I went off to work every day, thinking you were doing the same. And thanks for telling a total stranger, not me, that all my suspicions about your drinking were true."

No, there was nothing to say, so we went through the motions, quietly.

After I drove him back to the hospital, I spent my first night since our wedding alone. I sat at our kitchen table with a cup of scalding tea, staring into space, listening to silence envelope our house.

My mind wandered in circles as I relived key moments in our marriage. I saw for the first time the reality that existed right below the surface. Which of the thousands of sentences he'd spoken to me over the years had been lies? Which days had he come home drunk, taken a lengthy shower, put on cologne, and brushed his teeth an extra-long time so I wouldn't smell the truth? How many nights had he rolled away from me in bed, mumbling something about a stomachache when he was really suffering from self-induced nausea, alcohol mixed with Scope?

Hospital policy didn't allow patients phone calls during the first week, and although I'd thought that a little harsh, prison-like, I was now glad for the respite. I needed a few days.

At 10:00 p.m., I left a voice message for my boss. I knew she wouldn't get it until the next morning, but I told her I'd be taking the day off. Fridays were normally slow at our magazine's office, but two weeks before Christmas, you'd think the entire staff was shopping en masse at Macy's. They wouldn't miss me.

Around midnight I snuggled into bed. The darkness felt like an empty movie theater as I made myself think about things I'd spent the last few years avoiding or rationalizing. The slide show of my marriage played across the blank walls of my imagination, and I recalculated my new true north.

•   •   •   •   •

The two-hour family workshop was titled, "How Family Members Can Support the Recovering Alcoholic at Home." The expectation that I would attend the meeting hung over me like a raincloud. But that wasn't causing my hesitation. The title bothered me. It held the assumption that Eric was the fragile one, and I was the strong one; I didn't need assistance.

The message implied that I was okay and knew what to do; I should transition into this new life with ease. But if anyone had asked me—which they didn't—I'd have said the reality of living with my husband under these new circumstances was more than nerve-racking.

We had a comfortable, predictable way of interacting that I'd just learned was based on dishonesty. I was supposed to trust him again, just because he (and his counselors) said I should? What if our marriage was a dance of avoidance? I considered our history: Eric often side-stepped important issues, and I reeled him back in. What healthy pattern would replace that now?

The class surprised me, though. It focused on the challenges we would face as a couple, but it also encouraged family members to look at themselves. Some in attendance weren't ready to hear that.

Caroline, the counselor leading the workshop, began by asking the group how we were each related to the alcoholic we were supporting. The label felt like a stigma we were attaching to our loved ones' chests—a true scarlet letter, also in the shape of an -A, but representing their addiction, not adultery.

There were spouses, parents, and children (sixteen and older) present, as well as one man who looked down at the notebook in his lap. He shared that his partner of seventeen years was in the program.

The woman to my right might have been thirty-five or fifty-five years old. She was wearing too much makeup for whatever age she was, so I couldn't venture a good guess. Foundation weighed down the skin around her eyes, and her mascara was thick and flaking. But she was "well-put-together," as my mother would have said: manicured nails, a tailored navy pantsuit, and hair the shade of blonde that only comes with the help of a high-end stylist.

"I'm Kimberly," she spoke into the pause that followed the introductions. "My husband Don is here, but I don't think he should be." Her back was straight against the wood behind her, with her feet crossed at the ankles and tucked under the chair. Her rigid form gave the impression that she felt *she* didn't belong there, either.

"Why do you say that?" asked Caroline, eager to engage in dialogue that would get the conversation going.

"Well, he's an attorney," she said, by way of explaining the whole thing away. "The partners in his law firm told him he needed to come here, but he's not an alcoholic. They were worried about 'an incident' which happened a few weeks ago." She emphasized *an incident* by leaning forward and lowering her voice. "What happened had no bearing on the case he was working, so we don't understand how it's any of their concern." Her objection stated for the court to consider.

Caroline asked her next question in an even voice and maintained eye contact with Kimberly: "Do you know if your husband had been drinking the day of the incident?"

"Well, it was after work hours, so . . ."

Caroline nodded. "Was this the first time Don's partners had confronted him about his drinking?"

Kimberly recrossed her ankles in the opposite direction and cleared her throat, though there was no frog present there. "No. But this has been humiliating for my husband."

"And for you?" The compassion in Caroline's voice nudged Kimberly a little closer to accepting her new reality.

The rest of us, sitting in a semicircle facing Caroline, watched the scene unfold as if it were playing out on a stage. I sat transfixed as this well-coiffed woman, wearing two handfuls of precious gems on her fingers, teared up.

"I'm so embarrassed," she confessed. "Everyone in our town knows what happened. I feel like people are whispering behind my back every time I'm in the bank or the grocery store."

Caroline walked to Kimberly and produced a few tissues out of thin air. Like a magic trick, Kleenex boxes appeared on every horizontal surface in the room; I hadn't noticed them before.

"Kimberly, thank you for sharing with us. Your story will be relatable to almost everyone here, and it's important to feel those feelings in a safe place. This is a safe place." She looked around the room. "That's what the Twelve-Step support groups are about."

Caroline moved to a whiteboard on the wall. She wrote AA and Al-Anon in a shade of pink so cheerful it countered the shell-shocked mood of the room.

Now she was the teacher, and we sat as reluctant, but needy, students. None of us wanted to be in that room. No one wanted to share what had brought us to that place, literally and metaphorically. But each of us talked eventually, asking questions and offering snippets of stories that held shame or confusion. Heads nodded understanding around the room. The other people in that circle knew what we felt. Their eyes held the same secret fears and disbelief. Their hearts were injured in similar ways.

I was one of them. By the end of the meeting, I knew I belonged there, and I was ready to learn whatever could keep me from being vulnerable and naïve again.

Caroline explained the basics of the programs to us: AA was the lifeline for alcoholics. Al-Anon was support for those of us *in relationship with* an alcoholic, not recovering from the disease itself. But our "disease" also had a name: codependency.

Like Kimberly, I shrunk from the label. A *disease*. Really? Wasn't I merely a good wife who helped her husband however she could? Eric had a problem, yes. I knew doctors considered alcoholism a disease, but me? They think I have one, too?

Caroline introduced us to some basic concepts, including the most common symptoms of codependency: 1) Enabling the alcoholic to continue drinking, even when that's the last thing we want. 2) Staying in denial, refusing to see there's a problem with alcohol to begin with. 3) Being enmeshed with another person to the point where "two become one." Hollywood romanticizes such intimacy, but in the real world, that level of connection is unhealthy—to both parties. My perspective focused on marriage, but even between parents and children, such tangled closeness stifles growth.

The lessons continued. We learned about coping mechanisms designed to foster the alcoholic's recovery, tools that allow family members to live *alongside* loved ones, not for them. Caroline talked about detaching from another person's behavior, setting boundaries, and staying healthy in unhealthy situations. We learned the foundational tenet of the Serenity Prayer: Focus on ourselves (what we can control), and not on the alcoholic (whom we cannot— and should not—try to control). It felt like a seismic shift.

The phrases and concepts were a new language. With so much to learn, I welcomed the structure of the program and the presence of other people who had lived through—and survived—similar battles.

•   •   •   •   •

I approached the next chapter in my life as I had everything else since high school: If I do the work, I'll earn high grades. I read every book and brochure I could get my hands on about alcoholism, codependency, Alcoholics Anonymous, enabling, denial, setting boundaries, the roots of addiction. I became well educated in the Twelve-Step approach to recovery, the middle child syndrome as it relates to possible substance abuse, and on and on. I went to open AA meetings from time to time; I attended my Al-Anon meetings regularly; I went to the family support group that supplemented Eric's outpatient program. I listened on those occasions when he shared with me, and I worked my own recovery, eager to break old patterns and establish healthier ones.

When I first moved to Colorado, my parents and I set a routine of talking on the phone every Sunday morning. It was as close to church as we got. The miles between us made it hard for them to feel part of my daily life, so I shared with them what I was learning. The calls served as distance education for them, and the sharing helped me process new concepts.

"I don't understand how you've done anything wrong," Mom said, verbalizing her stance as Defender of My Daughter.

"Well, first, it's not a matter of doing something wrong, per se. Think of it more like this: Everyone has tools in their toolbox, right? You go through life knowing when you need a hammer and when you need an instrument with more finesse, like a screwdriver."

My mother intoned a neutral "hmmmmm," indicating she was hearing me, but didn't quite know where my analogy was leading. I continued.

"So, Eric and I both have our own toolboxes. His contained alcohol. It helped him feel more confident, less self-conscious. Sometimes it helped reduce stress or avoid conflict. Now he knows he needs to replace that tool with healthier ones, like asking for help from his AA friends, reading literature, writing down his feelings instead of ignoring them. He can go for a walk instead of reaching for a bottle; he can talk to me rather than feeling burdened by pressures at work and running away from them."

"Okay. I'm following." My dad was a silent participant on the call. I could hear him breathing, but he hadn't chimed in yet.

"I have to replace old tools that no longer work for me, too. Mine are a little harder to see. I'm working on opening my eyes when my instinct is to close them against things that aren't perfect-looking. I also need to accept that Eric isn't a copy of me; he's his own person, and he doesn't do things like I do. I'm working on letting him be himself and not judging that he's not 'doing it right' just because it's not how I would do it."

Dad found his voice. "I understand what you're saying, but how do you change those patterns? They're learned behaviors you've leaned on for a long time."

"That's a great question. We are creatures of habit, for sure, but we're also able to learn what's good for us and not. We can choose. Mom, you quit smoking twenty years ago, right? How did you do it?" It was a question I'd never asked her before.

She chuckled at the memory. "I kinda tricked myself."

"What do you mean? How?"

"I just didn't have the next cigarette. I didn't tell myself I was quitting; that was too much to imagine. I merely delayed the cig I wanted and expected to have the *next* one. But you know what happened? The craving passed. I'd never allowed my body the opportunity to miss the nicotine before, so I didn't know the urge would dissipate."

"That's cool. You see, you *chose* not to have the next cigarette," I said. "How long did it take before you stopped wanting to smoke at all?"

"Are you kidding? I still want a cigarette today!" She laughed at her own imperfection.

"Oh." My voice deflated like a day-old helium balloon. Not the answer I wanted to hear.

"But . . . the more months, then years, that went by without having a cigarette, I stopped noticing how long it had been between them. It's not that I don't still crave them occasionally—more than I admit—but I know I can resist them now. There's a compounding power that comes from making healthy choices over and over."

"Yes! The choice. I hope Eric gets to that point."

"If he wants it bad enough, he will," my dad said with authority. As I considered that, he added, "So what's the second thing?"

"What do you mean?"

"Earlier, your mother said she didn't understand what you've done wrong, why you need to change. You said 'first,' and you talked about the toolboxes. What's second?"

"Jeez, Dad, you should have been a lawyer." I smiled at him across the country through the phone line. "I guess the second thing is now I see how my tools weren't helping any more than his use of alcohol was."

"Go on."

"The Serenity Prayer is a good example. Not a surprise to you guys, but I liked to be in control of things around me."

They chuckled in unison, filling my earpiece. "Yes, we're aware," Mom said.

"Well, that included Eric. But I can't control him, and I shouldn't want to. It's not my place. I can only control myself—what I do and how I respond."

"That's a lesson we eventually learn as parents, too," she added. "You'll see."

"I'm sure. Trying to control people and events around me is stupid. Clearly, if I'd been able to control things in my life, I wouldn't have ended up in Al-Anon. Eric wouldn't have been sneaking booze behind my back."

"That's a lot to learn and to change," Dad said. "How's it going?"

Humility is a hard friend to share a life with, but I'd vowed to be honest in the work I was doing, so . . .

"Admittedly, my progress isn't linear. Sometimes my resolve weakens. I've snooped around the garage looking for bottles, and I've driven by his work to see if his car's there when it should be. Sometimes I count the money in our vacation savings jar. I feel guilty every time I check up on him." The confession felt good, which surprised me. I went on.

"But the good news is, I've found no evidence to incriminate him, so my search efforts have slowed down. When I remember, I tell myself to get busy working on my own recovery and stop focusing on his. But the goal is 'progress, not perfection.' I guess that sums up how I'm doing."

•   •   •   •   •

I'd never been a religious person, so I struggled with the "God talk" of the Twelve-Step programs. In fits and starts, I developed an acceptance of something bigger than—and outside of—myself. I was tired of trying to have all the answers, then falling short. One night, someone in my group said, "All you have to accept about God is that *you're not him!*" That felt right, so I began trusting more pieces of the program, too. Eventually, my shoulders felt less tight, and I noticed I was smiling more often.

It takes time and consistent effort to undo patterns that took a lifetime to establish. I continued to "work my program," as they say, "one day at a time," as they say, and Gwen, my sponsor, guided me through some harsh wake-up moments. I began to understand my role in covering up Eric's drinking. At first, I felt insulted: *I* wasn't the one hiding, sneaking around, or lying, but I came to accept that my responses to Eric's behavior had been unhealthy. I had helped maintain the very denial I was cocooned inside.

One memory burned like a rash: *I'd popped home at 10:00 one morning, having left my packed lunch on the kitchen counter before work. Eric was asleep on the couch. I was concerned, of course.*

"Eric? Are you okay?" I nudged his shoulder to rouse him. It took a second bump before he opened his eyes.

"Huh? What . . . what are you doing here?"

I chuckled. "Well, I live here, for one. Second, I forgot my lunch. Just came home to grab it. Why are you here?"

"Stomachache. Headache."

"Oh, honey, I'm sorry. Let me help you into bed. You'll be more comfortable there."

He lifted his head off the throw pillow like it weighed a hundred pounds and angled himself to a seated position. As he stood, he swayed and almost fell. I grabbed his arm and put it around my shoulders. Walking toward our bedroom, his movements were so careful that "walking on thin, cracked ice" went through my mind.

"Have you called in to work yet?"

He nodded in my general direction, and I took that as a yes.

His breath was more than sleepy-sour; I chalked it up to sickness. Covering him with our comforter, I planted a kiss on his forehead. He was asleep again before I left the room.

As I returned to the kitchen to grab my lunch, I noticed a bottle of peppermint schnapps by the sink. I frowned at it, waiting for the bottle to explain itself. Since the schnapps didn't talk, I settled on "Eric must have had a cocktail last night after I'd gone to bed to read. He forgot to put the bottle away."

As I worked with Gwen, that morning stood out as an early example of a time when I saw the truth, knew on some level what was happening, but still explained it away, choosing to believe Eric's words over my own senses. A brilliant illustration of denial. I had allowed the ruse to continue unchecked, helping perpetuate the pattern. Once I turned the spotlight onto the shadows of my memories, I saw more instances where my role in our problems showed itself. The process was humbling and necessary.

Gwen expected me to call her every morning, and we discussed that day's writing in our daily reader, *Courage to Change*. It felt unnatural at first, academic, like I was studying to pass a driver's test. But she was a master at helping me see how those words applied to my everyday life. One of the hardest concepts for me to grapple with was enabling. I'd thought my desire to take care of Eric was a loving gesture; I wanted to be his partner and help him when I could. Instead, I learned that when I did things for him that he could (and should) do for himself, I robbed him of the opportunity to experience his own success. I'd never seen helping as potentially negative before.

I told Gwen about a specific incident from a year before that highlighted my flawed behavior. We were supposed to meet his brother for dinner, and Eric got home from work late.

"Hey, I put some clean clothes out on the bed," I said, as he walked in the door.

"I can wear this. It's my brother Bill, not Bill Clinton," he answered, trying for a laugh.

"Come on, Eric. We don't get to eat out very often. Let's make it a nice occasion."

"Well, if you want me to change, I should take a shower—and if I take a shower, we'll need to call him to say we're running late."

"Already done," I said with pride. I'd thought of everything.

I often took charge of orchestrating our lives, leaving him with little to do except follow my lead. I felt good about myself for being so competent; I never stopped to think I might be implying he wasn't. Despite my intent to be loving, my actions were harmful.

The sponsorship relationship was strange to me. Designed to be inherently one-sided, Gwen was my mentor, rather than a friend. She, the one with experience, guided me, the novice, into a more enlightened, healthy way of thinking and eventually acting. Through those early weeks, I learned Gwen's story, too. Knowing how she'd come through her journey gave her "Twelve-Step street cred," and I was determined to listen and learn from her. The grace and serenity she embodied was inspiring; I wanted to feel the confidence and joy she exuded.

When she was fourteen, Gwen's father caused a car accident in which her mother died. Until that night, no one in their family suspected alcohol was a problem; however, the investigation revealed both parents had been over the legal limit, and neither was wearing a seat belt. Gwen's mother was thrown through the passenger side window; the impact with the cement caused her immediate death. Her father broke several ribs as he smashed against the steering wheel, and his spleen was removed during emergency surgery. His left arm was badly scarred—the welts serving as a constant reminder of the accident, a permanent accusation in flesh and blood.

Gwen never learned why charges weren't brought against her father, but he put himself in his own kind of jail. In the months following the accident, the man became increasingly despondent. He found release in the amber sweetness of bourbon. He pulled away from Gwen and her younger sister and eventually stopped going to work at all. Before she could even drive, Gwen was responsible for cleaning the house, doing the family's laundry, cooking all meals, and taking care of her little sister.

Her father's depression was all-consuming; he barely noticed when his daughters went to live with their grandparents.

Over and over in my meetings, people shared stories of how growing up in homes where substances were used as freely as salt on fries had a significant impact on children's lives. How some survived was a wonder. Ironically, addiction is a family disease, and the patterns people learn as children often replay themselves in adulthood. Many children of alcoholics either struggle with the same addiction issues or marry them—and the cycle of dysfunction and pain envelopes the next generation.

I continued to learn about my role in our marriage's unhealthy balance, and Eric also learned more about his own disease. He'd only ever known how to hide his addiction. It would take time to learn how to keep it out in the open, allowing me in as an ally in his battle.

As he progressed with reading his books, talking to new friends, and attending AA meetings, I noticed a new feeling: I respected him. How had I been with this man for so long without that before? His efforts were noticeable, and I was grateful he was making them.

In late March, as we sat on the couch together, each reading our separate "homework," I broke the silence. I wanted to connect with him about what I was learning.

"So, I think this program is going to help me be a better mom."

Eric put his book down on his lap and looked over at me. "How so?"

"Well, I see now how uncomfortable I feel when I'm not in charge. That makes me try to control what I can—even when those things aren't mine to control, you know?"

"Yeah," he said with a knowing smile. "One of those things is me."

"I know," I admitted, turning my gaze away. I hadn't meant this to be a confession, but the opportunity presented itself. "And I'm sorry about that. I didn't see I was doing it before."

"I appreciate you saying that, but I played my part, too. I was okay with you taking the lead most of the time. It let me off the hook. It also made it easier for me to blame you when things didn't go perfectly. I'm not proud of that." His confession hit its mark in my stomach, but I welcomed the self-awareness. He shifted the conversation.

"So, how do you think this will help you as a mom?" he asked with interest.

"Well, I don't know much about babies, but from what I see, *they're* the ones in control." I chuckled, and he nodded in agreement. "I'll get practice at letting go of the small things when they're babies, right? Then, I'll pick my bigger battles later, like who she dates when she's sixteen, or if he does his algebra before basketball practice."

We both burst out laughing at the same time. The idea of looking that far down the road was hysterical. We also realized the hubris of thinking we'd have more control over our kids' dating choices than we would about them picking up their toys as toddlers. We hadn't even learned how to change diapers yet!

"Maybe we need to take parenting one day at a time, too," he said, applying the famous Twelve-Step motto to our child-rearing days ahead. "You're right, though. I think these programs will help us along the way."

"I've been meaning to ask you something. It's delicate, so . . . okay?" I watched his reaction. His raised eyebrows told me to go on. "I'm wondering if impending fatherhood is bringing up thoughts or feelings about your own dad?" I'd never met Richard. He died two years before I met his son, and Eric didn't talk about him much.

Eric nodded and let out a slow breath. "I've been thinking about that a lot lately. It's impossible not to." His fingers played with the worn edges of the AA book in his lap, tracing the cover like it held the answers he was searching for. Maybe it did.

"I've been pushing down feelings about my dad for a long time. But I wonder now about his choice to start his own business. He wasn't home much. Maybe that's expected to make a business successful. But at what cost? I mean, he barely knew Bill or me as individuals, and by the time Trisha came along years later, he seemed tired all the time. And then he was gone."

"You're specifically talking about how much time your dad spent with you kids versus time at work," I said, putting my new paraphrasing skills to work.

"Yeah. I know that's not the only thing that's important to being a dad, but it's what creates memories. When I think about my childhood, Dad was a flash of color, literally—covered in different paints. He flashed into the house, then flashed out again. No wonder he had a heart attack and died at sixty."

"That was young, for sure."

"And now he won't be here to be a grandpa. That's sad, and it feels like it was preventable."

"What are some positive memories about him you can pass along to our kids?"

"He taught Bill and me how to fish. For a week every summer, my family went camping at Wolf Creek Pass. Man, my dad could tease trout out of a lake like no one else." Eric smiled, remembering.

"It'll be fun when you can teach our kids what he taught you."

"Yeah. Those are happy memories, but that was it. There wasn't any other father-son bonding that I remember. When I was in high school, he encouraged me to work at his shop after school. I wasn't thrilled with the idea. My friends were getting jobs at movie theaters and restaurants—but I wanted to spend more time with him, so I went along. And here I am now. I'm over thirty and still working there even though my dad is long gone."

"You aren't tied to that job, Eric. If you want to look at other options—"

"No, that's not what I'm complaining about."

"I didn't think you were complaining at all."

"Well, all I mean is, I want to do better for our baby. I want to be more present in his or her life."

"I'm glad. I think that's part of what creating a family is all about. We learn from what our parents did well, what they could have done better, and then push through with our own plans."

"Having this baby is making me more conscious of my choices. And doing this work," Eric held up his book as if presenting it at auction, "is a good start."

A few nights later, we lay in bed watching David Letterman. I was laughing at the Top Ten List, and I felt it: *squiggle, squiggle, bump.* I stopped laughing immediately and put my hand on my expanded abdomen. Eric continued to laugh at the screen, then noticed I wasn't. He looked over at me. Our eyes met, and I realized I was holding my breath, waiting for it to happen again. I was afraid to speak, as if my voice would hush the baby and make it not move again.

I reached out for his hand and placed it palm down on the little hill below my belly button. *Squiggle, squiggle, bump. Squiggle, BUMP!*

"Did you feel that?" I asked, my eyes large and hopeful. I'd noticed brief movements a week ago, but never what I'd called an actual kick.

He nodded and smiled like he had on our wedding day. He was beautiful.

The baby sent us "I love you" bumps for the next twenty minutes, and we giggled like kids. I wanted to describe to him what the sensation felt like on the inside, but I couldn't. There were no words.

As we turned off the lights, I realized Eric's hand on my belly was the first time he'd touched me in months. We'd been so focused on our respective psychological and spiritual growth that we'd failed to notice much about each other, physical or otherwise. But that night, we remembered what everything was for: the books, the meetings, the honesty, the struggles, the vulnerability. It was for us, our future, and our child.

Chapter Two: Hope

She was born by C-section an hour before midnight in the middle of June. The labor had worn me down for days—slow and unproductive—until my doctor persuaded me it was time to meet my child face-to-face. Most women relay their birth stories and end with, "It was the happiest moment of my life." I'm no different.

I'd longed for a daughter since I was a girl myself, and in the single breath it took my doctor to say, "It's a girl," my whole life's purpose was fulfilled. I felt complete. Any future blessings bestowed upon me after that would be superfluous, like a downpour in the middle of a spring rain: You're already wet; more raindrops can't make you any wetter.

Men meet their children for the first time on the day they're born; women already know much about the child long before their bodies deliver the infant into the light. Meeting Emma in her physical form was only a formal introduction. Like pen pals who've corresponded for years and finally fly cross-country for an in person visit, her arrival didn't begin our relationship, it merely added a new dimension to it.

Every cell in my body, every detail of my life, had been connected to this baby for nine months. Each breath I'd taken, every bite of food, every kick to my ribs, every prenatal vitamin. Every alcoholic drink I'd declined, every time I got up to pee in the night, every time my feet swelled, every daydream, and each nightmare. Each probing to measure my belly, each bout of heartburn . . . all of it. Every moment of the last nine months, I had not been alone. Everything was her. Everything was *for* her.

Eric and I spent those first few days unwrapping and re-wrapping Emma Grace in her hospital blankets, like a gift we wanted to receive over and over again. We gazed at her tiny body parts, commented on which facial features she got from him or me, and just watched her breathe. Her upper lip quivered right before she cried for a nursing, and we laughed when she got the hiccups. She mesmerized us, and we bonded in shared awe. We'd created this person! We felt magical.

•   •   •   •   •

Mom had flown in a few days after we got home from the hospital. I was overjoyed she would spend the first month of Emma's life with us. This was a huge blessing since Eric had to go back to work after only one week. My dad even flew out for a long weekend. He admitted he wouldn't be much help with the baby yet: "My contributions will come when I can read her Dr. Seuss and teach her to shoot baskets." Still, I loved having him meet his first granddaughter and wrap his arms around me for a few days.

All the books I'd read still hadn't prepared me for the nuances of motherhood. I didn't have the instinct to know what my baby needed. That worried me. I cried a lot (hormones?) and felt ill-suited to parenthood. But Mom assured me as only a mother can. She'd taught me to walk, ride a bike, and drive a car. Now she was teaching me to be a mom.

Those first few weeks were precious. Unlike work life, each day was a clean slate, open, with no expectations. All I had to do was tend to Emma. Once I healed from the surgery, my favorite time of the day was the three of us walking our neighborhood, feeling the summer sun on our faces. Mom and I chattered on and on about small nothings, but also about big things.

"How's it going with your Twelve-Step programs, both of you?" she asked one particularly hot day in early July. We were resting on a bench in the park under a cottonwood tree while Emma slept in the stroller.

"Really well. Obviously, since Emma's been born, I haven't been to any meetings, but I still talk to Gwen every morning and read my books."

"I wondered who you were talking to in your room early in the mornings," Mom chuckled. "I'd hoped you hadn't started seeing ghosts."

"Very funny. Why didn't you ask me?"

"Trying to be a guest and helper in your house, not a nosy mom— or worse, a nosy mother-in-law."

"That's silly. Eric knows you know everything, and he's grateful you're here to help us right now. As you've seen, he goes to his meetings three times a week after dinner. I hope that'll continue."

"I heard that. Why are you worried?"

"That's amazing. Will I be able to read my daughter's mind based on her voice inflection, too, someday?" I asked.

"Absolutely. It's a biological gift that keeps children safe. It goes back to our animal predecessors: When babies are in trouble, mommies know and respond."

I had no idea if she was pulling my leg or not, but it kinda made sense, and I liked the idea of it, so I let it sit.

"Everything's going so well right now. I don't want to jinx it with my worry, but the thought of going down that road again scares the hell out of me. I've learned how little control I have, and I feel vulnerable." As usual, honesty poured out of me and into my mother's hands. She always caught my pain, my tears, my very soul as it fell.

"I don't know much about the Twelve Steps, Kitty Kat, but I know you. You're strong and smart. But more than anything, once you've learned something, it becomes part of you. You've always been a good student." She nudged me with her shoulder and tossed me an I-know-you-so-well grin.

"You really think so?" I asked, voicing the insecurity of a ten-year-old.

"I do. Once you've learned the things in the program that will help you, if Eric takes a turn in the wrong direction, you'll be okay. Take the next right step, and you'll get where you're supposed to be. Dad and I will always be here for you—and now, Emma, too."

I don't care how old I get, I'll always need my mom, I thought as we started back toward my house. Emma was waking from her nap and would want "lunchtime boobie" soon. Eric had nicknamed the round-the-clock mealtimes I was providing to our infant: middle-of-the-night boobie, crack-of-dawn boobie, don't-want-to-sleep-yet boobie, etc. Clever, though I knew he was eager to feed her a bottle when the time was right.

Four weeks, two days, and five hours after my mom had arrived, she left to go back to her retired life in New York. I stood on our driveway with Emma in my arms, bawling like a kid going off to summer camp for the first time. *How am I going to do this without her?*

Somehow, I managed.

Eric's focus swelled as fatherhood enveloped him, and he concentrated his energy on being his best self. Our journey together had begun, the three of us, writing a story whose ending we couldn't see but knew would be wonderful. I had all the usual fantasies of a young married woman: growing old with my husband and conquering life's challenges together. I pictured our children growing, learning, advancing in careers; we'd put money aside for their college and our retirement. I saw myself dancing at Emma's wedding, becoming a grandmother, traveling the world . . . all with Eric by my side, surrounded by the love we'd created and built upon.

I was deeply in love with our daughter and slowly falling back in love with her father.

As our daily and weekly routines grew more comfortable, I found new confidence in my ability to keep my daughter alive and safe. I'd quit my editing job at the magazine a few weeks before Emma was born. Eric and I decided it made little sense for me to work when most of my paycheck would go to daycare.

Eric helped as best he could after work and on weekends. Being able to take a shower without watching Emma (in a bouncy seat on the bathroom floor) was a gift of immeasurable proportion—even if it came at 7:00 p.m. He also made dinner a few nights a week and played with Emma while I cleaned the house on weekends. He attended his meetings regularly, and at the end of August—once he felt comfortable being a solo parent—he suggested I go to an Al-Anon meeting once or twice a week. I felt like a puppy freed from her backyard on those nights; I even went out for coffee with some women after the meetings a few times.

I adored being a full-time mom and watching my baby girl change every day, but the one thing I hadn't counted on was the boredom. Not that *she* was boring, not at all! But I'd been accustomed to professional challenges, problem-solving, and regular pats on the back for work well done. No one was waiting to offer a "Hey, great job folding that laundry" at the end of my typical day now. I didn't want to slip into a gray space where I'd only be "Emma's mom" and forget Kat as a separate person.

Most of my friends had been people I'd met through work, so that was no longer a source of companionship. I needed to find other women who were going through a similar phase, and I found that support system at a Mommy & Me playgroup. We called it the MAM group.

Once a week, women and their babies or toddlers met at a nearby recreation center. The kids played with various toys and each other, while the moms exchanged adult conversation and advice. Many of us had college degrees and chose to stay home with our children for a few years. We often discussed the wisdom of that decision, but it never mattered for long. We'd traded climbing the company ladder for our children's first words and steps. The job market would wait for us; the kids, however, would wait for nothing.

Leigh was the first friend I made there who dug deeper than "What kind of work did you do *Before*?" We had nothing in common except for both being home with our babies, yet we were drawn to each other. She was a practicing Catholic; I practiced nothing. She got married at nineteen and had her first child within a year; I'd been a ripe old twenty-four when Eric and I wed, then waited four years before having Emma. Leigh had a son; I had a daughter. Blonde; brunette. High school grad; college grad. Republican; Democrat. Neat freak; comfort first. Read the newspaper; read novels. Beer; wine. Country music; classic rock. The list went on.

I loved her straightforward, no-nonsense ways.

"Don't you think some of these women here are pretentious?" she whispered to me in a corner of the playroom while we put toys away one afternoon.

"Leigh!" My shock wasn't so much that she'd said something judgmental; rather, it was that I had thought the same thing.

"Come on. You see it, I know you do."

It felt both freeing to be myself and also vulnerable. "Yes, I do, but we shouldn't say it out loud. Especially in the same room." I imagined teaching Emma such lessons in a similar Mommy-wise tone someday.

Eight years younger than I, Leigh became like a little sister to me. She was brave and bold; I balanced her out with my life experience and social caution. The friendship felt old and comfortable even as it was unfolding. The bonus was, we lived down the street from each other. We'd probably crossed paths at the cluster mailbox between our houses before and never noticed.

Emma was three months old in September when I started going to the MAM group. Her son Justin was seven months older, but we still called our get-togethers playdates. Justin would sit next to Emma, playing with plastic balls or building blocks. Despite Emma's uninvolved posture (lying on her back), he'd offer her a plastic cube occasionally, as if it were a prized heirloom worthy of bequeathing to her. He didn't care that she couldn't grab it; it went right back into his mouth for further exploration.

Seeing each other outside the playgroup became a priority. Sometimes we'd push our strollers to the neighborhood park or hang out at each other's houses for coffee and chats while the babies slept. I'd watch Justin when she needed a break, and she'd stay with Emma when I wanted to do errands alone.

It helped that our husbands liked each other, too. Keith and Eric chatted about "man things" as they took turns grilling most weekends: fishing, baseball, cars. They'd both grown up in Colorado, so they had some common ground there, too. Leigh and I often commented that they could pass for brothers: blondish hair, broad shoulders, and remarkably straight teeth despite never wearing braces. Keith wasn't much of a drinker, so passing on beer at our gatherings was easy. That was nice.

I wanted to mark Eric's first year of sobriety, and Leigh was an expert party planner. In December, with Leigh's help, I surprised Eric when he walked in after a meeting. He'd earned his one-year chip that night, a symbol of his yearlong achievement of abstinence.

With our close friends and family crammed into our cozy living and dining rooms, we celebrated Eric's healthier life and the challenges we'd overcome as a couple. After twelve months of mind-boggling changes, it felt like closure and a fresh beginning all in one. We raised our glasses of sparkling apple cider and toasted to good things yet to come.

And it *was* good, for a while.

PART II

A memory: The first time Eric flew east to visit Kat's parents, he was nervous. Not about them; he'd met Jack and Jillian a few months before in Colorado. He was anxious about The City. Images of getting mugged as he stepped off the plane taunted him from Hollywood's version of the Big Apple. Kat assured him she'd visited NYC multiple times throughout her life and never wrestled a stranger for her purse. At 6' 3", he was an unlikely target.

As they walked around Times Square a few days into the trip, Eric's shoulders relaxed the longer he remained un-mugged. But as they took their seats at the Winter Garden Theater to see Cats, new frown lines appeared between Eric's eyes. She asked what he was thinking.

"It's so noisy here in the city. And it smells. Do you notice?"

"Yeah, but that's part of the charm," Kat said with a smirk.

"Hmmm . . . guess I don't see it." He opened his Playbill and shook his head. "I wanted to like it here because you do."

Kat chuckled and reached over to hold his hand. "I only like it because I have great memories of spending time here with my parents. It wasn't about the city. I loved Yankees games, Broadway, and Chinatown with Mom and Dad. Always just the three of us, sometimes arm in arm."

"Whew. So, you'll never ask me to move here, then?" His face relaxed into the handsome, carefree one she'd fallen in love with.

"No way. If you recall, I left New York before I even met you. I like to think I was being called to Colorado for a reason. I just didn't know what that was until I met you."

"And I thought I was the romantic one here." He lifted her left hand to his lips and kissed it.

As the theater lights faded and the orchestra began the prelude, Eric leaned over and whispered in Kat's ear: "Your ring finger looks sad and empty. I'm gonna have to fix that soon."

The Slip & The Fall
Late May - November 1994

* Fork 3 *

Chapter One: Imperfection

Scientists say smell is our strongest sense. Pass by a stranger in a store, wearing the same perfume your mother wore when you were a kid, and time melts away. You're transported to the kitchen of your childhood home—Mom at the stove and you at the table, doing your fourth-grade word problems. It's a fantastic experience when good memories flood back.

But a lilac-infused spring evening had the distinction of bringing an unwelcome scent back into our home, and the memories it stirred were far from fantastic.

Seventeen months had passed since I'd smelled the bittersweet bite of alcohol on Eric's breath, seen the slight sway in his step, and detected the subtle slur of his speech. But it hadn't been so long that *my* illness, denial, didn't find its way back to the surface in an instant. My immediate reaction was, *I must be mistaken.*

The old, naïve part of me was desperate to turn away, discount what I was seeing and smelling. However, I'd learned enough through my own recovery to know that staying ignorant wasn't in anyone's best interest.

I made a conscious, forced effort, begging my eyes to stay focused. *Don't look away. Did he just bump into the counter?* I pleaded with my nose to breathe deeply, even though the odor stung not only my lungs, but also my brain. My fears were confirmed. There was no logical way to justify it into anything else: He was drunk.

They'd taught family members about the possibility of relapse at the hospital's outpatient education classes. (I assumed they'd educated the recovering alcoholics about it, too?) I remember Caroline, the counselor, writing on the whiteboard in big letters: RELAPSE IS OFTEN PART OF RECOVERY. A shared chill ran through the room as we shuddered at the thought. But Caroline had explained a slip was possible, and she advised us to be prepared.

One mistake didn't necessarily mean we'd be on the road to a daily problem. Often, the person in recovery was assessing his power to control the disease, checking to see if his drinking was really "that bad"—or even noticeable to others. He was also testing his own ability to "get back on track."

Like high school students in biology class facing a fetal pig dissection, we stared at Caroline in horror. The statistics were dire:

*85% of people relapse within a year of attending rehab
*36% of alcoholics recover (achieving daily sobriety) after a year (but that includes occasional slips)
*If a person remains sober for two years, their chance of staying sober rises to 60%
*Men are twice as likely as women to relapse after rehab
*Only 18% of alcoholics *are* able to achieve "low-risk drinking" following rehab (They can have an occasional glass of wine with dinner or a beer with the guys while watching a football game and not revert to daily drinking.)

The room had reverberated with the group's collective silence. What the hell were we doing there if the chances of having our normal lives and our sober loved ones back were so unlikely?

On that breezy but warm afternoon in late May, confronting the reality of a slip, I stood fixed in place and acknowledged the knots in my stomach. As I watched Eric put tremendous effort into walking a straight line down the hallway, I tried to recall what Caroline had said. *Do I confront him right now—let him know I know? Or wait until tomorrow when his head clears?* I knew I should remain calm, but I was also angry. A year and a half of sobriety and trust down the drain. A malodorous soup of feelings ranging from sad to scared bubbled up, and I couldn't deny the ray of disappointment curving above me.

His twenty minutes in the bathroom bought me time. I heard him throwing up and I was glad. Resentment reared its ugly head, and I heard myself mutter under my breath to no one, "Serves you right. Hope it burns all the way up." How quickly my own relapse showed itself! Where was my compassion? All I felt was righteous indignation.

I looked over at the playpen. Emma was snoozing, wrapped in a Peanuts blanket after tiring herself out while flipping through picture books. I took a few deep breaths to center myself for whatever would come next and took the casserole out of the oven. *I don't think we'll be eating soon.*

When Eric emerged from the bathroom, his face was pale and his eyelids heavy. I waited to see what approach he would take, as this would likely determine the strength and tone of my response. (How pathetic. Hadn't I learned not to live my life as a mere reaction to his behavior? But that was a concern for another day.)

He could have said any number of things at that moment: "I'm sorry. I had a bad day and made a bad decision"; or "I can't believe how shitty I feel; how did I use to do this every day?"; or "This is my boss's fault. Kaufman put so much pressure on me at work this week to make those sales calls; it was bound to get to me"; or "Don't freak out. I'll be okay tomorrow. I'll go call someone from my meeting."

But no. Each of those responses would have indicated admission of drinking, putting a name to the action that was his first slip. What I got instead was more than a physical relapse. Not only had he reached for a magic bottle and let its liquid seep into his life, like an old friend who only calls when he's in trouble. His relapse was also one of spirit: his conviction to be honest had failed.

"Man, I must'a eaten somethin' bad at lunch t'day," he said, his words bleeding into each other. Pure denial—or worse, a poor attempt to divert my attention as he used to do so expertly in our lie-infested past. Did he really believe his own falsehood, or was he simply hoping to deceive me?

"Bad hamburger, huh? Is that how you're gonna play this?" I said, stunned by his choice.

"Whatdya mean?"

"What I mean is, I can tell you drank today."

"I did not," he said with just enough affront to make me waver for a second.

"Eric, don't do this. Don't make it worse by lying."

"I'm not lyin'," he replied and started walking away from me. "I can't believe yer'accusin' me." I could feel him rolling his eyes, even though he wasn't looking in my direction. His previous defensive mode of communication was back: twisting everything around into someone else's fault, distorting what I said.

I paused to assess my next move and watched him reach into the cupboard for a glass. I was silent as he cracked some ice cubes out of the tray, dropping big chunks onto the floor and not picking them up. While pouring Pepsi, his reflexes proved too slow. Sticky froth spilled over the rim of the glass onto the counter. "Fuck," he mumbled.

Although anyone can misjudge pouring soda from time to time, not everyone looks at the glass and the liquid accusingly.

If the conversation didn't go another way, I knew that same look would soon be cast in my direction. Reaching into my mental archives, I tried for Honesty and Gentle Confrontation.

"Honey, we need to be honest with each other if we're going to get through this," I said.

"Get through what?" He gulped his soda down in thirty seconds.

I chose my words carefully. "Look, I can tell you drank today, and I think it's the first time in a very long time. It scares me, and I bet it scares you, too. We knew this might happen sometime, so let's talk about it."

"Yeah, we did know this 'might happen, so yeah, here it is. So what? If it happens, and it jus 'happened, then it's not a big deal, right?"

I tried to follow the logic of what he'd said but it hurt my head.

"Just because we knew it might happen doesn't mean it's not a big deal that it did," I said, trying a stab at my own line of logic. It went right over his intoxicated head.

"Whatever," he said. He placed the glass in the sink and left the kitchen. His shin grazed the coffee table in the living room. It must have hurt, but he kept moving. He walked right past Emma without a glance and pushed open the sliding door to our backyard deck. This was where he went to smoke—an accommodation he'd made since Emma was born. His exit was a deliberate attempt to avoid me. Part of me knew I should let him go. Leave him to his buzz and hold off the rest of the conversation until morning. But I wanted to get it all out in the open. I knew I was pushing it, but I followed him outside. He leaned against the side of the house, facing away from me into the fading light.

Since Honesty and Gentle Confrontation weren't working, I changed tactics: enter Concerned and Supportive Wife Who Sets Boundaries.

"What happened today?" I asked. "Did something catch you off guard or push you somehow?"

"I really don 'wanna talk about it," he said, dismissing me. "Why don 'tchya go to bed?"

"It's 6:15. And I want to know what happened; maybe I can help?"

"Didja 'ever think I don 'wantchu to know?" He took a long drag on his cigarette. "Or maybe I don 'want your help?"

I walked closer to him and smelled the booze through the smoke fumes. An image of his alcohol-drenched breath catching fire went through my head.

"I have a right to know. We're in this together, remember?" I put my hand gently on his elbow and tried to turn him around toward me. "Everything you do affects me. I love you, and I need to know what's going on." I was loving. I was firm.

"Together?" He spat the word like it didn't belong in his mouth. He pulled his arm away from my touch. "*I'm* the one out there workin'. *I'm* the one out there dealin' with stress every day. You don'understand what I go through." A little spittle built up around the corner of his mouth as he forgot to swallow.

"Yes, we *are* in this together," I reminded him. "No, I'm not working right now because we both agreed one of us should be home with Emma, remember? And I do understand about stress. *This* is stressful to me."

That was all he needed.

"It mus'be great to be you, Kat," he said with accusation floating in his red, watery eyes. "You always have all the answers, don'tchu? You get t'sit there and judge me and say how I fuck up all the time. Maybe *you're* my stress. You're always all over me 'bout stuff. Maybe *you're* why I drank today. Didja'ever think'a that?"

It was like a verbal orgasm. He had worked his way up to the exchange and climaxed with his anger turned outward at me. I wondered if this was only the alcohol talking. Were his words a jumble of consonants and vowels randomly tossed in the air? Or, had the drinking bolstered his confidence and diminished his inhibitions? Maybe these were his true feelings. Either way, his words hurt me, and I knew I wasn't reaching him.

As he flicked his cigarette on the porch and stomped it out, I stood silent. He had warped what I'd said and used my words to justify his poor choices. It made no sense.

Where was the Eric I'd been living with for the past year and a half? We'd been so happy, working on our programs and loving our daughter together. Time warped and knocked me back to life before his hospital stay, but even in those days, he never exploded like this.

The last year and a half of progress evaporated like sweat off a marathon runner's back.

My efforts to be understanding and accepting had been pushed away. *I* had been pushed away. How could he make me into some sabotaging enemy when one day ago he would have agreed we were on the same side in this war?

The truth was, he had sucked me in. I had fallen for the oldest alcoholic trick in the book: He was looking for a scapegoat— something outside himself—to blame for his slip. His Reason. He would have accused the sun of not shining bright enough that day if it could provide the excuse he needed to get his fix. And I had just stepped in and volunteered to be his cloudy sky.

I knew better. I should have walked away. "Discussing" anything with him in that state was useless. In his mind, I had proven myself to be The Nagging Wife, and he could now use that as his Reason to continue drinking for months. And he did.

•   •   •   •   •

I never knew which Eric was going to walk through the door. Sometimes, Remorseful Eric would shuffle in, head down, giving the impression he was repentant about his sobriety lapse that day. He'd apologize to me inside a vulnerable hug, whispering in my neck, "I'm sorry, babe. Be patient with me, okay?" He'd tried to resist, but before he knew it, he was at the liquor store. I fought my urge to feel sorry for him.

Other days, Angry Eric would chastise himself for "being weak and giving in." I heard him mumbling self-reproachments in the mirror as he brushed his teeth at bedtime: "You're fucking everything up. Stop it!" But Angry Eric also pointed at *me* occasionally. "Why do you keep asking me about work? It's fine. Leave me alone about it!" I tried to avoid being pulled into those arguments. My confrontation after his first slip had been a fiasco. I didn't recognize the Evil Kat he criticized. I fought my urge to resent him.

But most of the time, Guilty Eric was the one who found his way home at the end of the workday. He didn't talk about his shame and embarrassment. Those feelings stayed trapped inside him but propelled him into the next drink; they never led him back through the doors of an AA meeting. The self-defeating circle kept him trapped, as guilt drove him to drink more, and drinking more increased his guilt. I fought my urge to pity him.

Sometimes he apologized; mostly he didn't. After a while, any illusion of contrition was gone. By summer, he no longer talked about guilt or weakness or self-loathing. He'd even stopped blaming me for his need to drink on a particular day. His drinking just *was*.

It just *was* that he would get up late, citing a headache. It just *was* that he often came home early from work, noting a stomachache. It just *was* that he was tired and needed to rest for an hour before supper, then went to bed again right after we ate. It just *was* that he forgot entire conversations an hour after we had them. It just *was* that he was drinking almost every day, and not even trying not to anymore.

One day in early July when Eric *was* at work, Leigh and Justin came over for a playdate. After building blocks and make-believe cooking activities had exhausted them, the kids napped in Emma's room. Mid-afternoon, Leigh brought out her calorie-busting brownies.

"I thought you could use an indulgence. These will help take your mind off things," she said, addressing the unexpressed distractions in my head. Leigh sat at my dining room table, and I brought over two glasses of milk for us.

"Those look amazing. Thank you." I picked up a gooey square, chock full of walnuts, and savored the bliss of chocolate. "I was trying not to talk about my marital woes. Didn't want to ruin our time together." I spoke with an impolite mouthful.

"Kat, I'm not here for gossip—well, not about you," she chuckled. We often gossiped about other moms in the Mommy & Me group, then scolded ourselves for it. "I'm your friend. I know you're going through a hard time."

"I know. I'm grateful for that. You're one of the few people I can be real with, and that's very important to me."

"I promise I want to hear about Eric and how you're doing, but I'm bursting with some news of my own. Can I jump in first?" She was beaming like headlights shimmering in the rain.

"Of course. Especially if it's good news."

"I'm pregnant!"

"Oh! That's awesome!" I squealed and jumped out of my chair. I ran around to her side of the table and leaned down to hug her. "How far along are you?"

"About eight weeks. I have an appointment on Friday to confirm the due date, but I did my own calculation. I'm thinking early February."

"A new baby for the New Year!"

"True. We haven't told Justin yet. I'll wait a few more months. He won't understand it right now anyway." Justin was only twenty months old; she was right.

"Still. Keith must be excited, huh?"

"Yeah. I don't know what got into him, but he's been especially frisky this spring." She giggled like the teenager she was when she first met him. "I'm just happy we've been able to keep the spark going all these years."

"I'm really happy for you guys. I need you to be the stable couple in my life. My marriage surely isn't a good example."

"I guess I don't understand how things went bad so quickly," she said. "You guys were getting along so well. Both doing your programs."

"We were. I know. I have whiplash. He's so different these days. But then, in the middle of a shitty week, the Eric I love will show himself." I took another bite of brownie, relishing the sugar hit, and wondered if the jolt Eric got from his first gulp of alcohol might be a similar sensation. I continued chewing and talking.

"Just yesterday, Eric called me in the middle of the day—something he rarely does anymore. He told me he'd heard Whitney Houston singing 'I Will Always Love You' on the radio, and it reminded him of the winter we were pregnant with Emma. We went to see *The Bodyguard* like three times. Kept saying it was our last date before the baby came. It's a sweet memory, and I loved that Eric called to share it."

"But it's like his time being sober didn't matter to him." She said this with a shake of her head, but not with reproach.

"I don't think it's that easy. Something interesting I learned when we were going through the outpatient program has stuck with me. They said when an alcoholic stops drinking—whether it's for one year or twenty—the body doesn't know it. So, when that person picks up the bottle again, he doesn't return to the state of decline he was in the day he stopped drinking. Instead, the body acts as if the person *continued* drinking all that time."

"I don't get it." She was digging into her second brownie. Maybe I was talking too much?

"Well, for example, when Eric stopped drinking a year and a half ago, he was having stomach aches and missing work maybe once every other week. He also had the energy and mental control to hide his drinking. Now he's started again, we're not back at that state of things. He's drinking almost daily now, and he's got stomach aches and headaches much of the time. He's missing hours at work regularly each week, going in late, or coming home early. And he's not even trying to hide his drinking anymore. His behavior toward me is so Jekyll and Hyde. He wasn't like that before."

"I'm so sorry, Kat."

I shook off her sympathy because I was mid-roll in explaining. "From what I learned, his body thinks he's been drinking this whole time; the disease has progressed *as if*. This is where he would have been if he'd never stopped for those seventeen months. Plus, his tolerance for alcohol is higher now, so he needs more of it to get the same drunk feeling. That starts taking a toll on his organs. Not only the liver, but heart, brain, and pancreas, too."

"God, that's terrible. Do you think he understands what's happening?" Confusion etched her young face. Sometimes I forgot she was almost a decade younger than I.

"On some level, I guess. I mean, we learned all this together, but my fear is maybe he's too far along in the disease process to care. It's not that alcoholics can't get sober at this point in their disease. Many do. But the consequences of his drinking need to be more severe. You've heard of hitting bottom?" She nodded.

"At the beginning of his drinking, the idea of becoming a father was all he needed to choose a healthier path. It motivated him. But now, missing work, being distant from me, having a superficial relationship with Emma . . . even those aren't enough to jolt him into making better choices."

"What the hell has to happen before he'll choose to get sober again?" She asked the magic question. The one that kept me up at night.

"I'm afraid to find out."

•   •   •   •   •

Summer sputtered toward its conclusion, and although October was my favorite month, that year, the beauty of the changing leaves just looked like shades of death to me.

Self-indulgent, self-destructive, self-centered. Eric was so wrapped up in his own needs, it seemed I didn't exist in his world anymore. Emma and I became tangents, offshoots of his life. We were people who represented Obligation, Expectations, and the dreaded Responsibility. Our needs, when I bothered to express them, seemed unimportant to him—or at least not his concern. I'd tell him how lonely I was or that Emma missed her daddy, and he'd look at me like I was some other guy's wife. *Why are you telling this to me, lady? Am I supposed to do something about your sad lot in life?* We were roommates whose toothbrushes happened to lean against each other in the stand.

On nights when he was more present, we'd watch TV after Emma went to bed. He'd ask me about my day. My hope surged: *Maybe it's not as bad as I think?* But the next day, reality shoved me backward again. Hot and cold. Up and down. I couldn't figure it out.

Fortunately, the Al-Anon meetings I went to offered babysitting. Cara, the teenage daughter of one of our members, watched kids in a preschool classroom adjacent to our meeting. She considered this her volunteer work. We met in the basement of a Lutheran church, and there were toys and chalkboards available. Even though only two or three children came with their parents regularly, the church leadership made the room available.

Emma looked forward to seeing Cara and playing side by side with the other children. At sixteen months, she wasn't quite interacting with "friends" yet, but she tottered around the playroom with interest. I was grateful she didn't understand how not-normal it was for her mother to be opening her bruised heart to strangers in a chilly cellar beneath a gold-plated altar.

Those meetings became my lifeline. The people there—and the words of hope in the program's books—helped keep me on track with healthy choices. One of my favorite sayings was their definition of insanity: *doing the same thing over and over again and hoping for different results.* Nothing in my life would change for the better until I started making different decisions.

Conversations swirled around life-altering questions: *How do you maintain a relationship when one person is emotionally and physically unavailable? What's the point of marriage if there's no trust or honesty in it? What do you do when loving someone else becomes too costly to your own sense of self?*

And the question I battled with most: *How do you know when it's time to call the whole thing a wash?*

•   •   •   •   •

I was grateful when Bill invited himself over for dinner one night. Another person at the table might make for a more normal evening: I wouldn't have to carry the conversation all night.

Since Eric's father died, his brother Bill had assumed head-of-the-family status, a role he took seriously. He knew his little brother was on a bumpy road, and he seemed determined to help pave a smoother path for Eric, if possible.

Bill and I had been close when I first joined the family, but in the aftermath of his divorce the previous year, he was sometimes inconsistent in his approach to me. I knew he cared about me as a friend and even as a sister, but sometimes I got the feeling he thought I was too "strong" for his little brother.

Bill attended an evangelical church regularly and prided himself on being a good Christian man who practiced God's lessons in earnest. Part of those lessons, as he interpreted them, were sexist, in my opinion. Over the years, we'd had many theological and sociological conversations about how to translate the Bible in today's world, particularly regarding marriage. We always ended up agreeing to disagree, and we respected each other enough to hug away our differences.

Emma had been unusually irritable that afternoon—I chalked it up to teething—so I'd given her an early dinner and put her to bed before Bill arrived.

As I got busy chopping vegetables for our salad, I overheard the guys talking in the living room. I wasn't trying to eavesdrop, but an open floor plan allowed that "benefit."

"So, how're things at work?" Bill tossed a softball at his brother, opening the conversation with an easy pitch.

"Fine. You know. Same song, different verse."

"You find it boring? I thought you enjoyed the sales bit now?"

"Mostly. It's just kinda routine. Even the problems the customers ask me about are things I've fixed a hundred times now."

I walked into the living room and handed each of the guys an iced tea. "Sorry to interrupt. Dinner'll be ready in about ten," I said, then returned to the kitchen twelve feet away. Eric and Bill both said "Thanks" at the same time.

"You know, you've been working at that company for fifteen years. Maybe it's time for a change?" Bill's suggestion sounded both scary and exciting to me. I wondered how Eric would respond.

"Jeez. I hadn't realized . . . that's half my life! No wonder I'm sick of it."

Sick of it? I didn't think he felt that strongly about his job. Is this why he's drinking?

"You sound a little resentful. I always thought it was a good opportunity, solid benefits. I was even jealous that you got to work with Dad."

"In theory. But Dad was in his office most of the time. Treated me like any other employee when we were there."

"Did you ever talk to him about that?"

"No. But it's funny because I was trying to find a way to approach him about it, and then he died."

"Oh, Eric. I had no idea. What were you going to say to him?"

"Just that I was ready for more responsibility. I was hoping he'd teach me more about the finance side of the business. Accounting or payroll. Something like that."

"You must have felt a bit 'cut off,' for lack of a better phrase. His death prevented that conversation." Bill was doing such a great job of paraphrasing, I wondered if he learned that skill in marriage counseling.

"I guess. But I couldn't dwell on it. Mom needed me to step into the sales role to keep the company profitable while Uncle Eddie worked on the buyout. It didn't seem like the right time to tell her I didn't want to do that."

"Have you ever talked to Uncle Eddie about your interest in learning the finances? Maybe he'd be open to that now?"

"Nah. After I trained with Jerry and learned the sales part of things, I was settled there."

"Sounds like you've put your own interests aside for what you think other people need from you. What else would you be interested in doing—if you were to look outside the company?" Bill sounded like a therapist *and* a career counselor now.

Eric was quiet. The knife in my hand paused over a helpless cucumber on the cutting board in front of me. I waited to hear my husband's answer.

"I don't know. I like cooking, but I don't want to work fast food. Since I'm not professionally trained, I don't know where that would land me."

I bit the inside of my lip to stop me from laughing. Yes, Eric always talked about cooking, but besides pancakes and simple kid-friendly dinners, he hadn't prepared a proper meal for us in years.

"Would it be out of the question to think about going back to school? For culinary stuff or anything else?" Bill suggested this with hope dancing around the curves of his words.

"We can't afford that right now, not with Emma." It didn't quite sound like a poor-me statement, but close.

"There are loans . . ."

"Nah. I mean if I could get another job without going to school, that might be an idea. What do you think I could do?"

The salad was done, but I dawdled to hear the rest of the conversation, feeling like the sneaky wife I was being. I mixed an oil and vinegar dressing.

"Well, you have strong customer service skills now. Those would transfer to lots of other industries. You don't have to stay in manufacturing. What other kinds of businesses sound interesting to you?" Bill was on a roll and his enthusiasm was having a contagious effect on his brother.

I looked over my shoulder in time to see Eric shrug his. "Maybe banking? I'm good with numbers. Or . . . I saw a 'Help Wanted' sign at that nursery on Highway 7. Landscaping might be okay. Not sure what that would pay, though."

Landscaping? That's seasonal work. And have you seen our yard?

"Yeah, that may not be enough of an income for you as a family man, but banking sounds promising."

I walked into the dining room with dishes and set the table.

"Maybe. I'll think about it."

"Look, Eric. Ya gotta be happy, at home and at work. It's a balance. Remember how we always said Dad didn't get it right? You have a chance to do better. You deserve that."

"Yeah. I know. It's just hard to make such a big change. What if it doesn't work out?"

"But what if it does?" A big brother with words of wisdom. It was a perfect appetizer before our meal. I called the boys to the table with a tingle of optimism fluttering in my chest.

•   •   •   •   •

A week later, on Thursday afternoon, Mr. Kaufman called to see if Eric was okay. Was he feeling better after a few days at home? Apparently, there'd been no phone call on Monday, and the Human Resources manager had assumed illness. She'd given Eric the benefit of the doubt and chalked it up to his being too sick to call in.

But four days without contact was enough to cause the boss to get involved. I, too, became worried then because Eric had been "going to work" every morning that week. He had not, in fact, been sick at all (not counting his usual headaches and stomachaches). I tap-danced my way through the call, resenting being put in the position of covering for my husband. My Al-Anon friends' voices in my head told me I shouldn't, but this was his job. All three of us needed it.

Eric's uncle owned the company, but Mr. Kaufman was the General Manager. I'd only met him a few times. He was friendly, but he ran the business with precision and oversight, as if his name were on the ownership papers.

"I'm so sorry, Mr. Kaufman. I didn't realize Eric hadn't called in on Monday. He must have fallen right back to sleep after trying to get ready for work that morning. He's had a terrible flu of some kind for days," I said, amazed at how easily the lie crossed my lips.

"Of course," he said, believing me at once. "I'll let Mrs. Garza in HR know so she can process Eric's sick time paperwork. Has he been to the doctor yet?"

"Yes," I winced. "I'm sure he'll be back to work on Monday. The weekend should give him enough time to get back on his feet."

"Very good. Please tell Eric we're all hoping he feels better soon."

"Thank you, Mr. Kaufman. I appreciate your kindness."

I hung up the phone and stared at the receiver as if it held the answers to the questions reverberating in my head: *Where the hell is my husband? And where has he been going every day this week?*

I knew it would be a bad scene. There was no easy way to confront him about missing work all week. "Choose supportive words" was the best advice at the top of my mental Effective Communication Tools checklist. But I couldn't remember what those words were, and they felt far away, out of reach. Fear and anger simmered together throughout the day, ready to boil over and soil my tidy house.

I could have tried harder to use a gentle tone of voice, but the urgency I felt took over. I wanted answers. When he walked through the door at 5:30 p.m., I blindsided him with a barrage of questions, and then he blindsided me back with, "I'm moving out."

"What?!" I asked, my voice several notes higher than normal.

"I'm moving out," he repeated and brushed past me on his way into our bedroom.

Emma was engrossed in her pre-dinner *Barney* video, so she didn't hear our dialogue down the hall.

"Does this have anything to do with work?" I asked. It was a dumb question, but it was all I could think of. His job had been the primary thing on my mind until then.

"Yes and no. I hate that job, and I'm not going back. So, yeah, I guess so. But I need out of here anyway, so maybe not," he said, acting as if these words made perfect sense. I couldn't follow the logic. He added, "I've spent a few days thinking about this."

"I heard—from your boss! *Where* have you been thinking?" I asked, picturing a series of bars.

"Various places, mostly the park." His tone was calm. Where was the storm I'd been expecting?

He pulled a suitcase down from the top shelf in our closet and plopped it on our bed. He turned and finally looked at me. "Look, Kat, this isn't working. You hate me. I can see it every time you look at me. And I'm tired of feeling shitty about myself whenever I'm with you."

"What the hell are you talking about?" I responded at a volume I usually reserved for arguments with gun rights supporters. "I do *not* hate you. I *love* you, but you've been too drunk to notice. What do you think I'm doing here?"

His eyelids weren't heavy, and his words weren't slurred. I don't think he'd been drinking. No fight brewed waiting to tear us apart, but he'd made his decision. He was just letting me know.

"I don't know what either of us is doing here. We don't belong together anymore. We want different things," he said with a maturity I hadn't heard from him in ages. He went to his dresser and started taking out socks and underwear from the top drawer.

"I guess *so*," I said, sarcasm souring my tongue. "I want a husband, and you want vodka! But you used to want *me*, Eric. What happened? Only one of us has changed, and it's not me."

"You don't understand," he said, mostly to himself. Second drawer: T-shirts and shorts.

"I'm trying to understand, for God's sake. I've been trying to understand what you're doing for months now. Where have you gone? You act as if you don't want to be here with me . . . with Emma. Is it too much for you to be a part of this family? Am I so terrible to live with that you . . ." I couldn't finish the sentence. Tears blurred my eyes, yet when I searched his, they were bone dry. Was he feeling anything?

"I love Emma," he said, but added nothing more. Nothing about loving me. Third drawer: sweatpants and sweatshirts.

"Are you ever coming back? Do you want a divorce?" The sentence hung in the air like a thing apart from myself. The words were desperate, needy.

"I don't know. But I need a break," he said.

"A break from *what?*" Fury and disbelief rose beyond the confines of my body. "From what I've seen, you *have* been on a break. You glide through your days with no sense of responsibility except heading off to work—and apparently, you haven't even been doing *that* for a week! You barely help around the house or take care of our daughter." I knew I was focusing on the wrong things. His poor housekeeping skills weren't the issue; his unwillingness to stop using the crutch of alcohol was. But I couldn't stop picking the low-hanging fruit.

"I make pancakes every Sunday morning," he shot back, as if I weren't giving him due credit.

"Oh, excuse me. How will I ever manage if you're not around to do that *one* thing *once* a week?" I hoped Emma couldn't hear my rage in the other room. "Explain to me what it is you need a break *from?*"

"YOU, all right? I need a fucking break from you." He tossed a picture of Emma into the suitcase and glared at me. "You are so perfect, Kat. It's impossible to please you. No human man could ever live up to your expectations. I know I can't."

"That's such a cop-out. You haven't even *tried* to live up to your obligations to Emma and me lately. I've bent over backwards to give you time to figure this mess out on your own. I never expect you to be perfect, but I do expect you to show up. To try. To care." I was shaking. All the Al-Anon self-talk designed to calm me down was gone, like a book put away on a high shelf, forgotten. Months of pent-up frustration rushed out of me. Not my best mental health moment, but I couldn't stop.

"Have I ever asked *you* for a break? Who's been holding this house and this family together while you've been acting like a selfish sixteen-year-old all this time? Huh? You've got a lot of nerve."

In the middle of this crazy cross talk, I realized this was the longest conversation we'd had in five months. For a minute, I didn't mind what we were saying. It felt weirdly good to have a real exchange.

Closet: pants, button-down shirts, shoes . . .

He stopped packing for a minute, with a pair of sneakers in his right hand. He was suddenly calm. He looked at me straight on, tranquil as a yogi in mid-downward dog, and said, "You always have everything under control, Kat. You won't even notice I'm gone."

I sank onto the bed, resigned at last. There was no point in talking anymore; he wasn't hearing me. It was as if we'd both been watching the same movie, but each walked away from it with two separate ideas about its plot.

Maybe we *had* grown too far apart. Maybe we couldn't come back together again. The truth was, I'd been searching for good-enough reasons to leave, too. Maybe part of my anger was that he'd figured it out before I had.

"Where will you go?" I asked, my voice a demonstration of acceptance now. All the fight was gone from me.

"I'll stay at my mom's for a while until I figure something else out."

"Are you really quitting your job? I told Mr. Kaufman you were sick."

"Yeah, I'll call him tomorrow." He left the room. I heard the medicine cabinet open and close in the bathroom. He came back with his toothbrush, shaving kit, deodorant, cologne, and hairbrush.

I couldn't think of anything else to say. He zipped up the suitcase and lifted it off the bed. "I'd like to come by and see Emma on Saturday morning," he said, not looking at me. So, this was my daughter's future now: Saturday visits with Dad.

But not so quick.

"God, Eric, you're acting like I'm going to let you whisk her off to Dairy Queen whenever you call to say you want to come by. Have you forgotten you've been drinking almost every day for the last several months? I haven't let you drive Emma or me anywhere in all that time—or haven't you noticed? I'm not going to start now."

"Are you saying I can't see her?" he asked, registering a hint of genuine emotion for the first time in the conversation.

"Of course, you can see her, but you have to come here and play with her while I'm around. You can't take her anywhere." I said this as if I'd decided it weeks before, instead of ten seconds ago. I was making up the rules on the spot.

He paused, and I watched him calculate the fairness of the offer. Whether or not he agreed with its justness, he nodded. "I'll be here at ten o'clock."

As he turned to walk down the hall, I felt the earth shift. He was going to walk out our front door, and my life would never be the same. And he was leaving me to break this life-changing news to Emma by myself. Somehow, I was not surprised.

Chapter Two: Spiraling

Like most adjustments in life, the transition to single-parenthood was more than I expected. You can't prepare for these challenges; you face them the best you can when they stare you down.

Eric's departure didn't change much. After all, I was already taking care of our toddler and the house. What *was* different, though, was the stigma I felt. I tried to keep the news of our separation away from my small social circle, but gossip is juicy, and some stay-at-home moms are bored. Like reporters from *People* magazine, they wanted the scoop. It didn't matter that those details were *my life*, not a story for their entertainment. My real friends, of course, remained kind and present.

The first Saturday after Eric left our house that decisive Thursday night with suitcase in hand, he showed up for his "date" with Emma with a stuffed teddy bear. She oohed and giggled at it for thirty minutes before the two of them went upstairs to play in her room. She'd started taking an interest in my weekly shopping trips to Safeway. I found a make-believe kitchen—complete with pretend boxes and cans of food—at a consignment store on clearance. Only $7.00! Emma loved to pretend she was making dinner, though she just put the cans directly on the fake burner without "heating" the vegetables in a pot. I wished cooking were that easy.

I told Eric I was concerned about money and asked if he'd found any job leads yet. He shrugged and said, "I'm looking," then picked Emma up and carried her to her room.

When I went upstairs an hour later to tell them Emma's lunch was ready, I found them both asleep—my baby on a cluster of throw pillows on the floor next to her crib, and her daddy lying next to her. One whiff of the air in the sealed-off room confirmed that Eric was sleeping off an early morning binge.

The next Saturday, Eric showed up two hours late with no explanation. The following two Saturdays, he failed to show up at all.

Emma couldn't register his absence, per se, but one morning in early November she said, "Dada?" After lying to Mr. Kaufman on Eric's behalf weeks before, I'd made a conscious decision not to do it again, especially not to our daughter.

"I don't know where Daddy is, sweetie, but he loves you. It's okay to miss him." I wasn't sure if she understood my words, but I used my best lilting mommy voice to soothe her. Inside, I cursed Eric's selfishness. My resentment of his taking the easy way out hardened like a cake left uncovered on a kitchen counter.

I stretched our dollars at the grocery store. Emma and I ate a restricted diet of eggs, soup, mac and cheese, and whatever fruits and vegetables were on sale. When Eric called to talk to Emma, I asked how his job search was going. He was vague: "It's hard to find something right now," or "I put in a few applications this week, so we'll see."

In an effort not to panic, I told myself he wouldn't abandon us financially. He had literally and figuratively walked away from his other duties, but I believed he'd pay the mortgage and ensure we had money for food and health insurance.

When it was time to pay bills that month, the bank got the first check out of our savings account: I would *not* lose the house. With the cold air of winter knocking on autumn's backdoor, the utility company got the second. I stared at the rest of the envelopes on the table. *Which of these can wait another month? Cable? Car insurance?* I picked up the phone and canceled the newspaper and cable. Emma only watched videos anyway.

While reading the Sunday classified ads the day after his last No Show with Emma, I saw something with potential for Eric. I'd been looking for a part-time job for myself, but Colorado National Bank had an ad for a manager trainee program. People with an interest in finance, but no experience, could apply. After his conversation with Bill a few weeks ago, I thought he might be interested. I called his mother's house.

Helen had never warmed up to me the way I'd hoped, even after these many years and despite my role in giving her a grandchild. She came across as having done her maternal duty by introducing Eric to me. Since then, she was cordial, like a butler, but she rarely dove deeper than superficial conversation. I had the impression she didn't want to get to know me too well; if I left her son one day, she wouldn't be heartbroken about my absence. How could she have known back then, when she was promoting him like a ripe cantaloupe, that our relationship might not last?

This was the first time we'd spoken since Eric moved out, so I was expecting a little more consideration than usual. Maybe she would finally see how serious his drinking problem was (something she rationalized as easily fixable if he wanted to stop) or how fragile our marriage was (something she implied could be stronger if I didn't question her son's judgment so much).

But I didn't hear support in her voice, nor did she say anything encouraging to me. What she *did* say, however, shocked me speechless: "Eric isn't here, Kat. Why would you think he is?"

Did she mean, *He's not here at the moment,* or *Why would you think Eric would be here at all? It's not like he lives here.*

There was no way to respond without telling her the whole story.

"I guess Eric didn't tell you." I paused before adding, "He moved out of our house about a month ago."

"*What?!* Where is he? He called me last week and didn't say a thing about that."

"I don't know where he is, Helen. He told me he'd be staying with you until he found a new job and got a place of his own," I said with resignation. He had left me to break more bad news to people who loved him.

"He lost his job?" she asked with alarm.

"No. He *quit* his job," I clarified.

I told her the whole story. Since his relapse, Eric and I had kept a lot of our private lives separate from his mother, though she knew he was "working on" getting better. If asked, she'd have said she appreciated being on the outside of our drama. Helen wasn't the kind to share intimate details of her life, and she didn't want to know such things from other people, even her own children. Especially her children?

I wasn't that kind of person, however, and I didn't aspire to be that kind of parent. She was so different from my mother. I'd always had a little trouble relating to Helen, and it had taken me a while to learn how to live on the other side of her "appropriate" lines. Oddly, in this situation, I could see the benefit of maintaining a certain distance from your grown children: they should be able to live their own lives if you've raised them well. Perhaps part of Helen's aloofness during this relapse was symptomatic of some guilt: *If Eric's not living his life well, then perhaps I didn't raise him well?* Keeping her distance meant she didn't have to ask herself that uncomfortable question.

"I assumed he was with you, but now that I know he's not, I'm worried. Where could he be? Do you . . ." The words scraped against my throat. "Do you think he's with another woman?" There. The dark thread was out of my brain.

"No, Katharine, no," she said too quickly, mollifying herself or me, I'd never know. "He loves you. He would never—"

"I don't know about that. I don't know anything anymore. How can I know so little about my husband?" I started to cry. "He's been lying to me for so long now, I don't know what's real in my life."

Helen said nothing. She wasn't used to hearing emotion from me, and I wasn't used to sharing my feelings with her. But she was there, and this concerned her. Neither of us could ignore the ugliness of Eric's behavior anymore.

"What am I supposed to do?" I asked, then sniffled.

"I don't know, dear. I . . . I need time to think." This was hitting her hard, out of nowhere. She was handling it better than I would have given her credit for. "Let me talk to Bill. He'll have some ideas. I know he will."

"Okay," I replied, sounding small, like a child trying to be brave after scraping her knee. It felt good to lean on someone else; I was so tired of keeping everything together and trying to have all the answers. Eric accused me of that very thing the night he left. How wrong he was. I didn't know anything; this proved it.

After Eric's father died, Helen had shifted her wifely dependence on her husband to her eldest child with the ease of a gymnast flipping from one uneven bar to the other. There was nothing Bill couldn't handle, and Helen took credit for creating this capable statue of manhood. What a contrast her feelings about Eric must be.

But she was right. Bill would have some insight into where to look for his little brother. Maybe there was some telepathy he could use to hone into Eric's thinking pattern, distorted as it was with too much booze. Something I hadn't noticed before: Since Eric moved out, I'd stopped worrying about his drinking. He'd taken his daily chaos with him.

I'd been assuming Eric was staying at his mom's, going through the motions of looking for another job and a cheap place to call his own. My denial was so thick—it hadn't occurred to me he might be lying. I'd taken him at his word again and had gotten burned once more. Another lesson in humility. How many did I need?

•   •   •   •   •

When Bill arrived the next morning, he brought me a Mocha Grande from Starbucks. Normally, such a treat would start my day off with a happy jolt, but that morning, the coffee and the chocolate seemed thick all the way down. The sweetness contradicted my mood.

Bill's first suggestion was to look for a paper trail; we could find him if we knew where he was spending money. Because I kept the checkbook, there was no way Eric could use that account. I also knew the savings account was secure since I'd just paid the monthly bills from there—well, some of them.

When Bill asked me about credit cards, I told him we hadn't used any in over a year. I said this with some pride because we'd been conscientious about not getting into debt. When I'd stopped working to stay home with Emma, we decided we would only spend what we had in the bank. I'd seen friends splurge on things they didn't need and pay for them later with ridiculous interest rates. Bill's eyebrows arched as he looked at me, and I read his mind: Just because we *didn't* use the cards, didn't mean they *couldn't* be used. Those accounts were still valid and available.

I ran to the filing cabinet and found an old Visa card statement with the account number on it. I called the customer service number on the front.

The practiced pleasant voice on the other end of the line was more than helpful and accessed the account for me. "Ma'me," she said, "your current balance on this account is $6788.07. Is there anything else I can help you with today?" The color must have drained from my face. In an instant, Bill was by my side.

He lowered me onto a nearby chair and took the phone from my hand. "Hello?" he said to the bewildered woman from Citibank. "I'm afraid we've got a problem here. Can you help us?"

"To whom am I speaking?" she asked with hesitation.

"Oh, I'm sorry. My name is Bill Torrington. That was my sister-in-law you were speaking with. This is quite a shock. I'm afraid her husband, my brother, is missing. When you gave her the balance on that account, she realized he's using this credit card irresponsibly. She's concerned."

"I see. Has *Mrs.* Torrington been using this card at all this past month?" she asked.

"No, ma'me."

"Well, sir, I can help by providing some locations where this card has been used lately, and perhaps you can find Mr. Torrington that way. However, I'm afraid I can't release any information to you. Is your sister-in-law feeling better yet?"

Bill handed me the phone, and I saw my hand shaking as I reached for it. I asked why I hadn't received a bill for these charges. She checked the posting date and said the statement should have arrived about a week ago. She verified my address, and I visualized Eric taking the bill from the mailbox. Of course, he still had a key.

She told me most of the significant charges on the account were from the Quality Inn & Suites. Three miles from our house. Hotel room charges, restaurants, liquor stores, cash withdrawals from various ATMs around town. Gas stations, movie theaters, and even two visits to the Museum of Natural History in Denver. If I could assume he was *still* living this vacation-in-town, the next billing period would reveal another long list of charges coming in the next few weeks.

I'd lost sleep over which bills to pay while Eric was spending more than $200 a day without a second thought! I pictured him sitting by the indoor pool at the Quality Inn with a cocktail in hand, laughing like a carefree playboy who had nowhere else to be. My stomach roiled.

When I called the second credit card company we had an account with, I was relieved to learn that card had not been used. Yet. I tried to cancel it, but the soft-spoken man on the other end offered a scripted apology. In a phonetically articulated voice, he said, "I'm sorry ma'me, you'll have to put your request in writing. Also, since the card is in both your name and your husband's, you will both need to sign the letter." *Of course.*

By the time I'd learned the truth about Eric's careless use of our Visa card, the list of his offences added up like a criminal's rap sheet: Without his income, bills were accumulating that we couldn't pay; he hadn't seen Emma in over two weeks; his lounging at a hotel was lazy and self-centered; and he continued to lie and deceive his family.

We had no way of paying those credit card charges, and I needed to protect our savings. I knew little about the law, but watching *Law & Order* taught me one thing: Since we were married, *I* was equally responsible—legally and financially—for half of that debt.

I needed a lawyer, fast.

●   ●   ●   ●   ●

Charles Franklin Eberhardt was exactly what I expected from an attorney: clean-shaven, tall, piercing blue eyes, and just cocky enough to make you trust his ability. He wore a charcoal gray double-breasted suit that must have cost a few grand. Even his socks looked expensive as they peeped out from under his slacks when he sat down across from me.

Thank God my parents had agreed to pay for Mr. Eberhardt's retainer. Their ever-increasing concern for my future was keeping them up at night. I wouldn't have been welcome in that fancy office without their help.

We were not sitting at his desk, as I imagined we would. Rather, he had a beautiful sitting area boasting two love seats surrounded by several decorative tables and lamps. Along one wall was an impressive legal library, and at the far end of the large room, a wet bar completed the image of financial comfort. A beautiful series of enlarged photographs adorned the wall next to my chair. I recognized most as cities in Italy. Focusing on the colorful image of a Venetian gondola, I wished myself inside it.

After a brief and oddly formal introduction about his background, Mr. Eberhardt proceeded to shoot pointed questions at me, delving into the chaos that had become my life. When the interrogation was over, I felt drained. I never wanted to be on the other side of a courtroom fight with the man.

Charles, as he invited me to call him, not Charlie or Chuck, made a final recommendation: file for a legal separation. When I hesitated, saying that sounded awfully close to filing for divorce, he assured me the document would merely protect me from future financial debt Eric incurred. I would have a year to decide if the separation would proceed to the finality of a divorce.

I signed the necessary papers and left his office initiated in the ugliness of how quickly "'til death do us part" can morph into "I'd rather be dead than financially tied to you."

Chapter Three: Despair

I'd fought the urge to call the Quality Inn all weekend, though I knew the separation papers must have arrived at his hotel room by Friday afternoon. I didn't want an argument or accusations to ruin my weekend, so I waited until Monday.

"Quality Inn; this is Kristin. How may I direct your call?"

"I'm looking for one of your guests, but I'm not sure which room he's in. Eric Torrington."

"Just one moment, please," said the young woman. I imagined she looked like Britney Spears in a business casual skirt and blouse. "I'm sorry. Mr. Torrington checked out yesterday morning."

"Oh," I said, caught off guard. I hadn't expected this turn of events, and the hotel was my only connection to Eric. "I see. Thanks for your help."

Now what? I sat for a minute, then picked up the phone book. My guess was he'd gone to another hotel, having realized I knew where he was. I only hoped it was a less expensive one.

I called the Ramada, two Comfort Inns in different parts of town, and the Days Inn. No Mr. Torrington registered at any. It was a long shot, but I called the two bed & breakfasts I knew of, as well. Finally, I called a few of the dirtbag motels over by the highway. I cringed when the frail-sounding old man at one of them confirmed my fear.

"Ye-ah," he said with a drawl. "We got a Mis-ter Tor-ring-ton here. Checked in yes-ta-day. I rem-em-bah, seein' as how he paid in greenbacks."

"Okay. Thank you, sir. I appreciate your help," I said, speaking slowly into the receiver, as if his precise speech meant he wasn't bright, and I should slow down. Not a fair assumption on my part, I realized, but I'd made it, nonetheless.

I'd never been to the Hi-Way Haven Motel before, but I had a faint memory of where it was located. I'd passed by it once when I made a wrong turn off the interstate. I brought Emma over to Leigh's house, thankful for her willingness to be a last-minute babysitter, and I headed east.

The motel was in awful shape. Strips of paint had peeled off around the doors, and several broken windows caught my eye on the second floor. Those upstairs rooms looked vacant. I parked and walked into the office where a slow but friendly voice greeted me with a, "Hul-lo, Miss."

There was no mistaking he was the old man I'd spoken to on the phone an hour before. He looked me up and down, and I read his mind. I wasn't the typical customer he was used to serving.

After introducing myself, I asked which room Eric Torrington was in. I had a fleeting worry that Ray—his name embroidered, though faded, on his shirt—wouldn't disclose any information, protecting his client's privacy. Then I realized he probably cared little one way or another if I was a mad wife, a tax collector, or Meg Ryan.

I made my way around the corner to room 107 and noticed a slippery feeling in my stomach. Not only had Eric ended up in this terrible place (both physically and in his life), but a foreboding shiver told me something bad was about to happen.

I knocked on the dented beige door marked 10. An educated guess told me it was 107 because I'd passed 106 and could see 108 up ahead. "Hello? Eric? It's me, Kat."

Sounds from the TV were faint, but I could hear canned laughter from some sitcom. He didn't respond to my call.

"Eric? Open the door; we need to talk."

Again nothing.

I took two steps to my right and tried to peek inside the windows, but the curtains were drawn. I could only see a rectangle of light coming from what I guessed was the bathroom.

Maybe he was taking a shower or something. I decided to be patient and sat down on a banged up, graffiti-laden bench nearby. A BBQ grill with a broken top leaned askew in the courtyard, a ghost of happier times when families had gathered here for getaways at the doorstep of the Rocky Mountains. But now, this part of town was long forgotten as a vacation destination. The hotel had become home to transients, people down on their luck, or folks passing through for a one-night stop (or a one-night stand?). Folks who didn't have enough money for the Motel 6 down the road.

After a few minutes, I knocked again. "Eric, it's Kat. I need to talk to you. Please open the door."

"ERIC!" I banged louder.

A woman came out of 108, wearing a shiny red and gold robe. It hung more open than not, and she glared at me. "Hey, sist-ah, I'm tryin' to work over here. Ya mind keepin' it down?" She made no attempt to cover herself, and I saw her large breasts hanging low. There were gold pasties on her nipples, and her flabby tummy revealed a belly button pierced with a "diamond." She looked like a caricature of an old Las Vegas whore starring in a bad Western. Despite the November air, she didn't appear cold.

I offered a weak, "I'm sorry," as she turned to go back into her room. I tried to imagine what the man who waited for her there looked like. This was a sad place, indeed.

I knocked again on 107, but more quietly. I tapped on the window, too, and called Eric's name once more. After a few more minutes of nothingness, I walked back to the motel office, more worried than when I'd arrived.

Ray said he hadn't seen Eric leave the room since checking in. He'd made two trips from his car when he first arrived, carrying several grocery bags.

"Groceries?" I asked. "There's a kitchen in his room?"

"No, ma'me," said Ray. "But lots-a people load up here with munchie-type a food, ya know. And well, booze, of course. There's a li-quor store just up the block a ways."

"Can you ring his room from here?" I asked.

Ray nodded and dialed room 107 from his phone. It rang and rang. He must have seen the concern in my eyes as he replaced the receiver because the next thing he said was a verbalization of what was in my heart: "Are you thinking we should, uh, call the au-thor-it-ies, young lady? You seem to be wor-ried for this man's safety."

Our eyes locked, and I couldn't speak. I felt that familiar sting in my eyes, right before the tears come. I nodded, lowering myself onto a frayed and stained couch near his desk. Ray was a sweet old man who had seen his share of misery and human weakness, no doubt. But his worldliness had also taught him compassion and a nonjudgmental view of the people he encountered. He brought me a box of tissues. I felt safe with him.

Twenty minutes later, a police car arrived. No flashing lights or sirens. It delivered two officers who seemed all too acquainted with the motel.

"Hiya, Ray. What seems to be the trouble today?" asked the female cop, who wore her hair very short and very blonde. She was probably my age, but she was "rough around the edges," as my mother would have said. Nevertheless, she had a kind face, and I could tell she hated coming here because it usually involved bad news.

"Well, Officer Lange, it seems the mis-sus here came by to talk to her husband. He checked in yes-ta-day, but he won't answer the door or the phone. She's a might wor-ried about him now, ya see," Roy explained it better than I could have. His experience in these situations was probably extensive.

"What's your name, ma'me?" asked the other officer, coming closer to me with a notepad in his hand. He was tall and carried a hefty beer belly in front of him. This made his back sway and reminded me of a horse that's seen better days.

"Katharine Torrington," I whispered. "I go by Kat."

"Do you have reason to believe your husband is in danger, Mrs. Torrington?" asked the tall policeman. He opened the pad and started jotting notes.

"Well, I don't know for sure," I spoke honestly. Pushing my embarrassment aside, I offered, "We separated a little over a month ago."

Officer Lange sat next to me and placed a hand on my left shoulder. "How did you know your husband is staying here? Have you two been communicating?"

"No. I tracked his use of an old credit card. He had charged up several thousands of dollars before I found out. I went to an attorney last Tuesday to file for a legal separation. Eric was supposed to receive those papers by Friday. Then, he didn't show up for a visit with our daughter, Emma, on Saturday, so I tried to call him. They told me he'd checked out of the Quality Inn on Sunday morning. That's where he'd been staying before."

The story came out in one long whoosh. The officers both listened carefully, and the man nodded for me to continue.

"I figured Eric must have checked into another hotel to delay my finding him, so I just started calling places around town." I looked down at my hands and added, "I never thought he'd come to a place like this. I'm sorry, Ray." I looked up at the old man, apologetic for calling his place a dump without saying as much. I wondered how he'd come to manage this seedy stop in the middle of nowhere. Had he ever been married? Was he retired from a "real" career along the way?

Ray's upper lip slid into a crooked half-smile, and he nodded once at me. He understood that my husband and I were considered "middle-class folk" until this month. Normally, we wouldn't have patronized his facility.

The big and tall officer, whose name I never learned, spoke next. "Mrs. Torrington, what else can you tell us about your husband's situation that will help us here?"

"He's been struggling with a drinking problem," I confessed. "It's caused our family terrible trouble this past year. He quit his job out of the blue last month and moved out. He said he was going to stay at his mother's while he found an apartment and looked for another job, but he ended up staying at the Quality Inn instead. I don't think he was looking for another job at all," I said, more to myself, still trying to understand.

"Has your husband ever threatened to hurt himself?" asked Officer Lange.

"No!" the word exploded out of me without restraint. "Eric's in a difficult place right now, but he loves Emma."

The male officer took a small step toward me. He made direct eye contact before asking the next question as peacefully as possible. "Before we enter the room, ma'am, is there a chance Eric might have a gun with him?"

"Oh, God, no! He would never. He's not a violent man. Please, I just need to know he's okay."

"We understand," said Officer Lange. "Let's find out. We'll need you to stay here while Ray lets my partner and me into the room, okay? We'll be back in a few minutes."

I could tell from the way Ray walked ahead of the police with the master key in his hand, he'd made this "room-check walk" with the law before.

Waiting in the office alone was torture. I was fidgety. I paced the ancient brown carpet and twisted my watch around and around on my wrist. It felt like an hour, but the clock on the wall registered only three minutes. Officer Lange entered the room with Ray trailing behind like a kid being dragged into church.

Although her eyes were big and brown and warm, I gasped out loud before she said a word. I would have testified that she'd stuck a sword in my chest and twisted it; that's how certain I was of the pain her unspoken words inflicted.

I don't remember how I got out of there. When my head finally cleared, Bill was sitting next to me, and Helen was on the other side of him. I looked around. We were in a waiting area, but not a nice one. It was sterile and chilly. Undecorated and unpopulated. Hospital waiting rooms were not this way.

The fog in my head started to clear when I saw a familiar face. Officer Big and Tall, Officer Lange's partner, walked toward me. Words came from his mouth, but I couldn't make sense of them: "Never . . . terrible . . . note . . . report."

Bill spoke next, and his words came together a little better. "I think I should go. I don't want them to go through this." He squeezed his arm around my shoulder in an awkward sideways hug, then stood. Before he walked away with the officer, he bent to kiss Helen's cheek.

"You need more Kleenex," Helen said and handed me a crumbled wad. Her own eyes were red and puffy; I wondered why she thought *I* needed tissues.

She continued talking to me, as if we'd already been having a conversation, but I didn't remember any of it. I tried to get my brain to catch up, to follow the path of her words.

"We can't blame ourselves, Kat. I once knew a woman who . . . and after, we all looked back and saw how troubled she'd been. But you can never know how much pain someone else is in." She dabbed at her eyes.

"Helen, where's Emma?"

"Don't you remember? You said you dropped her off at your friend's house before you . . . before."

"Yes. Leigh. I should call her." I looked around and found my purse under my chair. I fished out some coins and looked around for a pay phone. When I saw a phone on a wall down the hallway with a sign that said, "Courtesy phone," I was surprised. I dropped the change into my pocket. The sign directed me: "Please limit your calls to three minutes. Dial 9 to get an outside line."

"God, Kat! Are you all right?! Where *are* you? It's been hours since you left here. What's going on?"

"Is Emma okay?" I asked, suddenly worried something was wrong with my baby, and I hadn't been available.

"Yes, of course, Emma is fine. She and Justin are playing with his train set. They both napped a while ago, then I gave them applesauce and graham crackers after. She's fine. Where the hell *are* you? Did you find Eric?"

"Eric? Oh—ERIC! Oh, God. Oh, no. Eric!" It all came back in one glaring flash: the ambulance, the stretcher, the sheet covering his face, the smell of the room, the bottles of booze—there were so many! And most surprising, several plastic prescription pill containers. Where had he gotten those? What was in them? *Why?*

"Kat? What? *What?* Tell me. What?" I heard my friend's voice on the other end, strangled by dread, and it stirred the panic in me.

"He's dead, Leigh. Oh, God, I saw him. He's dead." *Aaawwhhhhhhhhhhh. Uhhhh.* Animal sounds escaped me, like the ones I'd made when I was in labor before the blessing of the epidural. Primal and guttural noises that scared me. They seemed to come from another dimension, certainly not from inside me.

"Oh, my God!" she said. "What . . . what happened?"

"I don't know for sure," I sobbed into the phone, holding the receiver close to my mouth. Then I remembered. "There was a note. He wrote . . . he left me a note, Leigh. I can't read it. I can't." I coughed and slobbered and could barely catch my breath. The room started spinning, and I felt light-headed. I knew I was going to pass out. "Wait," I said into the phone.

I slid with my back against the wall, down to the floor and tried to take in deep breaths. *Slow down*, I said to myself. *Breathe. Breathe.*

I stayed on the floor and was glad the phone cord stretched that far. I heard Leigh crying before I said anything else.

"Kat, what can I do? Are you okay?"

"Well, I didn't faint, so I guess that's a good thing." I couldn't believe I was making light of something so horrible, but Leigh chuckled, too, and it felt all right. "I'm sitting here on the floor. It's cold. God, Leigh, I don't even know where I am!"

"Is anyone there with you?" she asked with alarm.

"Yes, when I first woke up, Bill and Helen were here. Bill went somewhere with one of the police officers I met earlier, and Helen's right down the hall."

"When you first *woke up?* What do you mean?"

"Well . . . maybe I *did* faint? Earlier, I mean. I don't remember. I just know I don't remember anything after I saw Eric in the room, and the bed, and . . ."

The note. The note. The note!

I dabbed away my tears and sniffled into the phone.

"Look around you. Tell me what you see," she said.

"The walls are green, like a hospital green, but they're cinder block, not regular walls. And there's no carpet. It's like this isn't where people usually hang out."

"Is it the police station? You said you saw an officer there."

"I don't think so. I've only seen a few people, and they're not in uniforms," I said, genuinely confused. "Wait, there's Bill. I should go find out what's going on." I stood and wiped my eyes again. "Can Emma stay with you a little longer?"

"Of course. Don't worry. She can stay here all night. But you shouldn't be alone tonight, Kat. Why don't you come here when you leave wherever you are, and stay over with Emma here, okay?"

"Yeah. You're right. I will. I don't know when that'll be, though."

"Whenever you get here, we'll be here. Don't worry," she said. "And Kat, I'm so sorry about Eric. I'm here for you and Emma. You won't be alone."

I couldn't even say "Thank you" or "I know" or "I'll be there soon." My throat choked any words I might have tried to say. I hung up the phone and ran down the hall toward Bill.

I was in the morgue, of course. The basement of the hospital is not as welcoming as the upper floors. They don't expect to host the living for more than a few minutes, and those who visit aren't particular about the décor when they do.

Bill had identified Eric's body, saving Helen and me that unbearable task. But I had already seen him from a distance. I'd waited with the police outside the hotel room for the ambulance to arrive. The officers wouldn't let me go in, but I leaned in through the doorway, needing to see for myself. My husband was really gone.

All of it, surreal. The reality of this fork in my life jabbed me like a knife threatening my jugular. And the mental pain, so sharp. Beyond anything I could have imagined. Sadness, guilt, and regret filled me. If only—

Emma's life would never be the same. Neither would mine.

How could he? How could he have been so desperate? Was there anything I could have done? Was the letter from the lawyer too much for him? Even if I wasn't enough to live for, wasn't Emma? Couldn't he see another way out of this mess?

The note. Suddenly, I wanted to read it. But not there.

•   •   •   •   •

I drove to the lake we'd visited often when we were dating. The beautiful walking trail around the circumference offered gorgeous mountain views from every angle. We used to spend hours there. Sometimes Eric stopped to fish, and I'd sit on a nearby bench and watch him, daydreaming about our future. Part of that future had come true when Emma completed our family.

Our walks had continued, and we took turns carrying our bundle in a Snugli or backpack. When Emma got too heavy for those, we pushed her in the stroller, and she giggled at the birds. She loved watching the "big kids," who couldn't have been more than four or five, as they swung or slid or ran around with balls. Those were perfect days. He was sober, and we were happy. It was a lifetime ago. Emma's lifetime.

I walked to a bench on the east side of the water and looked at the back range topped with snow. November in Colorado. The sun was warm, though the air was crisp. I pulled my jacket tight around my chest, but not because of the weather. The chill I felt was coming from within.

I was thankful to be holding a copy of the actual note. To touch the real paper Eric had held in his last moments would have been like touching sandpaper on fire.

My whole life I've felt like I didn't belong. I kept trying to be what I thought everyone wanted me to be, but half the time I didn't know what that was. I'm a fake, but I wasn't even good at that, so now I'm a fake and a failure.

I thought when I got married I would finally "get it," but even then I was acting. I kept looking around, trying to be like the guys I knew who were grown up. All I got was frustrated. I know you love me, Kat, but I could never understand why. That doesn't mean I didn't love you, too, cuz I did. But I also know I didn't love you enough. I always felt like I was doing it wrong. I'm sorry for that.

When Emma was born, it was like a piece of me decided to survive. I always knew I wouldn't, but I'm so glad I got to know her, even a little. I know I've been a lousy father and that's part of why I need to leave. But it's not because of love. I love her more than anything.

I know this isn't making a lot of sense. But I don't think it really can, not to you. I just can't stay here anymore. I keep making mistakes and hurting people, and I don't know how to make it right. It'll be better this way. I'm ready. I'm tired of feeling bad about myself all the time. I'm just tired.

Please tell Emma, every day, that I'm with her. All she has to do is look up to the stars, and I'll be there. Thanks.

But what if his slip hadn't become a full-fledged relapse?
What if he hadn't given up on us? On himself?

The Slip & The Fall
Late May - November 1994

* Fork 4 *

Chapter One: Tested

Scientists say smell is our strongest sense. Pass by a stranger in a store, wearing the same perfume your mother wore when you were a kid, and time melts away. You're transported to the kitchen of your childhood home—Mom at the stove and you at the table, doing your fourth-grade word problems. It's a fantastic experience when good memories flood back.

But a lilac-infused spring evening had the distinction of bringing an unwelcome scent back into my home, and the memories it stirred were far from fantastic.

Seventeen months had passed since I'd smelled the bittersweet bite of alcohol on Eric's breath, seen the slight sway in his step, and detected the subtle slur of his speech. But it hadn't been so long that *my* illness, denial, didn't find its way back to the surface in an instant. My immediate reaction was, *I must be mistaken.*

The old, naïve part of me was desperate to turn away, discount what I was seeing and smelling. However, I'd learned enough through my own recovery to know that staying ignorant wasn't in anyone's best interest.

I made a conscious, forced effort, begging my eyes to stay focused. *Don't look away. Did he just bump into the counter?* I pleaded with my nose to breathe deeply, even though the odor stung not only my lungs, but also my brain. My fears were confirmed. There was no logical way to justify it into anything else: He was drunk.

They had taught us about the possibility of relapse in his outpatient education classes, and I knew a one-time slip didn't necessarily mean we were back on the road to a daily problem, but it still scared the hell out me. Flashbacks of his passed-out form on the couch and memories of my unacknowledged tearful pleas tore at me like someone ripping off a Band-Aid when you're not expecting it. I stood fixed in place and acknowledged the knots in my stomach.

As I watched him put tremendous effort into walking a straight line down the hallway, I tried to recall what the family counselor had said. *Do I confront him right now—let him know I know? Or wait until tomorrow when his head clears?* I knew I should remain calm, but I was also angry. A year and a half of sobriety and trust down the drain. A malodorous soup of feelings ranging from sad to scared bubbled up. I couldn't deny the ray of disappointment that curved above me.

I checked on Emma; she'd fallen asleep in the playpen. After taking the casserole out of the oven, I carried Emma up to her crib. The distance would be good for Eric and me, and watching my baby's sleeping form always put things in perspective. I smiled as she repositioned beneath the cheerful mobile and found her way back to the kaleidoscope of her dreams.

When she was awake, Emma took in the sights and sounds and texture of everything with an innocence and joy that helped *me* remember the awe of those things, too. As she regenerated for another day of adventure, she breathed evenly. Her favorite stuffed animal, a music-making goose my mom had given her, lay next to her. Ensuring peace in my daughter's life mattered more than anything else.

In Al-Anon I learned to ask myself, "Is it really important?" This simple phrase helped prioritize what I should focus on, as all the slogans did. The beauty of the program was how the principles worked—if you remembered to use them.

In the past year and a half, I had learned so much, but I hadn't been tested on any of it yet. *Easy does it; Keep it simple; Live and let live;*

One day at a time. These little mantras grew to have depths of meaning I never imagined before, and although they each sounded simple, they were not easy. Time to put all that theory into action.

Eric's tumble from sobriety had certainly caught me off guard, but how else would it happen? It's not something we'd planned for. Still, I had to concentrate, think, not just react. I settled into the comfy rocking chair in Emma's room and gave myself a good talking to.

We knew this could happen one day; that day is here. He knows what he's done; you don't need to confront him. Let him sleep it off, and we can talk in the morning. Okay? Okay.

I recalled the "Relapse Lesson" Caroline, the counselor at the hospital, had given family members. She'd scared the shit out of us with a long list of statistics that didn't bode well for those in recovery. And yet, what choice did we have? We had to focus on the possible, the hope. It didn't mean we couldn't also carry pragmatism in our back pocket.

Caroline had also told us about the triggers that often lead to a slip. They vary per person, but several were common to most people: stress, fatigue, loneliness, boredom, temptation (being with people or in familiar places where past drinking occurred), and lack of a positive support systems—or disregarding those. Eric had never been a drinking-with-the-boys type, and the bar scene didn't attract him, so the recovery advice to "change your playmates and playgrounds" was immaterial. But what had triggered this slip?

Stress was part of his job—anyone's job—but he'd been handling that well for over a year. Even though I thought of myself as part of his support system, maybe he didn't feel it. Maybe I was too busy with Emma? Could he be bored with the predictability of our routines? He might feel isolated or lonely. He'd never had many friends—something I'd wondered about over the years. His attendance at AA meetings was (mostly) regular, but he hadn't sought a sponsor yet. Maybe that would help?

At the end of this simplistic self-pep talk, I had no real answers other than two things: One, Eric was an alcoholic; that's why he drank. His recovery was a commitment to *not give into* those triggers. Two, this was Eric's problem to solve. I knew enough to accept I couldn't—and shouldn't try to—fix it for him. He had slipped, for whatever reason, and he alone had to choose to get back on the path to sobriety. Ensuring this slip didn't turn into a prolonged relapse was a solo journey. I knew it, and he knew it. My role was to give him space to figure it out and to support him by accepting the path and timeline it might take.

I left Emma's room, hoping my actual conversation with Eric in the morning would be as straightforward as the one I'd just had with myself.

When I went back downstairs, he was already asleep. It was 7:00 p.m., less than an hour since he'd come home. He'd taken the opportunity of my brief absence to go to bed.

It doesn't take an education in the Twelve Steps to know that's called avoidance.

•   •   •   •   •

The next few weeks brought similar scenarios, not frequent at first, but enough to keep me guessing which Eric would walk in the door. On good nights, the three of us would have dinner together; Eric and I shared the highlights of our days. Emma had ventured beyond cereal and baby food in jars. As she tested her fingers and exercised her taste buds, we watched her face register new foods: peas (yuck), peaches (yum), and tiny bits of hamburger (just okay, but better with ketchup). We noted her preferences and wondered if she'd like crab legs one day, our favorite indulgence.

After dinner, Eric played with Emma in the living room while I did the dishes. The open floor plan allowed me to listen to my baby's giggles and "moh da!" (Emma-talk for "more, Daddy.") I relished the musical sounds, especially when Eric laughed back with her.

We took turns giving Emma her evening baths. (It was my task alone when he'd been drinking, but he didn't seem to notice the restriction.) And we usually sat together and read her bedtime stories before kissing her goodnight.

But on evenings when he wobbled into the house and plopped down on the couch, the routine was different: I bit my tongue and kept my distance. Emma played *around* him, and sometimes he slept through dinner. We'd play in Emma's room before bath time and stories, and goodnight kisses only came from Mommy on those nights.

The morning after that first slip, I tried to talk to Eric about it, but he brushed past me on his way to work. "We'll talk about it later," he said. Later never happened.

At the beginning, the odor would follow him home only once or twice a week. But as spring heated up to a dry, hot summer, I resigned myself to seeing glimpses of the Eric I used to know only on Sundays. He didn't drink on the weekends, so he spent Saturdays withdrawn and sleepy, medicating his stomachaches and acting as if he'd had a hard week. By Sunday, he was feeling lucid enough to make pancakes for Emma and me, and he smiled easily as we walked to the park or shopped for the next week's groceries. We'd chat about some upcoming event or holiday. He'd tell me stories about his job, and I'd share gossip from the MAM group. Sitting on a bench together, we'd watch Emma cross the playground. She was newly vertical and as unstable as . . . well, someone who'd had too much to drink. I was happy on those days. They were enough to sustain me through the next week. Most of the time.

The path I took through the Twelve-Step program was typical. I started with "fake it 'til ya make it." You don't have to believe what you're doing at first, you just go through the motions. Your beliefs and feelings follow in time.

The routine of going to meetings helped. The people I met in those rooms never made me feel "less than," and I found in them an acceptance and support which amazed me. The group discouraged pity parties, and no one ever said, "Oh, I've been there, this is what you should do . . ." Instead, the quiet nods of heads, the deep knowing look in their eyes, told me they *did* know how I felt. Whatever I was feeling was okay. Most of us stood as examples of "progress, not perfection," and that was a fine goal. I worked hard to learn their language and their way of love.

The changes came. I thought before I spoke. My actions became more about me, and less about merely reacting to Eric. The place I felt improvement most was in my stomach: the knots had loosened.

Another routine that helped was talking with Gwen on the phone every morning. Her experience, strength, and hope grounded me. As my sponsor, she was a safe place to dump my fears and "process out loud." She didn't tell me what to do, but she guided me to trust the program—and myself. Not easy when I doubted the person in the mirror.

One day she suggested we meet in person—a real treat! Emma and I met Gwen at a coffee shop that offered toys for children to busy themselves with while grown-ups talked. I assumed most friends chatted about movies, jobs, and politics, not the threads holding their marriages together.

"What do I do with the sense of betrayal I feel?" I started with the bottom line and worked backward.

"Tell me, specifically, what you feel betrayed by?"

"Every time he comes home with that smell on him, I feel like he's been cheating on me, but with a bottle. I know it sounds ridiculous—and impossible—but isn't it like that? He's choosing this other thing instead of me, and it brings him a kind of pleasure I can't." I picked up a napkin and started tearing it into tiny shreds. Emma was "reading" a hardback book about farm animals. "If he were in love with some gorgeous woman—a size six blonde—I might be able to compete somehow: dye my hair, lose weight. But this way, it's hopeless. There's no way to make myself into that something else he wants. I'm only human."

I'd started imagining his obsession akin to what he used to feel for me, but better. The tingle alcohol produced on his lips and the warmth it spread through his belly was something like the love we'd once shared, but this lust required nothing of him in return. It was pure and selfish, and it enticed him away from me every time it won a daily battle. It offered respite and unconditional love; it didn't question him or demand he live up to his responsibilities.

"You feel frustrated because his choices are out of your control. What *can* you control about this situation?" Gwen's face was an illustration of serenity. I wanted that peace and the equilibrium it represented: a calm center in the middle of a storm.

"I know I'm supposed to say I can only control *my response* to his behaviors. I should focus on my own choices and actions, not his: eat healthy, read my literature, meditate, get enough sleep. I know what I *should* do, but there are days when I want to scream at him: 'Stop this self-destructive behavior! You're ruining our lives!'"

Gwen chuckled and shot me a "been there, done that" smile.

"That's what I'm here for. Say those things to *me*, but *do* those healthier things when you're with him. You've listed a few; you know what they are. It's a matter of choosing to act on those healthy options instead of giving in to less beneficial ones."

It sounded easy, but it wasn't.

"Tell me how you're detaching these days." Gwen nudged me to focus on things I was doing well so I'd stop "shoulding" on myself.

"Well, on nights when he's been drinking, I put distance between us. Sometimes Emma and I go for an after-dinner trip to the playground or over to my friend Leigh's house down the street until bedtime. There's a 7:00 p.m. Al-Anon meeting with free babysitting on Wednesdays, so I go there if his drinking coincides with those nights." I watched Emma pick up a shape-sorter and try to push the square plastic piece into the circular opening. *Like mother, like daughter.* "I don't mention why we're leaving the house; he already knows and doesn't want to hear my reasons. I simply kiss him goodbye and say, 'We'll be back in a bit.'"

Gwen nodded her approval. "That shows you're not labeling his behavior as 'bad.' You're focusing on making good decisions for you and Emma."

"Other times, we stay home, and I busy myself with laundry. I teach Emma how to sort by colors." I smiled at the memory of her trying to say blue; it came out *boo*. I confided in my sponsor, "I even wash clean clothes sometimes just to have something to do."

My coffee was gone, so I swept up the tattered remnants of my napkin and tossed them inside the empty cup.

"What else?" she asked.

"I guess I'm also getting better at not enabling." I felt a flicker of accomplishment about my budding Al-Anon skills.

"Give me an example."

"By the time I'm done keeping my distance those nights, Eric's often asleep—usually upright on the couch. I don't wake him anymore to move him to our room, and I never pick up after him. After waking between 2:00 and 5:00 most mornings, he wanders to our bed. He doesn't say anything to me about it the next day, but I imagine he makes the connection between that and why his neck hurts in the morning. I supposed he also realizes he's waking up in his clothes?"

"Great job. Those are natural consequences. You can't make him learn the lessons, but you're not standing in his way of discovering them." Gwen's verbalization of what I'd been doing right felt like I'd passed my final exam in physics. Her last pat on the back summarized the benefit of detaching. "This takes nothing away from Eric, yet it strengthens *you*. It's a perfect self-preservation tool when others around you are self-destructing."

In meetings and Twelve-Step literature, I learned the adage *you can still love the alcoholic while hating the disease*. While I understood that in theory, reality kept knocking on my brain: One of these days, I will detach myself from Eric so much that our love will be stretched too thin. Eventually, the ties that connect us will break.

• • • • •

"I'm wondering what you'd think of us going to counseling together?" I braved the question while we sat on a blanket at the park. Two days after the Fourth of July, we were enjoying a picnic of leftover chicken fingers and watermelon. Emma was busy exploring the sandbox; I watched to make sure most of the sand ended up in her hands, not in her mouth. The new shovel and pail she'd received for her first birthday the month before sat next to her unused. Her hand-eye coordination wasn't quite ready for them, but they served as colorful companions. Bath time would be a gritty one.

"It's funny you bring that up. Someone mentioned it at a meeting last week."

"Really? In what context?"

"The topic was having a strong support system and keeping the struggle out in front of you. Being open with the people in your life who matter most."

"The struggle?" I asked.

"The battle for control over the disease. You know how some days I'm successful at that, and other days, not so much." His eyes darted to the horizon, in the opposite direction of mine. "It's back and forth. I'm trying."

"I know you are, and I can't imagine how hard it is. I see you making the effort. And feeling frustrated when . . . well, when the disease wins some days, as you said."

Emma grabbed our attention when she squealed at a butterfly in her vicinity. "Oooh!" she said with her mouth the shape of a perfect circle. We, her adoring parents, chuckled at her enthusiasm.

"I'd be open to counseling, I guess. But I've never done anything like that. What would you want to get out of it?" Good question. I wasn't entirely sure myself.

"I feel distant from you sometimes, like we're not 'in this' together. I mean, I have my meetings and things I'm working on, and you have yours. I wonder if we could support each other better—or at least better understand what we're each going through?"

"That makes sense. I want to talk to you about things, but sometimes I don't know how. Maybe a counselor can help."

I was more than happy with his willingness to give it a try. "Thanks, honey. It can only help, right?" I leaned over to kiss him on the cheek, and he smiled at me. "I'll make some calls in the morning."

•   •   •   •   •

I made an appointment with a male counselor. I thought that might feel more comfortable for Eric, and I found someone who specialized in both substance abuse and marriage counseling. His name was Tom Benedict, and even though a Ph.D. followed his surname, he declined having us call him doctor. Very approachable.

He appeared younger than I think he was. A round, boyish face peered out from a fringe of old-fashioned "bangs," for lack of a better word. His light brown hair flopped down casually over his left eye. He flipped his head occasionally to move the strands away, presumably so he could see. But there were deep laugh lines around those half-hidden eyes; they added a sense of wisdom I usually attributed to a more advanced age.

Our first meeting with Tom was a general fact-finding mission: He wanted each of us to provide some background on why we were there. I found that surprising because I thought it was obvious. *How could our perspectives be different when we both knew Eric's relapse was the undisputed problem?*

But, as I continued to learn on my marital journey, situations were never cut and dry. I expressed a desire to feel more connected to Eric as he regained his footing and got back on track with his recovery. I was concerned that my detaching (though necessary and healthy for me) might create a permanent chasm between us, one I feared we couldn't bridge.

Eric shared how he felt "on the spot," as if he were supposed to be doing his recovery according to some unknown playbook I possessed—one he was unaware of. He expressed hesitation to share with me because he worried about disappointing me.

As interesting as that was, the cynical part of me saw it as a diversion—a way to shift focus away from his relapse. We'd soon find out the quality of the addiction counseling education Tom Benedict had earned from Minneapolis College.

The next time we met with the counselor, Tom talked us through the basics of paraphrasing and mirroring—communication techniques I remembered learning in college. Active listening and repeating what the other person says feels unnatural, but it slows people down. The goal is to hear and validate what your partner is saying before you jump in and counter or move the conversation in a different direction. So, we practiced.

"What I hear you saying is, *You worry I'm judging you and expecting you to work your Twelve Steps as I do. That makes you feel inadequate or incapable.* Did I get that right?"

Then he tried. "What I hear you saying is, *When I don't share what I'm learning with you, you feel left out. That makes you feel distant from me, disconnected.* Did I get that right?"

And so it went, back and forth: Each of us saying something on our minds that we couldn't—or hadn't—said in the privacy of our own home, and the other person feeding it back. It was robotic, but I felt heard.

At the end of the second session, Eric accurately paraphrased my bottom line: "*What I hear you saying is, you're worried I'm still having slips. You're afraid I might never get and stay sober again. That makes you feel scared about our future—for us and for Emma.* Did I get that right?"

It was surreal hearing him utter those words—fears I'd only said aloud to Gwen, Leigh, and my parents. I prayed he understood this was more than a wordplay exercise. I needed him to *hear* me.

As we settled into bed later that night, Eric said, "It's cool to tell each other those things at Tom's office. I mean, it's a weird *way* to say them, but I can see why it helps. Do you think we can do it by ourselves without him?"

"That's the goal. I hope so. It would be awkward for him to move in with us just so we can have a conversation, right?" I grinned over at him, trying for some levity.

"Ha ha, funny pants. But for your information, I thought I was better at the active listening thing than you were."

"Oh, really? Do tell."

"Well, since it's a well-known fact that you talk more than I do," he paused for effect and raised his eyebrows high, "I'm used to listening to you."

I nodded. "Fair point. But I'd probably shut up if you talked more. Deal?"

"I'll work on it." He extended his hand, and we shook on it. "Deal."

It felt like a start, a beginning to a new openness and vulnerability between us. I slept better than I had in two months.

•   •   •   •   •

The following Wednesday was our third session with Tom. Eric was coming directly from work that day, so we drove separately.

At 4:15, Tom said, "Should we start?"

"Without Eric? Can't we wait a few more minutes? I'm sure traffic's just making him run late."

Tom looked at me with an expression worthy of a king who isn't buying whatever joke his jester is tossing out. "Is it possible Eric isn't coming today?" *Is that pity in his eyes?*

"Well, anything's possible, but . . ." The sentence drifted away. "We had a good talk after our last session with you. He said he liked the exercises we were doing."

"I'm glad about that. Those are great tools you guys can continue practicing—especially when you want to make sure you're hearing each other."

"But?" I asked, waiting for the disclaimer I heard coming.

"Yes, but marriage counseling can only work if both partners participate equally—and if they both want to be here. Otherwise, this is *individual* counseling. I can do that with you alone, but I don't think that's what you were looking for."

"What if he has a good reason for not being here?" I said in a pathetic and defensive tone.

"As you said before, 'Anything's possible.' But there are telephones; he hasn't called. My assistant would have buzzed me by now." He folded his hands in front of him on his color-coded desk calendar. "Look, Kat, I know you're working your Al-Anon program—and it shows most of the time. But your willingness to believe what you want to see when Eric's actions are saying something else is part of your codependency. You know that."

I was being called out. He was right. I nodded, allowing him to continue.

"I think you also know doing counseling as a couple while he continues to drink won't work. Eric needs to be sober—and not just a day here and there. Sober. *In recovery.* Working his program as earnestly as you're working yours."

"How can he say last week's session helped him connect with me, but now he's not willing to try again?"

"You know how flight attendants give those safety announcements on airplanes: *Place the oxygen mask over your own mouth and nose first, then assist children or others next to you?* That's because you can't take care of someone else if you're not breathing yourself."

"And? I don't follow."

"Eric must be breathing on his own, taking care of his most basic need first—being sober—before he can focus on committing to your marriage. I know it's painful for you to accept, especially since you put him—and your daughter, of course—first. But until Eric can get and stay sober, everything else in his life is secondary."

I knew he'd seen patients cry in his office before, but I was still embarrassed. I reached for a tissue from the box on his desk and said, "Pretty naïve of me, huh?"

"Not at all. You care deeply for your husband and your family. There's no shame in that. But marriage counseling is a waste of time at this point. And that's okay for now. I'll be here to help you both as soon as he's ready."

"*If* he's ever ready." I thanked Tom for his time and candor—not to mention his ethics for discontinuing sessions (and declining income) when he knew he couldn't help us. As I left the office, I glanced at the framed certificate on his wall and made a mental note: For a relatively unknown institution, Minneapolis College did a good job educating this particular student.

I couldn't see how our story would end. Maybe Eric would get Sober—capital -S—for good. Maybe I'd find a way to be healthy inside a marriage marred by madness. All I knew for sure was Emma needed at least one stable parent. By default, at that time, it had to be me.

I thought of that time as The Downward Spiral. It wasn't a linear drop, like a jump from a cliff, but rather a one-step-forward, two-steps-back pattern. It followed the shape of a coil: We'd push our way up over the first bowed edge, then slide down the twisted curve on the other side. We'd struggle back upwards and descend into the muck again for a while. Riding the downward arc always lasted longer.

Though it was gradual, I could feel the descent, like an airplane decreasing in altitude, drawn out over the span of several miles. I wondered if the landing would be soft or if I'd be freed in a crash echoing from the Rockies to the Atlantic Ocean. At first glance, the smooth landing appears to be the better option. But the truth is, if your life as you know it ends and you don't even feel the pain of it, isn't that sadder than burning up in a sea of flames that leaves you screaming?

•   •   •   •   •

When he started throwing up blood at the end of July, I knew we were in trouble. He wouldn't admit it was alcohol-related, so we spent a fortune in doctor's bills, trying to find out "What's wrong?" And he missed a lot of work.

Orders were given for upper and lower GIs, an MRI, throat cultures, blood tests, and stool samples. Anything related to digestive tract illnesses was explored: ulcers, cancer, acid reflux, irritable bowel syndrome. When Eric's primary physician learned of the terrible cramps and stomach pain Eric was experiencing, he prescribed Paregoric, a derivative of opium! But the good doctor didn't have all the facts: Eric never mentioned the several bottles of vodka he drank every week. He never offered the possibility that such high ingestion of alcohol *might* be a contributing factor in his discomfort. He also failed to acknowledge that adding a narcotic to his weekly intake of booze just might not be a great idea.

The combination of the prescription along with his self-medicating could have been lethal, but it only proved to be extra damaging. The stomach ailments persisted, and the doctor continued to scratch his head. I guess the buzz was worth the risk for Eric, but when I found out about his lie of omission (by being a snoop and doing a little pharmaceutical research—very un-Al-Anon of me!), I called Dr. Hubbard for a private consultation.

To say he was embarrassed would be a terrific understatement. The doctor was relieved to know the truth, yet ashamed he hadn't put it all together. He had taken Eric at his word and never pressed him about his alcohol intake. (Eric hadn't told him about his two weeks in the hospital and the subsequent outpatient treatment for substance abuse.)

I didn't blame the doctor; I was an expert at not seeing evidence right in front of me. Besides, most patients *want* to feel better, so they help their doctor by providing accurate information. Addicts have different motives: attention, self-pity, punishment, deception. For Eric, add in the bonus of a new high, and he had plenty of reasons to keep the truth from his doctor.

But this physician was not about to be deceived and taken advantage of once he knew the truth. He did some research of his own about how he could best help Eric, and then he called for an intervention. With the help of a psychologist friend, Dr. Hubbard orchestrated a scene out of a Tennessee Williams play.

I'd gotten pretty good at detaching by then, so being an active participant in his plan required me to push through some resistance. But if the doctor's plan went as he hoped, Eric might have a real chance of confronting his alcoholism, getting the medical attention he needed, and maybe, just maybe, I'd get my husband back.

•　　•　　•　　•　　•

My job was to get Eric to the doctor's office that day. I'm a lousy liar, so I had to harness my inner Meryl Streep to make the ruse believable. Dr. Hubbard was in practice with my primary care provider. I told Eric I had my annual OB/GYN exam, and I asked him to come along and watch Emma in the waiting room.

There were several holes in my story. He could have asked, "Why can't my mom watch Emma?" or "Can't I watch her at home?" But, fortunately, (or un-), he wasn't into logic those days and didn't seem to notice or care that my request made little sense. He trudged home a little early that day, and we all piled into the car.

When we checked in at the receptionist's desk, I signed the requisite intake sheet and winked at Misty behind the desk. She knew about the charade and said with microscopic innuendo, "I'll let the doctor know you're here." Eric and Emma were already deeply involved in a puzzle game in the children's waiting area. Except for Eric's size, they looked like playmates, concentrating on finding the straight-edged pieces together.

When Al Kaufman walked into the lobby a few minutes later, Eric glanced up and did a double take. "Oh . . . uh. Hi, Al. Didn't know your doctor was in this practice, too."

"Yes. Same insurance plan, ya know."

"Guess so," said Eric. He stood, then bent over to pick Emma up off the floor. "Have you met my family? This is Katharine," he said, nodding his head in my direction.

Al Kaufman walked the three feet between us to shake my hand. "Pleased to meet you, ma'am." He could barely look me in the eye, as our recent phone conversation had been difficult for both of us. The dear man was nervous about what he was about to help facilitate.

"Please, call me Kat," I said as we squeezed hands.

He was a handsome man in his early sixties, with graying hair along his temples. His face was weathered from years of hard work in the outdoors, but his body had endured the work well. He appeared fit and strong enough to keep up with the men he supervised who were half his age. Al Kaufman wore a wedding ring, and I wondered about his wife. What kinds of struggles had they faced together over the years?

"Oh, my," he said in a more relaxed voice, turning to address Emma. "Who is *this* little beauty?"

"This is Miss Emma," said her proud father. Next, he spoke to the toddler on his hip. "Emma, this is Mr. Kaufman. Can you say 'Hi?'"

Emma produced a huge smile, showing off her new teeth in varying stages of descent. She turned away and buried her face in her daddy's neck, shying away from the stranger's grin. The two men shared a chuckle at Emma's dramatics.

"She's a real cutie, isn't she? You're a lucky man, Eric. A lovely family you have." He nodded in my direction.

Emma went back to her puzzle with her father in tow, and Mr. Kaufman sat down across the waiting room from me, a magazine in hand. I flipped through my purse, trying to look casual while my stomach churned. I searched for ChapStick and Tums, not necessarily in that order.

I snuck a glance at Al Kaufman, whom I imagined was trying hard not to sneak a glance back at me. I thought about what I'd asked this man to do when I called him three days ago. I'd only met him a few times, briefly, at company parties. The conversations were never deep. During our phone call that week, I'd shared the sad and candid details of my husband's secret.

"I know this is highly unusual," I said, "but Eric's doctor stressed how we need as many people as possible—from all areas of Eric's life—to be present at this meeting. Eric needs to see how his actions are affecting people all around him. His mother and brother will be there, and of course, I will be, too."

Kaufman let out a long breath, and I waited for him to speak.

"I really like Eric, and most days, he's still a good employee, but . . . I have noticed lethargy in the afternoons, and he's used a lot of sick time over the past few months," he admitted. Then, more to himself than to me, he added, "My own brother went through something similar a few years back."

I took the opportunity of his pause to explain the intervention process, and I asked if he would participate.

"I've never done anything like this before. I'm worried it's not my place."

"I know it feels like an invasion of his privacy, Mr. Kaufman, but hasn't Eric already invaded yours? He's already brought this problem into your workplace. He's probably drinking on his lunch breaks some days and coming back to work drunk. You're paying him to be unproductive."

"Maybe, but won't it embarrass him to be confronted like this?" he asked, genuinely concerned for Eric's sake.

"Yes," I agreed. "But this is a matter of life and death. I don't mean to be dramatic, but it really could be. And what would happen to your company and your insurance rates if Eric had *or caused* an accident there while under the influence? Couldn't the law also hold you legally responsible in some way?"

"I imagine you're right," he said, conceding the point. I pictured him shaking his head in the quiet of his office.

"You shouldn't have to take that chance, Mr. Kaufman. If you can help Eric turn his life around now, he could be a great employee again. But this way, he's a liability and a worry." While Al Kaufman absorbed that thought, I continued.

"Look, you have every right to fire him, but I'm asking you to consider another option. You seem like a kind man, and I hear the concern in your voice. If Eric had cancer, wouldn't you tell him to get the treatment he needs—to take the time off work required to get healthy? Is this so different?"

In the doctor's waiting room, Misty spoke up. "Mrs. Torrington, the doctor will see you now."

•　　•　　•　　•　　•

When I walked into Dr. Hubbard's office, my mother-in-law and brother-in-law were already there. Bill hugged me and asked how I was holding up.

"Okay, I guess. I'm really glad you're here. Thanks for coming." I looked over at his mother to extend the thanks to her, as well, but I was met with significantly less warmth. Helen was there against her better judgment. After hours of arguing over coffee, Bill had convinced her that Eric needed help. This was the best way to get it.

Over the past few months, I'd been able to have serious conversations with my brother-in-law about Eric's drinking. He was open to hearing about it and trying to resolve it. Bill felt an obligation as the senior male in the family to get Eric the help he needed. After his own divorce the previous year, Bill wanted to spare his kid brother that pain, if possible. He'd assessed our marriage and found it salvageable, so far.

My mother-in-law was another story. I'd heard many parents in Al-Anon confess their feelings of failure regarding their grown children's alcoholism. It was a double burden because not only did they suffer watching their child battle the disease, but they also had the added burden of wondering what their role might have been in "giving" it to them. Jewish, Catholic, agnostic; it didn't matter. A mother's guilt is a religion all its own.

So, Helen was there, but with a chip on her shoulder and blind faith in her pocket. "Eric could stop this if he really tried," she'd told me shortly after his relapse three months ago, voicing her wholehearted belief in her son's character. "He just needs a little more time. He's under a lot of stress right now, being the sole supporter of your family." I ignored the jab to my stay-at-home mom status. Somehow, her years at home with her children in the '60s and '70s were not the same.

"But I need him sober, Helen," I'd said. "And Emma deserves a daddy who doesn't fall asleep for the night before she does."

"Well . . ." she'd said, but it never went beyond that.

At least she'd come to the intervention. Bill must have spoken magic words to get her to attend because not only did she believe Eric would "figure this out" on his own, but she was also a very private person. She believed family matters should stay in the family. Period. Bringing Eric's boss and doctor into the mix made her quite uncomfortable.

A medical assistant I didn't know escorted Mr. Kaufman into the room, and I walked over to shake his hand again. I thanked him one more time for coming and then introduced him to Helen and Bill. "Please, call me Al," he said to all of us.

Dr. Hubbard popped his head into the room and said, "I'll go get Eric."

I was glad I didn't have to see Eric's face when the doctor called him in from the waiting room and explained that Misty was going to keep an eye on Emma while they visited. I'm sure he was confused, but he didn't protest. He followed the doctor down the hall and into his now-crowded office.

I fought tears when I saw the terror in Eric's eyes. Instinctively, he took a step backward toward the door he'd just come through, but Dr. Hubbard was there, not by mistake, blocking his escape. "What are you all doing here?" he said, looking from one of us to the next in quick succession.

"Eric, let's sit down, and I'll explain," Dr. Hubbard said, leading Eric to the sole remaining seat in the room. "*I* invited everyone here today," he began. "The people in this room care about you very much."

Eric sat as still as a cat ready to pounce, trying to figure out how he'd ended up there. It seemed his mind wasn't working fast enough to catch what was going on. Nervous energy radiated off him as he waited for The Explanation that would put it all together for him.

"Am I sick? Is that why I'm here?" He looked across the room, directing his question into my eyes, searching for support from his wife. I held his gaze, but he broke it when he looked back at the doctor. "You found something on the MRI or the lab tests?" he asked, his voice skirting the edge of hopeful. If he were truly ill with a physical something, maybe no one would talk about what he dreaded we were going to talk about.

"Well, in a sense, yes, you are sick. But it's nothing that can't be treated. You're going to be fine. I assure you." Dr. Hubbard had a paternal voice, calm yet authoritative.

No one else spoke. We sat as voyeuristic and awkward observers in the doctor-patient exchange.

"What's wrong with me?" my husband of five years asked with a thread of fear wrapped around urgency. For a moment, he forgot the rest of us were in the room, until—

"And why are we talking about whatever's wrong with me in front of all these people?" My heart thumped like a rabbit trying to escape a hutch; I was sure others could hear it. I resisted the urge to yell, "I am not 'these people!' I am your *wife*, and I'm trying to save our marriage and maybe even your life!"

"Eric," Dr. Hubbard said, maintaining control of the conversation. "As you know, we've done many tests, and I've examined you several times over the past few weeks. The good news is there doesn't seem to be any primary medical reason for your symptoms. I've been able to rule out all diseases or disorders of the digestive tract and various kinds of cancers."

"So, you're saying it's all in my head? I imagine throwing up blood, the cramps, and the burning in my stomach?" Eric said this with his voice slightly elevated in pitch and volume.

"No, that's not what I'm saying. I know you have those symptoms, and they're real. In fact, you do have a small ulcer on the lining of your stomach, but I believe your alcohol intake is what's causing these troubles."

"Oh, great. I *knew* this would come up," he said and turned with accusation in his eyes, looking only at me. "What the hell are you doing, making this into something so big? You're such a drama queen, Kat!"

"This is not about Katharine; it's about you," said the doctor, redirecting Eric back to the matter at hand. "We're here to talk about you, about this relapse you've been dealing with."

"I was sober for seventeen months," he said as a way of explanation, but it fell flat.

"I know. We all know that, and that's why we know you can do it again. We came together as a group today to let you know we all care about you. This relapse has taken its toll on you, and we all want to help you regain sobriety and good health." It sounded so simple coming from Dr. Hubbard; I almost expected Eric to be convinced. But that didn't happen.

After a beat, Bill found his voice.

"Eric, we didn't bring you here today to embarrass you, though I know it did. I'm sorry about that. But you're hurting yourself every time you pick up a bottle, and we want you to know it hurts us, too."

"How am I hurting *you?*" Eric asked with a sneer usually reserved for surly teenagers.

"You've been sick. You're missing work, losing touch with your wife and child. I want better for you, brother. I want you to be happy and healthy. I don't see that happening right now, and it's going to get worse if you keep drinking. So yes, it hurts me to watch what's happening." Bill was passionate in his delivery. I thought for a moment he'd gotten through to Eric, but the younger brother turned his icy gaze back toward the doctor without saying another word. Bill's face registered an anguish that I recognized from looking in my own mirror. He'd been dismissed.

"I know this is very difficult, son," said Dr. Hubbard. I noted the affectionate address and wondered if it made Eric think of his own father. "Please try to hear what everyone is saying, even though you want nothing more than to disregard all of us. This is hard for us, too."

"Hard for *you?*" Eric snapped. "From what I see, *I'm* the one in the hot seat. How is it hard for you to sit there and tell me all the ways I'm fucking up?!"

Al Kaufman couldn't take that without speaking up. "Now, you hold on right there, Mr. Torrington," addressing Eric with a respect I was certain he didn't feel at that moment. "I will not allow you to speak that way in front of your wife and mother. What kind of man are you?" Al uncrossed his legs and leaned forward in Eric's direction before continuing.

"I have to say, it was more than difficult for me to come here today, because I wasn't sure it was my place. But after seeing this side of you, I'm convinced you *do* have a serious problem. A right-thinking man does not act this way. A clearheaded man takes responsibility for his actions and tries to better himself with humility.

"From what I see," the seasoned manager said, "you're in a room full of people who love or genuinely care about you, and all you're doing is spitting in their faces. Grow up, young man," he said with the force of a cop no one should argue with. After a pause, he lowered his voice to a whisper, looked Eric straight in the eye, and added, "or you're going to lose everything . . . starting with your job."

The threat hung in the air like an unexpected rain cloud. Eric made no response.

Somehow, I felt it was time for me to speak. I was grateful Mr. Kaufman had reeled in Eric's emotional escalation before I had to face it.

"Honey," I started, "I've been patient for several months, letting you try to handle this relapse on your own. But all I see is how we're growing farther apart, and I'm scared. I don't want to lose you, but I feel you slipping away." I paused, trying to read his reaction, but his face was blank, an empty canvas taunting an artist to leave a mark. "Emma and I need you, but we need you sober. I can't live this way anymore. Please . . ." I couldn't put the rest of the sentence together.

Finally, Helen spoke. "Eric, I hate being here like this, and I'm more angry with you than anything because you should be able to shake this off. I do not appreciate your problem being everyone's business. But that's not what I wanted to say." Helen refocused. "I know what it's like to want to escape from responsibilities and stress; I felt that way after your father died, leaving me with piles of bills and legal matters I didn't know how to handle. But running away from things never solves them. You know that. It only delays having to deal with them. You have a family to care for, and you're not doing it. It's time."

Eric had been quiet since Mr. Kaufman's straight-shooting comments. Could it mean he was listening and hearing our concerns? Dr. Hubbard took the opportunity to bring the meeting to its conclusion.

"Here's what needs to happen next. I've arranged for you to be admitted to a substance abuse treatment center about an hour from here. It's a residential facility, which means you'll be staying there. I've checked with your insurance, and it will cover thirty days."

"Thirty days?!" Eric's voice cracked and his eyes grew wide with shock. The reality of what was happening found its target. "How can I take that much time off work?" I marveled at the irony: He hadn't been concerned about missing work because of his drinking before.

Al Kaufman's voice was softer when he spoke this time, addressing Eric's concern. "Don't worry about that, son. I'm making you a promise: You will have your job when you return next month. You need to take this time and get better. I'll support you as long as you're doing your part to get back to the company as your old self." Then he added, as if reading Eric's mind, "And I'll do my best to make sure your business stays your business. No one will know where you are, only that you needed a leave for medical reasons. Most of the guys already know you've had stomach problems. We'll let them think you're working on fixing those, okay?"

Eric looked relieved at the plan, and I almost thought Helen would lean over and kiss the man, but that would have been far too emotional for her. Instead, she offered a polite, "Thank you for your discretion, Mr. Kaufman."

Helen spoke again, this time to Eric and me. Although her voice was tight, businesslike, the sentiment was generous and unexpected: "I'm planning to contribute in the one way I can. I will pay your mortgage and utilities the month you're gone." I was more than surprised at this offer. Eric somehow managed to look both grateful and resentful at the same time. I imagine the bitterness came from swallowing the distasteful truth that his mother was stepping in to do what he should be doing—providing for his family.

We each stumbled through our thanks for her support and extended the same gratitude to Mr. Kaufman for doing his part on the job front.

Bill had been quiet since Eric's earlier rejection, but he took a chance at speaking again. "I don't want you to worry about things at home, either. If Kat needs anything while you're away, she can

call me. I'll also plan to see Emma every week for some uncle time."
I smiled at him across the room and mouthed a "thank you." Eric
nodded in his direction, still not able to face being "shown up" by
his brother. *It must be chilly living in that shadow.*

The room fell silent. The weight of all the emotions lifted. The
elephant had been acknowledged, confronted, and was being led out
of the living room. Eric was still in shock, but he wasn't fighting
anymore. I imagined he was trying to envision being "locked up for
a month," as he would later call it.

And then I realized: He would not be missing *me* for those thirty
days; he would be missing his vodka.

Chapter Two: The (Damn) Ray of Hope

The drive to Serenity House took us along one of the most stunning stretches of highway in Colorado. Unsubtle twists in the two-lane road urged us to hug the sides of the mountain as we followed the creek in the ravine below. I wondered at the power of that tiny stream of water and how its persistence over the millennia had forced the valley between the tons of rock above it.

I'd driven into the backcountry many times before, but this time I focused my mind on *a new start*, and the scenery was more breathtaking than usual.

I smiled remembering Emma's excitement when I opened the front door of our house earlier. She jumped up and down and danced around the living room, welcoming Cara, the babysitter from my Wednesday night Al-Anon meeting, into our house. Emma appeared thrilled to have the doting teenager all to herself. I knew "the girls" would have a fun day together, and I'd given Cara money to order a pizza for a late lunch/early dinner. Emma was unlikely to take a nap with all the extra stimulation, so it would be an early bedtime for her.

On the Friday of Labor Day weekend, the sun was strong. The mountain air was a reprieve; it fanned my face and blew my hair around as we drove with the windows halfway down. I was enjoying the ride, lost in my own reverie about how this was the beginning of a new, healthier chapter of our lives, when Eric's voice interrupted my thoughts.

"There are some bottles in the garage you should probably throw away. I didn't have a chance," he said.

"Oh," I said, shaking my head slightly at the ugly reality he'd thrown into my hopeful daydream.

"I think there's also some under the porch out back and a few in some upper cabinets in the kitchen." There wasn't a hint of shame in what he said, only resignation, like a child caught sneaking quarters from his dad's dresser after getting away with it for months.

"I'll look around," I said, trying to imagine how strange it would feel snooping around my own house, finding hidden "treasures" I never knew were there. *What if I don't find them all, and he discovers one later?* I pushed the thought away.

I asked him to pop in a CD. We were losing the radio station from Denver. We drove in conversational silence for another twenty minutes, listening to Simon and Garfunkel sing about "making love to Cecilia" and that famous "Bridge Over Troubled Waters." That song felt especially ironic.

I wondered what Eric was thinking but couldn't bring myself to ask. Maybe he was just trying to focus on getting where we were going without fighting with me—a pretty good short-term goal for someone who'd gotten drunk in our basement the night before checking into rehab. I'd chalked it up to a farewell pity party of sorts, like saying good-bye to a friend before going on a long vacation.

When I turned onto the long, unpaved road that led up to the facility, the jagged points of Rocky Mountain National Park's back range caught my attention. Formidable against the cloudless sky, they didn't seem real—like a convincing backdrop painted on the set of a Broadway play. The Serenity House stood in front of the always snowcapped mountains and practically dared you not to say, "Wow." So, I did.

"Wow. It's beautiful here, Eric. A perfect place to focus on—" I paused, not knowing the best way to phrase it, "things."

"You act like it's going to be a vacation up here," he said with a hint of self-pity.

I resisted the urge to argue and instead said, "What I mean is, if you have to be away from home for a month, this looks like a beautiful place to be. That's all."

He changed the subject with one statement: "Let's park over there," pointing to a few empty spaces marked by a "Visitors" sign.

He grabbed his suitcase from the back seat, and we walked up the steps to a wraparound porch covered by overhanging logs. The whole design and decor of the building was "woodsy," which reflected the forests surrounding the complex. Inside, you could tell the place had undergone renovations more recently than not; the artwork and furniture welcomed guests in a fusion of rustic and modern.

A woman wearing a name tag that read Tracy Pierce greeted us. I noted the R.N. after her name, though she was wearing regular clothes, not scrubs. She shook our hands and welcomed us as if we were the most important people she'd speak to all day. "It's very nice to meet you both. Dr. Hubbard is one of our favorite referring physicians."

She led us over to the admitting area and asked us to make ourselves comfortable, though I imagined Eric was anything but. As we started the paperwork, Eric excused himself. I assumed he went to the men's room—a passive-aggressive protest to his being forced into this situation.

As we started on the forms, Tracy handed me a large packet. "I'm sure you have many questions. This folder will address most of them. But if not, feel free to call our family support office at this number." She pointed to the digits on a business card stapled to the inside of the front cover.

"Also, here's a flyer about our family weekend. You're invited to attend during Eric's last weekend here. We strongly encourage you to attend, if possible. It's a wonderful opportunity for you to learn more about your husband's recovery process and how you can focus on your own well-being during this challenging time." The way Tracy respected my needs as equally important to Eric's made me feel less invisible. I'd grown used to being the unseen victim in this whole mess; I was grateful Serenity House seemed to understand that. The fact they even *had* a family weekend addressing these issues confirmed I mustn't be the only "support person," as she'd called us, to feel that way.

By the time Eric returned, we were done with the admissions process and were chatting about our children—her twins were a year older than Emma. Tracy took us on a tour of the campus, leaving Eric's suitcase with an imposing man named Mark. He would inspect its contents for alcohol and illegal substances, as well as anything that could be used as a weapon. The reality of a "secured environment" was a little scary to me, but also reassuring. Eric, however, just looked annoyed. I heard him mumble something under his breath about privacy.

In addition to "The Mess Hall," what residents called the cafeteria, the main building housed several meeting rooms where group discussions and activities took place. Upstairs, a large loft housed the counselors' offices. All guests attended daily individual therapy, as well as group counseling and AA meetings. There was also a two-story A-frame lounge with overstuffed chairs, smooth wood coffee and end tables, and an expansive stone fireplace in the middle of the room, open on both sides. Subtle lighting created a cozy atmosphere. I envisioned people sitting around in the evenings reading, playing cards, or writing letters home to people they regretted hurting on their way to this place.

There were no TVs on campus and no newspapers, as the whole point of rehab was introspection and redirection. Game shows and sitcoms didn't help with that process, nor did politics, sports, or crime stories. In that spirit, each resident was restricted to one phone call a day, incoming or outgoing. Staying connected to family was important, but personal healing and growth was the priority.

We walked across an expansive lawn with stripes, announcing a fresh mowing. Our destination was The Alley, the row of three identical bunkhouses designated for sleeping and bathing. The building we entered was undecorated, but functional: Ten shared bedrooms dotted the hallways, with two large bathrooms on either end.

In Building C, Tracy knocked on door number eight and said, "I want to introduce you to Bruce, your roommate." After a brief pause, the heavy door opened. Though Eric was 6' 2", Bruce towered over him. His disproportionately bushy dark beard further minimized his already-thin frame. He looked to be in his fifties, but I had a feeling he was chronologically much younger. His eyes showed no age lines; his skin, however, told the tale of his dedication to alcohol. As we shook hands, I imagined he might not be able to account for a few of the years showing on his ruddy cheeks.

"How ya doin'?" he asked as he took Eric's hand. "Welcome to the West Wing, as I like to call it." He grinned slyly, making a small joke in reference to the White House.

"Hi," Eric said shortly, not in the mood to make a friend quite yet.

Bruce was savvy enough to read his new bunkmate's state of mind and didn't push it. As he stepped past us on his way out the door, he offered a warm smile to my husband and said, "Hey, we'll talk later, okay?" He nodded in my direction and left.

As Tracy chatted about mealtimes and exercise sessions, Eric and I looked around the room which would be his personal space for the next month. The unoccupied side was a mirror image of Bruce's: a twin bed pushed against the opposite wall, a separate closet with a dresser inside, and a small desk with a table lamp. Eric's desk was under the room's only window. Tracy explained that a full-time janitor lived on-site and cleaned the bedrooms and bathrooms twice a week, but residents were expected to do their own laundry, sheets, and towels every week. The washers and dryers were free, but in high demand, so "Expect to sit and read for a while when you go over there," she said in Eric's direction. "It's actually a good time to get some homework done."

I thought about my own college dorm days, the whole waiting-for-a-washing-machine thing. But Eric had only lived in his parents' house and then ours. There were always machines available to him, and he never had to hoard quarters. He'd be experiencing a lot of new things over the next four weeks.

By the time Tracy had brought us full circle to the main lodge, Mark had finished going through Eric's personal things. He handed me a gallon Ziplock bag and said to Eric, "I'm sending these items home with your wife. We can't allow cologne, Swiss Army knives, or drugs of any kind."

"It's just Tums," Eric said, looking through the clear plastic. "I get a lot of heartburn."

"I know, man. That's part of why you're here. This place will help you get rid of that. But if you ever need over-the-counter stuff, we have a nurse who can give it to you," Mark was polite, but there was no room in his demeanor for further discussion.

"Why no cologne?" I asked.

"It's not so much the cologne, ma'me, although it does have alcohol in it." Mark addressed me with a professorial tone, instructing me of The Rules. "It's actually more the glass bottle."

The image of a depressed or violent resident breaking a bottle of cologne, using the glass as a weapon, made me queasy. Also, I knew cologne had alcohol in it, but really? Would someone *drink* it? I couldn't comprehend that kind of desperation, but that's why they have The Rules, I told myself.

Tracy came up behind me and put a hand on my shoulder. Her touch was firm but assuring. "Kat, it's time to say good-bye now. Eric has his first meeting with Mr. Gaines, his counselor, in a half hour. I'd like him to put his things away in his bunkroom before that."

"Oh, of course," I said, suddenly feeling out of place.

"I'll give you two a few minutes, but just a few. Eric, please come get me at the admissions desk when you're ready," she said, then reached for my hand. "I know it'll be difficult for you to drive home alone today. Try to concentrate on all the good that will come of this."

Tracy's words silenced any of mine that might have tried to escape, and I held back tears I didn't know wanted to come. She'd verbalized my unacknowledged fears, and her compassion made me feel fragile.

And then Eric and I were alone. The program offered weekly visiting days. Emma and I would come up for three hours on the following Sunday, nine days away. They asked us to wait a week, allowing Eric more time to adjust to the center before a visit.

To me, it seemed like a long time. But as I looked at my husband, with the floor-to-ceiling rock fireplace behind his broad shoulders, it didn't seem this separation was going to bother him at all. He was focused on the unknown, concerned about the demons he'd be forced to confront before he could go home.

We mumbled a few pleasantries and fumbled through an awkward hug, but he didn't kiss me good-bye. I accepted it as a combination of punishment and disinterest. I tried to assess which part was worse.

I'd driven up the mountain picturing a ray of hope encircling us. As I drove home down the curvy road, my hands clutched the steering wheel with intent. I seized the control I had over that hunk of steel, aware it was the only thing I had any real, immediate influence over. The rest of my life was spinning, caught up in movement all its own. I had a vested interest in the storm's outcome, but I was unable to shape the winds that blew.

•   •   •   •   •

Emma looked adorable, wearing a navy jumper with splashes of primary-colored flowers. My outfit was less cheery: jeans and a maroon knit top. I'd studied the blouses in my closet that Sunday morning for longer than I should have, trying to decide what to wear. But it wasn't a date, and Eric wouldn't care how I was dressed.

We arrived early at Serenity House, but a crowd had already gathered near the parking lot. Visiting day was a big deal. Energetic noise and movement greeted family members as they sought out their "residents" for hugs.

After a nap in the car, Emma was full of energy; she insisted on walking as soon as I pulled her from the car seat. Her wobbly gait was an endearing distraction from the awkwardness that stood between Eric and me like a saguaro cactus. He knelt to scoop her into his arms, covering her cheeks and forehead with countless kisses in quick succession. Her unfiltered giggles were his reward. I noticed his scruffy week-old beard and wondered if it tickled Emma. The new look worked on him. Very mountain man.

Several of Eric's new friends came running up to us, saying "Ooooh, Eric, she's beautiful!" and "This must be Emma! Hello sweetie. I'm a friend of your daddy's." Eric lifted her high in the air. She landed with a *whomp!* on his shoulders, her chubby legs hanging down on his chest. He held her safely in place with his big hands, supporting her back. The perch provided her with a vantage point away from the crowd's attention, and she enjoyed steering Daddy to new places with the mere command of her pointed finger.

The welcome I received was far less affectionate: a platonic peck on the cheek. I wasn't sure how I'd become the bad guy in all this, but I interpreted Eric's aloofness as blaming me for his confinement. He'd conveniently forgotten Dr. Hubbard's primary role in his admission to rehab—not to mention the relapse itself which bore Eric's name alone.

We bumped into people he knew all over the campus, but Eric never introduced me. Maybe he assumed everyone would figure out who I was? I sported a plastic smile and stood to the side when people chatted with Eric and Emma; I might have been a hired nanny if someone didn't know better.

By lunchtime, I wanted to melt into the wall. Until then, I was only being ignored. But as I walked through the cafeteria line alone (Emma sat on Eric's lap at a nearby table eating a PB & J), I noticed people looking at me with a familiarity that seemed suspect. It finally dawned on me: Eric had been *sharing* during his week in the program. Obviously, some of those stories were about me—his perspective of me.

I tried to act normal and unconcerned, but I felt self-conscious: How was I walking? Too stiff? How'd my hair look? Did I look like a controlling wife? With a jolt, I realized Eric might have felt a similar scrutiny for a long time, like a specimen under the microscope. I'd been confiding details of our marriage to close friends and my parents—and only my perspective. I carried new compassion for him through the meal.

This ritual repeated itself two more times, and each Sunday was very much the same, with one exception. After the third visit, Eric called midweek. It was the first time he'd called to talk to me, not Emma. We hadn't had a private conversation since before he'd gone to the mountains, and those weren't quality chats. He'd been drinking like a bridegroom the night before his wedding at the time—every night for weeks. This call was different. He was sober, of course, and his usual aloof attitude was missing.

"So, I met a guy here who's from Poughkeepsie," he started. An olive branch.

"Really? That's a small world moment, huh? How long has he been in Colorado?"

"Only a few years, but he mentioned your high school. He played football back in the day, and apparently, his biggest sports jock moment happened at an away game on that field."

"Wow. Strange. I wonder if I was there at the time, though you know I didn't go to many football games. Is he about our age?"

"Nah. He's older. Probably late fifties. Talked about drinking with his grandson, though the kid wasn't of age yet. Got him in trouble with his daughter, the boy's mom."

"Hmmm." What was I supposed to say to that? I changed the subject. "Do you have a lot of homework each night?"

"Yeah, a bit. It varies." I didn't hear any defensiveness in his voice. "Some is about the Twelve Steps, but other assignments have to do with the counseling. Mr. Gaines is pretty cool, though it still feels weird calling him that since he's younger than I am."

"Why do you have to?"

"Not sure. It's just expected. A respect thing, I guess? They call us by our last names, too: Mr. Torrington. Miss Avery. I don't mind, though I keep looking around for my dad." He chuckled. It was the first hint of relaxation and humor I'd heard from him in months. A glimmer of my old Eric!

He shifted the conversation. "How are you?" It was the first time since we'd tried counseling in July that he'd expressed the slightest interest in my well-being. It was so jarring that I didn't have an answer for him. I babbled through an "okay" and "staying busy." But before I could get anything meaningful out, he asked, "What's Emma doing?"

"Do you mean right now or in general?"

"Both, I guess."

"Well, she just finished having a snack—mandarin oranges and American cheese. I pointed out that they're both orange, and she tried to say it. It came out *owan.*" Emma was in her highchair, trying to master her pinching skills: only some of the slippery fruit made it into her mouth. "I think we'll head out to the driveway next for some chalk drawing. Maybe we'll keep the orange theme going—or we'll be adventurous and discuss blue or green." I heard his smile.

"God, I miss her." A catch in his throat.

"I know. You wanna talk to her?"

"Next time. There's someone waiting to get on the phone, so I'd better go. Give her a kiss from me."

"I will. It was good talking to you, Eric."

"It was. I'll see you Sunday."

The conversation was nothing more than banal, but I played it over in my mind after I'd put Emma down for a nap. I thought about all the different things I could have said, but in the end, they were all trivial. Well, not everything would've been trivial: I'd just learned we were expecting another baby in April.

•   •   •   •   •

Family Weekend was a time for spouses, parents, or adult children to stay at the Serenity House complex for a Friday and Saturday night. We would attend support sessions as a group to learn more about Alcoholism/Addiction (several residents were being treated for drug abuse). For those not yet initiated in the ways of Al-Anon, there were on-site meetings with fellow "codependents." Most of us wore the label with resignation, if not acceptance. After all, as the program teaches, "Our best thinking got us here, so . . ." The end of that sentence is "another way of thinking might get us somewhere else." Somewhere better, healthier.

After a graduation ceremony on Sunday afternoon, we would bring our recovering loved ones home, with Hope and Apprehension riding in the back seat.

My mom had flown out the Monday before to prepare for her weekend stay with Emma while I was away. We'd had a wonderful girls' week, including a fun "high tea" at a cute salon that catered to little girls. Mom and I wore white gloves, and the three of us donned fancy hats. At fifteen months, Emma was the youngest there as we ate scones and drank tea from pretty little cups. Mom and I adopted English accents, held our pinkies up as we sipped, and Emma giggled at our antics.

During my mom's visit, I slept deeply, knowing she would listen for Emma's mumblings in the middle of the night. In the mornings, I woke to happy chattering between the two of them as Emma watched a *Barney* video and her Bubbie prepared breakfast. What a joy to share those parenting tasks for a few precious days.

After checking in at the Serenity lodge, a staff member escorted me to a studio cabin on the opposite side of the grounds from Eric's bunkhouse. Knowing I'd have time alone—without having to make small talk with a roommate—was a gift of epic proportions. I'd have time to journal, read, and process in the privacy of my own space.

Family members ate meals as a group, crowding into the dining hall at a different time from the residential guests. Conversations floated through many topics with ease. Like soldiers who bond through common war wounds, physical or emotional, we were comfortable with each other. We discussed various Al-Anon principles, everyone preparing to navigate *detachment* and *boundaries* once they got back to reality. We also braved the Big Question on everyone's mind: What if rehab doesn't work?

Eric and I were alone only once, for a few minutes before "lights-out" on Saturday. It reminded me of sleepaway camp when I was thirteen. I wasn't interested in sneaking around the grounds after hours to meet boys on the other side of the compound back then, and I wasn't interested in more than conversation with Eric that night either. At thirteen, I was too young. Now, I was too old. When had I been the *right* age for it, and how had I missed it?

"I'm not sure what to talk to you about. So many topics feel off-limits right now," I said. We sat on a bench overlooking a small pond boasting a fountain in the middle. The only light came from the moon and sidewalk lamps a distance away. "I'm very interested in what your days have been like here, but I don't want to sound like I'm interviewing you—or worse, grilling you." I zipped up my jacket, thankful I'd brought it. The first weekend of October was pleasant at home, but at 7,500 feet, the mountain air at night felt like Thanksgiving.

"Yeah, I get it. It's been important to keep what I've been learning here, here. I'm not sure how to talk about it with you either, so I haven't."

"Sharing it in bits and pieces over the phone in fifteen-minute chats probably hasn't been enough time." I looked up to see an expanse of dark sky peppered with an unimaginable number of stars, so bright and clear without city lights intruding.

"It's not only that. I'm not sure yet how to blend these two worlds. I'm just starting to feel comfortable looking inside myself. I'm worried about what it'll be like at home, trying to do all of this on my own." Eric followed my gaze upwards to the heavens and added, "I'm also not sure how to let you in."

Ouch, but honest. In fact, more honest than I expected to hear from him that weekend.

I gave him a truthful response that matched his candor. "I wish I knew. It's what I want, though, and I hope it comes naturally at some point. But I understand it may not happen right away. My plan is to let you figure it out. But know I'm on your side, okay? I always have been." I ventured a look at him in the darkness that sat between us.

"I know that. I do."

We sat in a silence that reminded me of when we first met: He'd been reserved and hesitant, and I'd waited for him to notice me. Maybe not much had changed since then.

"I've been working on my Fourth Step this week. *A fearless and moral inventory of ourselves.*" I couldn't see his hands well in the night, but I knew he'd made quote marks in the air. "Jesus. It feels like a cruel assignment made up by a madman." He chuckled, but the tone had a twisted edge.

"Yeah, that was an intimidating one for me, too." The Twelve Steps of the AA and Al-Anon programs were mirror images of each other.

"Obviously, I won't finish it here since I'm going home tomorrow. I guess that's what a sponsor is for. Gotta do that soon." It seemed he was talking to himself more than to me.

"Gwen has been a helpful sounding board for me," I said, showing my understanding of the process. "The sponsorship relationship is interesting—unlike a typical give-and-take friendship. I'm sure you've learned that here. But her guidance has been important as I've worked through the first few steps this year. I hope you find a great guy to partner with." The programs wisely encourage only same-sex sponsorships. Too risky to be vulnerable to the possibility of attraction hovering above the duo.

"Me, too." He seemed to be thinking about what I'd said. A comfortable pause. "I've been thinking about my dad a lot up here." I wasn't expecting that jump, but I followed along.

"In what way?" I was careful not to show my surprise. He usually only talked about his father with his brother.

"I think I've been angry at him. But since that felt wrong—because he's gone—it was easier to be mad at myself."

"About what, if you're okay telling me?"

"He kinda pushed me to work at the shop. I've always told the story in a kinder way, like he 'encouraged me' to work there. But the truth is, he expected it. There was pressure. I was only sixteen. What could I say? All my friends had jobs after school, so it was just a way to make money. But not being asked if I wanted to work there . . ." He let the end of the sentence float up toward the stars above us. "It didn't seem fair. Bill was off at college. No one ever asked me if I wanted to go that route. I didn't feel I had a choice."

"I can see why that didn't feel good. But what do you mean it made you angry at yourself?"

"Well, I never confronted him about any of it, and then he was gone. I was pissed at myself for missing the opportunity. He may have been pushy about it when I was young, but I never stood up for myself. Not even as an adult." *Wow, he's really digging deep.*

"That's a big 'ah-ha,' Eric." We both sat with the revelation. "Have the counselors or other group members suggested how you can move through that?"

"Yeah. I'm actually working on a letter to my dad. Obviously, I can't give it to him, but a lot of people here have similar issues with people from their pasts that they can't confront. Writing it down helps, so they say."

"I really hope that works for you." I wasn't sure what else to say. He was battling demons I couldn't see. "Thanks for telling me about this. It means a lot to me."

"I'm still working through it, but that's the gist." I felt the air shift as he searched for an easier topic. "So, has it been nice to have a cabin to yourself these few days?"

"Definitely. I can't remember the last time I was alone." We both chuckled. "But I know Emma's having a great time with my mom. I talked to them this afternoon. Emma's making you a card to welcome you home."

"I can't wait to hold her. To be home."

"We both want that."

"Kat?"

"Yeah?"

"I don't have all the other words yet, but I'm sorry."

The air escaped my chest. I hadn't realized how much I needed to hear that.

He leaned over, kissed my cheek, then stood. "I'll watch you walk back to your cabin. See you tomorrow."

•   •   •   •   •

I woke early the next morning. I tried to go back to sleep after the heat of the sunlight warmed my eyelids, but no amount of tossing would make it so.

After showering and dressing, I walked around the grounds and thought about my conversation with Eric the night before. Possibility cracked open a door that had been shut, locked, and bolted. I dared myself to peek inside.

As I settled on the same bench we'd occupied hours before, I thought about how I'd gotten to that point in my life. I also reviewed the insights I'd gained during the weekend, pondering what it all meant as Eric and I geared up for The Next Chapter.

The scenery was worthy of a Colorado mountain calendar, the atmosphere serene. Second chances were possible in such a place. The Twelve-Step programs call it a spiritual awakening: the moment when you recognize an "ah-ha" thought and sense your life will never be the same for having acknowledged it. I felt my first one on that mountaintop as it happened, not as a thought I reflected on later. As it formed, I *thought* it and *felt* it and *shivered* at the significance of it right then.

My "ah-ha" was simply this: No matter what happened between Eric and me, *I had to choose to be okay.* Love and commitment weren't the issues; I'd proven my devotion a thousand times. From that day on, my own well-being would guide me. I had to choose to be happy, even if he didn't. I had to decide to be healthy, even if he wasn't. I had to move forward into the light, even if he chose to sit in the dark waiting for someone else to flip a switch.

And if he drowned—in sorrows or inside bottles—I had the power and the right and the *choice* to swim for shore. Even if it meant leaving him behind to float endlessly in his own sea of inaction. Even if it meant he went down in a wave of self-destruction.

The fork had shown itself, and I couldn't unsee it.

As the sun ascended over the horizon, it lit the new path I'd envisioned. Serenity comes with a price: no room for acquiescence. The road I aspired to would require making choices because they were right, not because they were comfortable.

The sad, unavoidable reality was that although I might be willing to make those tough choices, Eric might not be. And if he didn't choose to come along with me on that path, we might end up traveling down different forks, into separate futures.

I'd never been able to picture my life without him, until that day.

●　　　●　　　●　　　●　　　●

I wasn't sure how much Emma noticed Eric's absence from our daily lives during the month he was away, but she seemed especially excited to snuggle in her daddy's arms as we sat in Grandma Helen's living room. The father-daughter and mother-son reunions were livelier than our twisting ride down the mountain which had held more silences than words. We weren't angry, just nervous.

A dinner of grilled salmon helped us celebrate the special occasion, and Bill stopped by to give his personal "welcome home." Eric was receptive to his brother's hug when it came, and we all tried to settle into the new normal: optimism fused with caution.

I had no idea how to tell Eric about the baby. Conversation had been strained between us for so many months, I didn't trust my words to do the job. I had to find another way.

I'd kept the pregnancy test stick from when we found out we were pregnant with Emma; it had a forever-home in a pretty box that lived in my underwear drawer. I loved to take it out and look at it—a talisman that connected me to the apex-high moment of joy I felt when I first saw it.

Now I had a second one to match, and it, too, made me smile. I couldn't help but wonder about the baby growing inside me: Who would this child turn out to be? And how was it possible I already loved it so much, but couldn't picture his/her face?

Both test results rested in a small box, wrapped in sunny yellow paper. When we got into bed on his first night back, I handed the gift to Eric. He looked at me with a "What's this for?" question sitting on his eyebrows. He opened the box slowly, like a birthday present to be savored. Two bright pink plusses announced themselves in their respective hard plastic containers. "I guess we're starting a collection," I said, my words floating on uneven breath.

I wouldn't have placed a single nickel on a bet if you'd asked me what his reaction would be. I had absolutely no idea. We'd been distant, in every way, for so long. It was a minor miracle we'd gotten pregnant again at all. While Eric was at Serenity House, I spent a lot of time remembering the details of that day.

Emma was taking her afternoon nap. I'd suffered a terrible sunburn the last Saturday in July when we took her to the lake. My stupidity revealed itself the next day as crimson skin flashed beneath my lightweight summer dress. I wasn't peeling yet, but oh, how it burned!

I tried for a casual tone when I asked Eric to put the cool aloe on my back and shoulders. But we hadn't been intimate for several months, so it came as an awkward request—no matter how matter-of-fact I said it. The heat that radiated from my skin made the salve melt in his hands and dissolve within a minute. Before I knew what was happening, I'd forgotten how much my skin hurt. My dress was on the floor. Eric was rubbing me all over, and there was no more lotion involved.

It only happened once the entire summer, but as we learn in high school: it only takes one time.

He held those pregnancy test results, one in each hand, and a hundred years went by before he looked up. When he did, his eyes betrayed his calm voice: "The sunburn?" Then he smiled, and I could breathe again.

We didn't talk about the baby anymore that night. We didn't talk about anything. It was a silent homecoming, but a warm-enough one. Even though it seemed we should make love to celebrate his return, the start of our new life, or our expanding family, we didn't. We couldn't yet. There was still too much unresolved. But it was okay.

We lay in bed, side by side, no angry wall between us for the first time in so long, both imagining a house with two children inside it. I listened to him relax. The air around him did not smell of alcohol; his speech did not roll sloppily off his tongue. We just were. We were together. And it was nice.

•   •   •   •   •

Hope can be a terrible thing, though it shouldn't be. It camouflages reality by painting the here and now in feel-good pastels and brave rainbow colors. It tricks you into trusting that things really are as they seem. That (Damn) Ray of Hope comes gallivanting into your house, seducing you into believing, then slaps you across the face. She leaves you full of anger, scolding you for being foolish and vulnerable again.

He says, "I didn't." You say, "I know you did." Hope says, "Be patient."

He says, "I'm sorry." You say, "I'm scared." Hope says, "He's trying."

Hope says, "It'll get better." The Slap says, "Sucker!"

After a month of soul-searching, endless counseling sessions, scores of AA meetings, and thousands of dollars, Eric fell off his symbolic wagon and plunged with a splash back into the comfort of his bottle. It had only taken three weeks.

Our baby on the way had slipped his mind. Emma, with her God's-gift-to-the-world-smile, somehow disregarded. And every vow of being better, feeling better, doing better, was silenced in mid-gulp. Gone. Deleted from his mind and from my life with the ease of an erase button on a tape recorder.

Something ugly started growing in my spirit that day. I felt the first slash of hate scratch my heart. Like a piece of coal scraping along the inside wall of a cave, it would leave a black mark that would never fade away. Unseen, but ever present.

The (Damn) Ray of Hope told me not to panic, that Eric knew he had too much to lose this time. The (Damn) Ray of Hope begged me to believe in my husband, that he would get back on track quickly. But I was smarter this time. I knew The Slap was coming. This time, I turned my face away—and my heart followed.

PART III

A memory: Before Kat opened her eyes, she knew it was later than she normally woke. The angle of the sun was different as it lit the bedroom.

Stretching her arms above her head and taking a deep breath, she felt . . . relaxed. Well-rested. How was that possible when she had a baby in the house?

She dared to glance over at the clock on her bedstand: 9:15! Smiling to herself and feeling decadent, Kat realized she hadn't slept in that late since Emma was born eleven months before.

As she pushed the covers down toward her feet and sat up on the edge of the bed, she noticed the silence. She wasn't worried, however. She assumed Eric was keeping Emma entertained, quietly, as a lovely Mother's Day gift. It certainly was.

After a quick stop in the bathroom, Kat walked out to the living room and saw a vase full of flowers on the kitchen counter. A note in Eric's handwriting leaned against the glass: "When you're ready, come out back, Mommy."

When she opened the sliding door to the back patio, her baby girl, who sat on a blanket spread on the deck, greeted her with squeals of giggles. Emma raised her arms up, her wordless way of communicating her needs. Once in her mommy's arms, Emma puckered up and waited for a return kiss that Kat was happy to provide.

Eric stood and walked over to wrap his arms around both of them. "My two favorite women." He kissed Kat with purpose on the lips.

"Maybe let's hold off calling our baby a woman for a little longer?" Kat smiled up at him.

"For now. But Miss Emma and I have a surprise for you," he said, as he turned Kat around so she could look out onto the lawn. "Happy First Mother's Day."

During the extra ninety minutes she'd slept, Eric had set up their camping pop-up tent, strung Christmas lights around it, and prepared a picnic of bagels, cream cheese, an assortment of donuts, and an all-important thermos of coffee. A perfect outdoor breakfast right in their backyard.

As Kat settled under the tent and sipped her coffee, she breathed in the sweetness of the morning. Her husband had marked sixteen months of sobriety, and their daughter was healthy and happy, a month away from her first birthday. Kat was twenty-nine years old, and decades stretched out ahead of her, like unwritten pages in the novel of her life.

Biding Time
Winter 1994 – 1995

* Fork 5 *

Chapter One: Hubris

"Biding your time" is an interesting expression. I don't know where it comes from, and I don't know its historical context, but I know the connotation: It means waiting. Waiting out a terrible situation until you can make a change.

It seems harmless enough. It shouldn't hurt at all. There is no action to take and no action to avoid. It's a passive thing. An *IN*action, if you will. Doing nothing. Sitting on the sidelines. Watching the world go by. Kicking back. What other clichés can I toss out?

But waiting, biding your time, is an inhuman task when it's *your life* that's moving forward without you.

•   •   •   •   •

In the months after Eric's return from Serenity House, our lives were anything but serene. In addition to the mess that had become our home life, we were also enduring a cold and snowy autumn. I looked toward April, ready for it to deliver us into its warmth, and our baby into my arms.

By Thanksgiving, I couldn't remember what the mountain treatment center looked like, nor was I feeling grateful for much. The promise of peace that rehab had represented was long gone, leaving in its wake a series of poor decisions on Eric's part that had only led to more poor decisions. Most of the time, I sat in the metaphorical passenger seat "riding shotgun down the avalanche," the title of a Shawn Colvin song. Had she once been in the same helpless limbo?

Although I'd had a hard time believing in God when I started in Al-Anon, I did a lot of praying during those chilly months: prayers for Eric's recovery, prayers for my own strength to deal with his reborn passion for drinking, and prayers for courage to do the right thing—once I gained clarity to know what the right thing was. I concentrated on this one solace: If I did the right thing for me, it would inherently and inevitably be the right thing for Emma and Baby T, my child I didn't know yet.

The most repeated solemn whisper to my Higher Power during those days was *Thank you for keeping him from hurting someone else the morning of the accident.*

He'd gone to work one blue-gray morning at the beginning of November, told his boss he forgot something at home, but drove to a liquor store instead. After parking at a nearby playground to sample his purchase, Eric drove back to work. The delusions born of his denial were these: 1) He believed no one at work would notice he was shit-faced, and 2) He didn't think anyone would notice he'd been gone from work for two hours!

Obviously, he was wrong on both counts, and his boss confronted him within minutes. For weeks after, Eric would blame Mr. Kaufman for embarrassing him in front of his co-workers, causing him to "drive away so mad." But no one else was to blame for his decisions that morning. No one else put him behind the wheel with a .19 blood alcohol content, and he alone overcompensated for a squirrel crossing the street. In an instant, weeks of bad choices came to a screeching halt, but not before his

Toyota 2 x 4 had sideswiped a Honda Civic carrying two grad students on their way to class at the university.

A legal nightmare rivaling a John Grisham movie began that afternoon when I got a call from an Officer Sherrick saying they had my husband in custody.

Panic shot through me like a lightning bolt hitting a swimming pool: *Was I expected to bail him out of jail? Would I be enabling his drinking if I did—or not supporting his recovery if I didn't?* I was lost in a myriad of Twelve-Step "shoulds," and I stood paralyzed in the middle of my living room. I didn't know what to do, but my fingers dialed Gwen before my brain could argue.

"There are no 'shoulds' in this program, Kat. No one can tell you what to do or not do. There are, maybe, healthier choices than others. What is your gut telling you?"

"That I can't trust my gut!" I was scared, weepy, shaking. Mostly, I felt pressure: Every minute I waited to decide what to do, Eric was sitting in a jail cell downtown.

"Okay, first, breathe. Take a few centering breaths. Get some oxygen to your brain and let's talk through your options." The calm she exuded, even through the phone, was like a palm tree swaying on a beach. I clung to her voice and tried to feel the breeze in my hair.

"Right. Okay. That's helping."

"Good. Now. Here's a mantra I've heard many times and tried to live by: 'If you're going to resent it, don't do it. If you do it, don't resent it.'"

My heart raced again. "What the fuck does that mean?!"

"Deep breaths, Kat. Come on."

"All right, yeah." I breathed. Silence on the phone as I concentrated harder. Air going in my nose and out my mouth. Three times. Gwen waited.

"Explain the resentment thing so I can understand it," I said, feeling like a freshman on her first day of college classes.

"Whatever you decide to do is acceptable. There's no right or wrong. If you think it makes more sense to bail him out so he can go back to work and face his boss, then that's okay. But if you do that, be at peace with the decision. Don't resent it or him. It's your choice." I nodded, even though she couldn't see me.

"Go on," I said.

"On the other hand, you can also choose *not* to put up the bond and let him face difference consequences. Again, own your decision; no resentments."

"But how do I know which choice is best for him?"

"You don't, sweetheart. But remember, you're not making this decision based on his needs. You're making it based on *yours*."

"I keep forgetting how to do that. My instinct is always to keep the peace. Make things better for him."

"Yes, that's your codependency at work, right? You respond by putting your own needs second to his. You *react* to his decisions and his demeanor. But now, you've said you want to break that pattern. What that looks like is doing what's best for you. He will adjust—or he won't. You can't control his response."

"UGH! I hate this! Why isn't what's best for me the same as what's best for him?" The whine in my voice was grating, even to my own ear.

Gwen chuckled. "I don't know. Sometimes it is, and sometimes it isn't. But that's a discussion for another day. Today, Eric made choices: He drank alcohol, then he drove his car and caused an accident. Those decisions landed him in jail. That's not on you. Your choice is a different one, and you're in control of it. You are."

After I hung up, I called Bill and asked him to come have dinner with Emma while I went downtown. He was as shocked about the day's events as I'd been, but he was also angry.

"Are you comfortable bailing him out? Maybe a night in jail will do him good?"

"I have no idea. I really don't. But I worked through this with my sponsor, and I feel as sure about it as I can. There will still be consequences for Eric; I'm not standing in the way of those."

"I get it. There's no good choice here. But Kat, you're pregnant. When is he gonna get it together?" It was a rhetorical question. After I didn't answer, he added, "I'll be over soon with a pizza."

"Thank you. I owe you."

"No. Eric does."

A first DUI in our beloved state amounted to little more than a "Gee, you shouldn't do that" admonition, especially since the victims of the crash were, thankfully, unharmed in any serious way. Our insurance would be affected, of course, and we owed the injured parties for damages. But after a minimal bond—well, minimal for most people; it hit our checkbook hard—Eric was home before bedtime. One consequence followed him home from the jail: He was required to attend twice a week alcohol education classes for two months.

I was an emotional mess the rest of that sleepless night, but he chalked it all up to "that fucking squirrel" and never once verbalized any responsibility, regret, or renewed focus on recovery. I was appalled. And he never mentioned my bailing him out. It never crossed his mind that I could have made another choice.

But things weren't as easy as he thought they'd be after the accident. Mr. Kaufman was furious about Eric's lack of concern for his job, especially after supporting him during rehab. Kaufman put Eric on a sixty-day probation and made it clear that any infraction during that time would result in his being fired. In the meantime, Eric's work tasks were reassigned so he wouldn't be driving any company vehicles until he completed his alcohol education classes.

Ms. Callahan, the counselor who ran the alcohol education class, closely monitored attendance, so when Eric played hooky one night, he got a call from the DMV the next morning. Unless he had a doctor's note, his next unexcused absence would lead to a substantial fine and further penalties. For the next two weeks, he bitched and complained, but he went. Then, the third week, he bitched and complained, *got drunk*, and then went to class.

When Ms. Callahan saw Eric's glassy eyes and caught a whiff of his breath, she dismissed him and told him he needed to call someone for a ride home. He said he was fine and sat down at the table. She reiterated the rule: "Students must be alcohol-free in class. Call for a ride home."

Eric stood up, swaying a bit, and said with dramatic flair, "Fine, I don'wanna to be here anyway. I'll juss take myself home then."

Ms. Callahan clearly stated, "If you get in your car, Mr. Torrington, I will call the police."

Good judgment was not to be found in my husband that night, and I got another call from Officer Sherrick a few hours later. It was his fate to be on duty both times my husband made dreadful choices that autumn.

•   •   •   •   •

The state of Colorado was less tolerant of a second DUI, and the repercussions impacted Eric in ways he couldn't ignore. First, he was forced to spend the night in jail. With an arraignment hearing scheduled the following morning, bail wasn't an option. He told me later he was in a cell with three other men. He didn't sleep a wink.

When I'd called Helen the night of that arrest, I heard a mixture of sorrow and resignation in her voice. She had moved past anger and her usual stance that Eric could "fix" his problem if only he tried harder. I was a little surprised to see her the next morning at the hearing. Each of us lost in our own swirling, dismal thoughts, we didn't talk to each other beyond a cordial greeting. We sat next to each other like immigrants from different countries arriving on the shore of the same, unknown country: strangers with more in common than not, but still unable to speak a common language.

I sat in the courtroom with bitterness thickening on my face like spoiled milk. Although I was grateful Eric had qualified for a public defender—we certainly didn't have the funds to secure a private attorney—my hands shook at the prospect of Eric losing his job in the aftermath of this second DUI. I was ashamed by my neediness; I hated depending on his income. On him. How had our mutual decision for me to stay home with Emma turned into a dependency I was embarrassed by? And what if he lost his job? What would that mean for our family?

I looked to the state to set consequences that would keep Eric in line.

Judge Randall Simmons wore thick glasses; the black frames gave him an owlish appearance. This seemed fitting, as I assumed he was a wise man. The silver in his hair was the only indication of his age.

"Mr. Torrington," the judge said. "Please stand."

Eric rose from his seat. The pear-shaped woman beside him stood, too, leaning on the desk in front of her for support. She wore a brown plaid suit ten years out of fashion. This matched her "librarian shoes" perfectly. (In middle school, my friends and I were unkind when gossiping about our librarian, Ms. Chapin. She was an unmarried woman "of a certain age" who wore squishy, bland colored shoes. Similar footwear held the substantial weight of Eric's public defender now.)

"Ms. Barber, do you wish to have the Court recite the charges being brought against your client today?"

"No, Your Honor, we have discussed them. Mr. Torrington is prepared to enter his plea of guilty."

"Very well," said the judge. "Will the court reporter please enter the plea into the record?"

Eric stood before the judge in the clothes he'd worn the day before. His hair was greasy and messy. His eyelids were heavy—a combination of hangover and a lack of sleep, I assumed. Looking at my husband in that moment, I felt equally dirty. A guilt-by-association stench seemed to connect me to him from my seat three rows behind where he sat. I wished I could blink myself back to my college dorm room and make different decisions every day since then. I assumed Helen was having similar desolate thoughts as she listened to her youngest son face consequences she couldn't have envisioned just a year ago.

The judge was stern when addressing my husband: "This is your second alcohol-related infraction in the past month, Mr. Torrington. The state cannot accept that behavior without serious penalties. I hereby revoke your driver's license for a period of no less than one year."

I saw Eric's knees buckle, but he said nothing to the stout woman standing next to him. She didn't say anything to him, either. Frankly, she looked bored.

"Additionally," the judge continued, "the Court requires you to attend Alcoholics Anonymous meetings twice a week for six months. You will make sure someone from those meetings signs off on your attendance each time you go—your attorney will have that form. Also, you are required to attend your alcohol education class for an additional three months." His Honor paused to catch his breath, as if all the sentencing was exhausting for him. "Finally, when you attend those classes twice each week, you will submit to breathalyzer tests."

After court, we learned how the handy contraption detects even a drop of alcohol on someone's breath. The person blows into the straw on one end, and at the other end, a digital screen displays the reading: 0.00 = no alcohol. 0.01 or above reads as a violation.

Judge Simmons's next words to Eric were a grave warning: "If your breathalyzer registers any amount higher than 0.00, Mr. Torrington, I will report it to the DMV, and you will face additional charges. Jail time *will* be an option at my disposal." The judge paused, then added, "I hope you make better decisions during this time to ensure a more stable future."

Ms. Barber turned her head slightly toward Eric, and I heard her quiet directive. Eric heard it, too: "Thank you, Your Honor," he said with his head more bowed than upright.

In response, the judge said, "Since you entered a guilty plea today, I will reduce your cash bond to a reasonable $1000, payable to the Clerk in the courthouse lobby. Once paid, you will be free to leave. Again, I encourage you to follow all the conditions of your bond with no exception. Good luck to you, sir."

We were dismissed. However, I felt tears on my cheeks before I found my feet: We didn't have "a reasonable" $1000 in our checking account at that moment. When Eric walked toward me, I looked away; without a friendly face for his eyes to land on, he pivoted to his mother.

"Hi, Mom. I'm really sorry." He found himself wrapped in her hug. "I appreciate you being here, even though I'm ashamed you saw all that."

"I know, son. But how could I not come?"

"Still . . ."

I found my voice, though it was soft and sounded pathetic to my own ears: "We don't have money for the bond, Eric. I don't know what to do."

Eric hadn't been paying attention to our bills over the past year, so he registered more surprise than he should have. "Really? How is that possible?"

The snotty wife inside me answered *Maybe because you've been drinking your paycheck?* But instead, Mature Kat shrugged and shook her head. "Bills. Groceries. Life."

We didn't have to wait long before our problem was solved. Helen took Eric by the elbow and started walking him to the courtroom exit doors. "I've got it."

And even though I was loath to accept money from her, and the Al-Anon inside me screamed *We shouldn't fix this for him,* I bit my tongue. I thought about our upcoming mortgage payment due in a few weeks. I said, "Thank you, Helen" with humility that, well, humiliated me.

Eric said nothing.

•   •   •   •   •

I don't know who Murphy was, but his Law says, "Anything that can go wrong will go wrong." Mr. Murphy is right a surprising number of times, and in our house, the adage came true: Eric was fired the day after his court appearance.

Having missed a day without calling in, Mr. Kaufman had called Eric into his office first thing the next morning. Eric had no convincing explanation other than the truth. The experienced manager followed through on his previous warning. He expressed his hope that things would get better for my husband, but he still escorted Eric out the front door.

To me, it was the other shoe falling. To Eric, it seemed a get-out-of-jail-free card . . . despite the pun.

After turning in his license at the courthouse, Eric had studied the bus route map the night before heading into the office. Typical of many middle-income people, we were not used to public transportation, but we were grateful it was available. Unfortunately, from that day on, Eric only used the bus to get to his AE (alcohol education) classes and AA meetings, not to a job.

The judge's admonition hung over our house like a neon sign warning of imminent danger. Eric followed the rules outlined at the arraignment, but only like a C student. He didn't *stop* drinking, which an A student would have done; rather, he *cut back* on his intake, drinking when he wouldn't be monitored.

The days were endless that month as we waited for Christmas and then the New Year; we'd never been at home together during weekdays. I continued with my daily routines that revolved around caring for Emma and maintaining the house; he puttered, trying to stay out of my way. He played with Emma or took her to the park sometimes, but mostly he wandered from room to room, tinkering with "projects" he'd been putting off. I waited for him to talk about looking for another job, but it never happened. Time to toss my hat in the ring.

"I've been thinking," I broached during a commercial break. We were sitting on separate couches watching *Seinfeld* one Thursday night. "Maybe I should see if any of the other moms in my MAM group would be interested in me watching their kids for a few hours a day?"

"Why would you do that?" Oblivion sat like a veil over his face.

"Well, it would be fun for Emma, and I could bring in a little money, you know, until you find something permanent again."

He glanced over at me like I'd asked him to mow the lawn in the middle of a snowstorm. "I guess . . . but I'm gonna find something after New Year's. No one hires in December," he said with the authority of a congressman on the House floor.

"I know," I agreed good-naturedly. "I really don't think it will be difficult. I'll be doing all the same things I do with Emma now, just for a few more kids."

"If you want to. Money does seem to be tight. I'm not happy about going into our savings for bills." I ignored the tone, as if I'd been sneaking off to place bets at the racetrack instead of grocery shopping.

"I know, but at least we have some savings. As you said, it'll only be for a while. I'll make sure the other moms know it's temporary. Some will be happy to pay for a respite."

I floated the idea at our next group playdate, and as I suspected, two of the moms popped up in their chairs right away. "Put me down as a big, fat YES," Karen said. "I'll drop Kaylee off at 9:00 on Tuesday. Will that work?"

Georgianne piped in without a beat. "I know Sammy would love some one-on-one time with you, Kat. You're his favorite mom here in the group . . . no offense, ladies." She chuckled to the women around her. "I think my boy has his first crush."

"I'm flattered," I said. "Only male attention I'm getting these days." I made my voice self-effacing and teasing, careful not to reveal the truth under my "joke."

"Well, your husband managed to get you pregnant a second time, Kat, so something's going on at your house," Karen teased.

"Fair point."

"I'll bring Sammy over on Tuesday at 9:00 also, Kat," added Georgianne. "I can't wait to do some Christmas shopping *alone!* What a gift."

•　•　•　•　•

Chanukah was early that year, but a late present from my parents arrived in our mailbox the week before Christmas. The envelope was addressed to me alone. Cardinals adorned the beautiful card, some flying and others resting on a bare-limbed tree. My mother loved red in everything: birds, scarves, roses, and even cars. You wouldn't think an older woman would favor the color in autos, but she teased: "I was an Italian movie star in a past life. Ferrari red is classy, sexy, and independent, just like me." Oh, how she laughed at herself then.

When I opened the card, a check for $5,000 fell to the floor. I gasped and picked it up with careful fingers, as if it might break. But that wasn't the only gift. An inspiring poem was taped inside:

Keep Going by
Edgar Guest (1921)

When things go wrong, as they sometimes will,
And the road you're trudging seems all uphill,
When the funds are low and the debts are high,
And you want to smile, but you have to sigh,
When care is pressing you down a bit,
Rest if you must, but don't you quit.

Life is queer with its twists and turns,
As every one of us sometimes learns.
And many a failure turns about
When he might have won had he stuck it out.
Don't give up though the pace seems slow,
You may succeed with another blow.

Often the goal is nearer than it seems to a faint and
faltering man.
Often the struggler has given up when he might
have captured the victor's cup,
And he learned too late when the night slipped down,
How close he was to the golden crown.

Success is failure turned inside out,
The silver tint of the clouds of doubt,
And you never can tell how close you are.
It may be near when it seems afar.
So stick to the fight when you're hardest hit.

It's when things seem worst that
You musn't quit.

•   •   •   •   •

On nights Eric went to his AA meetings—as required by Judge Simmons—I waited for his return, hoping he'd share some insights like he used to. But reality kept proving he was only going through the motions. I imagined the wisdom of the program swirling like music in those rooms as he sat in the middle of it all with cotton balls in his ears.

Sometimes he rallied, as if pushing through a toothache. He even came home after AE class one night with flowers for me. I had to bite the inside of my lower lip to stop from laughing. Certainly, a sweet gesture, but if there were ever an illustration of putting a Band-Aid on a severed limb, that was it. Even so, I thanked him with a kiss, a gesture of positive reinforcement—like a parent does to encourage a child's good behavior.

I wanted to believe he could make the changes he needed to. I wanted to believe that having the state watch over his shoulder for half a year would make those changes permanent. I wanted to believe that I still loved him, but I was having doubts.

To create balance in my life, I attended my meetings regularly, and I also spent time with my friend Leigh. I didn't want to wallow in the muck of my marriage all day long, so the four of us would venture in search of playdate distractions. The outings allowed the kids time outside our houses and provided a change of scenery for us mommies.

On an extra-cold afternoon just days before Christmas, Leigh and I bundled up the kids. We went to an indoor venue that boasted child-sized mazes made of giant plastic tubes, ball pits, and mini trampolines surrounded by soft foam. Watching the older kids squirm and giggle inside the cylinders with windows, I imagined them as stoned mice trapped in a scientific experiment. *Where's the cheese?* they seemed to say to each other, as they searched aimlessly for the exit.

At eighteen months, Emma was too small for some of the play zones designed for "big kids." Justin might have managed some of those obstacles, now a month past his second birthday, but he preferred to play near Emma. Leigh and I found an open area with squishy carpet squares in bright colors on the floor. We watched as our toddlers interacted with children more their own size. Emma favored interactive equipment that made musical sounds, and Justin stacked up colorful foam shapes, then tested and retested gravity as he knocked them down. I tried not to think of Eric, but the burst of destruction felt like a foreshadowing of our house being flattened.

Condensation blurred the windows as I watched the snow fall outside. Inside, thirty warm children and their parents emitted lots of hot air.

Leigh excused herself to use the bathroom, and I watched my friend waddle away. She was seven months pregnant, but if I'd been asked to guess, I would have said she wouldn't make it to the New Year.

"Some days, I swear I must be carrying twins," she said when she returned, lowering herself to the mat next to me with the grace of a gorilla, "but I saw the ultrasound. One baby. How am I so HUGE?" She laughed from her enormous belly and glowed from her beautiful face. We both loved being pregnant, and it was a joy to share the journey with her this time—especially since I felt so distant from Eric.

"You look amazing. The embodiment of womanhood," I said. Five months along, my own belly wasn't boldly announcing a human life inside yet; I only looked fat.

"I keep telling myself if we were living in the 1500s, I'd be considered sexy like this. Those Renaissance men liked their women round."

I rolled my eyes at her. "I don't think they were all pregnant, Leigh. Society just had a broader appreciation of female beauty. Women were beautiful in all sizes."

"Still. I wish our culture were more accepting of those variations."

"Totally," I agreed. "How are you feeling, besides unsexy?" I winked at her.

"Mostly great. I have better energy in the mornings, of course. By this time of the day, I'm beat. Keith will take dinner and bedtime duties tonight, so I'll go to bed early."

"He's awesome. I'm so happy for you." And I meant it. I didn't let myself wallow in comparisons or jealousy when I saw others in stable marriages. It helped me remember that what Eric and I were living through wasn't normal. In a weird way, that was helpful.

Reading my mind, Leigh asked, "How are you doing these days?"

"I started watching a couple of kids during the week. Two on Tuesdays and just one on Thursdays. It's only for three hours each day, but it brings in a little extra cash. Eric isn't exactly pounding the pavement looking for a job."

"Is it awkward with him around when the kids are there?"

"Nah. He disappears most of the time. He's trying to build a new bookshelf for Emma, for her new 'big girl' bedroom. We're keeping the nursery where it is and moving her next door into the office. Can't remember the last time we used that room. We have a few months to pretty it up for her. Anyway, Eric's spending a lot of time in the basement."

"And what about taking care of you? Are you making time for that?" The concern on her face was genuine.

"My meetings help a lot, and I talk to Gwen every morning. It stabilizes my priorities for the day, even before I leave my bedroom."

"I'm so glad you have her. I'm always here for you, too, but she really understands what you're going through firsthand."

I nodded. "I can't imagine doing this without her and the other people in the meetings. Also, we go for a walk every day. Emma loves it, of course, but it really clears my head. It certainly helps this pregnant body."

"I can't wait to see you as big as I am now. Isn't it weird that we weren't pregnant together last time? Feels like I've known you all my life."

"Me, too." I looked over at my friend, this person I didn't even know a few years ago. I'd never felt this close to another woman before, not one I didn't call Mom. "I know I said I couldn't get through this time without Gwen, but you know I feel the same about you, too, right? You're truly the sister I never had. Thank you for everything you've done for Emma and me."

"It's nothing. But it's also everything. I'm here for you, and I know you're here for me. I feel lucky about that every day," she said with a smile emanating from her heart.

I reached out to pat the mountain in front of her. There were other words between us that didn't need to be spoken aloud.

•   •   •   •   •

Christmas was anything but merry. Helen hosted the family, and Eric's sister flew in from Toronto. It had been a few years since we'd all seen Trisha, so catching up with her filled some of the awkward lapses in conversation. Except for watching Emma open presents and the treat of eating crab legs—a Christmas Eve tradition in the Torrington clan—I sat apart from most of the family waiting to go home.

Helen had bought me a nursing nightgown (ever practical, that woman), but in a color I hated: lime green. I mused at how little she knew me. And for Eric, she bought a refillable monthly city bus pass, continuing the theme of giving gifts more utilitarian than fun. She'd loaded the pass with three months' worth of unlimited rides, so at least there was a financial benefit.

The whole evening was a manifestation of make-believe: Let's pretend we're a normal family! Let's imagine no one here has to take a breathalyzer test tomorrow—yes, even on Christmas day. Let's agree to ignore that Eric and Kat haven't said more than ten words to each other all night—and let's assume that's perfectly normal for a couple expecting a baby in four months.

A whole holiday event filled with Oscar-winning performances. It was exhausting.

On New Year's Eve, Eric's AA group hosted a speaker meeting. Different from typical Twelve-Step gatherings, at those meetings, the member shares his personal story, from hitting bottom to the journey through his recovery. The speaker, Tim—a guy Eric had known in high school—asked Eric to be in the crowd as a familiar face for support. Afterwards, they'd all have snacks, and then a regular meeting would follow.

Not surprisingly, we had no plans, so I encouraged Eric to go. I'd been to speaker meetings before, and they were always powerful, inspiring. I hoped he would find something in Tim's story to connect with.

I spent the night thinking about the spiritual awakening I'd had on that inspirational autumn morning on a mountaintop. *Was that only three months ago?* I'd decided I had to be okay, no matter what Eric chose for his life. The truth was, I had to wait. My life was on hold, but I clung to the possibility of escape like it was an invisible passport only I could see. My parents asked me about that very thing when we talked on the phone. Bearing down on the arrival of 1995 in New York, it was still 9:30 in Colorado.

"You know how we feel about doing whatever you can to preserve your marriage, Kat. From what we've seen, you've done a great job. We know it's been hard. But have you thought about what you might do after the baby's born if Eric doesn't pull himself together for good?" Dad said this with a mixture of paternal pride and fatherly fatalism. How could he pull off those contradictory emotions in the span of a few sentences?

"I'm not sure. Every time I think of raising Emma and this baby alone, I see Eric drowning in a sea of loneliness and self-destruction. Could I really do that to him?"

"But you're not doing anything *to* him. He's doing all of this to himself—and to you and your kids. You're only responding, considering what you can do to salvage your future."

On the extension in their den, Mom chimed in. "Your dad's right. I know you don't want to think about taking the kids away from their father, but what choice do you have? You can't let them grow up in a house with so much chaos."

"I do my best to shelter Emma from the ups and downs of Eric's behavior," I said, defensiveness infusing my words.

"We know, Kitty Kat." The nickname felt like a warm hug. "I don't know how you've managed, and I'm so sorry you've had to. But I blame Eric."

"Blame isn't helpful, Mom, though I understand that feeling." I was sitting on our love seat, snuggled under a crocheted afghan my grandmother had made back in the '70s. The zigzag design in orange, blue, and green was ugly as hell, but the blanket wrapped me in love. "I'm just trying to get through the next few months and deliver this baby. I can figure out what happens next *if* Eric hasn't found his footing by then."

I continued with a new point. "I agree that the kids witnessing their father's inconsistent sobriety would be less than ideal, but there are families that make it work. I've seen in it my meetings. *But* . . . I also know I don't want my kids learning about love in a marriage where one parent runs away from his responsibilities, and the other runs after him. I don't want Emma and this baby to think I condone Eric's choices—especially the legal consequences he's facing. That's all weighing on me."

My father's voice turned quiet as he spoke next. "We don't envy the decisions you're facing, and we want you to know something else, Katharine: We're sorry. We talk about this a lot, and we realize now how unhelpful we were to you at the beginning of all this." My father rarely apologized, so I listened with concentration to whatever came next. "We were so worried about you being a single mom that we failed to consider how hard being in that marriage would be. Maybe the lesser of two evils, but we should have judged less and supported you more."

My mother piggybacked on his sentiment: "You're an amazing mother. You'll be able to raise these children alone if that's what happens. And you know we'll always be here to help in whatever way makes sense. You have the freedom to do what's best for you and the kids, whether that's staying with Eric or not. We're just sorry we're late in expressing this to you."

I was stunned into a rare silence. My parents had been the loudest cheerleaders in the "marriage forever, no matter what" camp when Eric first revealed his drinking problem and all the deception that implied. I'd doubled down on staying in the marriage and worked to "fix it" not only because my parents felt strongly about it, but also because I believed I had to commit to the road I'd chosen. More than two years later, the course had been tiresome, exacting, and often hopeless.

"I'm grateful you said all that. It means everything to me. Knowing you're not looking down on my decision—whatever it may be—will help me more than you know. It's hard watching him flounder, but I'm doing my best."

"We know you are, sweetie. And we love you so much," Mom said. I could see her at the desk in my dad's office. She would be looking at the wall of family pictures there as we talked, cutting through the two thousand miles between us in her mind.

"Happy New Year, darling," Dad added. "We hope it brings you peace in every way."

I hung up the phone in time to watch the ball drop on TV—Times Square in New York City. Despite living in Colorado for several years, to me, the shifting of years was still marked by that giant neon globe descending in the Big Apple, not according to the clock on my own wall. So much of my heart remained in the state of my birth. I wondered where I'd be spending New Year's Eve the following year . . .

Chapter Two: Descent into Hell

The *third* and final time Eric and alcohol and the law met up was the day we went for our ultrasound. Because of the holidays, we were catching our first glimpse of Baby T at twenty-two weeks, a little later than usual. The small curve of my abdomen had started to swell right as January welcomed us. I was thrilled, of course, for a miracle cannot be minimized by the banality of our human frailties.

My eyes focused on the display. I scanned the small moving creature ignorantly, looking for formations I could recognize: Leg? Spine? Heart? It took the doctor's expertise to point these out, and I watched in awe, just as I had when looking at Emma in that state. How perfect it all was. My child, safe and protected deep inside me, was unaware of the emotional turmoil our family endured as we awaited his or her arrival.

Eric stood next to me, as transfixed by the blurry images on the monitor as I was. My husband—the father of the baby developing inside me—and yet . . . If someone had been watching us through a two-way mirror, I feared they wouldn't know we shared a bed, let alone the DNA on the screen.

If Dr. Blake sensed the emotional distance between us, she didn't say. She seemed to love this part of her job as much as the actual deliveries. Her voice sounded like soda pop—little bubbles coming up to the surface. She asked us the magic question: "Do you want to know if this bundle is a boy or girl?"

Although I wasn't sure I wanted to know, Eric jumped in and said yes. He turned to me as an afterthought. "If that's okay with you?"

I didn't have a strong feeling one way or another, so I accommodated his excitement. Why not? It would help me with shopping.

•   •   •   •   •

For the first time, *good* news was his Reason for imbibing.

Eric walked through the door that night after his AA meeting, carrying a bottle of champagne and wearing a huge smile. The insanity of the paradox was lost on him. I cringed at his making a mockery out of the Twelve-Step program I had come to trust. But there were other things wrong with the scene: Not only could we not afford such a luxury, but also, I wouldn't be able to share a drink with him in my gestating condition. And . . . he must have taken a cab home from the meeting instead of getting a ride with one of his "meeting mates," Sean or Danny. A stop at the liquor store was nothing unusual for a taxi driver, but it revealed another unnecessary expense.

I looked at the bottle, then aimed a quizzical expression toward him.

"What better way to celebrate our new baby, baby?" He laughed too loud at his own bad joke and came over to kiss me on his way to the kitchen. "A son! A baby boy! Snips and snails and puppy dog tails . . ." I heard him singing as he closed the cabinet door where the glasses stood ready, waiting to be useful to someone.

I pulled myself up from the couch and edged toward him in time to hear the happy *POP!* As he poured two glasses to their rims, I said, "Honey, you know I can't drink that now."

"Yeah, I guess," he agreed. "But if you're *eating* for two, I guess I can *drink* for two, huh?" He took both glasses in hand and alternated sips from each. "To us and to our growing family!"

He hadn't even gotten a nonalcoholic drink for me so we could at least "toast" together. There was a brazen selfishness in this solo act; it left me alone on the other side of his solitary party. Besides, it wasn't like we'd just found out we were expecting. Months had passed since I'd presented him with the pregnancy test result. Learning the baby would be called Evan instead of Erika was his *raison du jour*. Eric used the event to "celebrate" and justify indulging.

I faked a little nausea (though maybe I *was* queasy) and went to bed early after checking on Emma. I must have been more tired than usual because I didn't hear him come to bed.

The first thing I noticed when I started waking up was his breath: hot and sour and loud in my ear. Then I felt his erection pushing hard on the outside of my left thigh. I was barely awake and quite surprised at being "romanced" while I'd been asleep! This was not typical. In fact, during his entire relapse since October, we hadn't had sex at all. Alcohol usually made him uninterested in, if not incapable of, having sex. Then again, he wasn't used to champagne. It seemed to have a different effect.

"Honey, I . . ."

"unnhhh."

"I, I'm kinda still asleep, honey," I said.

"I know. Gonna wake yu'up," he said, trying to sound sweet. Instead, he sounded like a caricature of a drunk in a cartoon.

"Eric, wait." I stalled, trying to think of a polite way to tell him I didn't want to make love. He stunk!

"Don'wanna wait, Baby. Want'chu now." He moaned into my hair as his left hand found my right breast. He squeezed it suddenly and much too hard. I gasped, but he made the mistake of thinking my sound was born of pleasure and squeezed too hard again.

Before I knew what was happening, he rolled on top of me. Thankfully, he wasn't putting his full weight on my swollen abdomen; that was all I could think about.

As he fumbled below to push my panties down, he pressed his mouth down on mine. He thrust his tongue unlovingly inside, his teeth clinking against mine. I tasted stale alcohol on his breath, mixed with fresh cigarettes. I tried not to gag. I worked to take air in as his lips formed a tight circle around mine. I pushed my hands against his shoulders to move him up enough so I could speak.

"Eric, slow down. I'm not ready," I said, but he was in the bed alone, unaware of my responses. Even more frightening, unconcerned.

He kept trying to kiss me, but his aim was off. His tongue licked around my lips. I turned my head away, but his mouth followed. It was disgusting, and it distracted me; I couldn't think of what to do.

His legs were strong, holding mine open. I tried to pull my knees together but couldn't. I struggled to wriggle out from under him. His right hand had my hair pinned to the pillow—I assumed by accident—and it hurt more than I thought it would. Suddenly, I felt his fingers push inside me. I cried out. I wasn't close to being wet; my body instinctively tightened against the intrusion. I'd never seen him like this before, and I'd never been forced to have sex with anyone in my life. I couldn't believe it was happening to me now, with Eric.

He pulled my arms up over my head and held them tight with his own. He looked right into my face. I thought for sure he would stop because how could he not see I was crying? I didn't yell or scream. I stared into his eyes and said in a shaky voice I didn't recognize, "Eric, stop. I don't want you to do this. You're hurting me. Please stop." But he wasn't there. Instead, he closed his eyes, and with an urgent push, thrust himself hard at me. I was so dry, he had to be quite forceful to get inside. It took several tries.

I stopped fighting his legs; I let mine open. It was the path of least resistance, and I hoped it would decrease the friction. And just as he had not been there when he'd looked into my eyes a moment before, I let myself fade away then, too. I couldn't feel the pain anymore. The stinging, the stabbing. They turned into numbness, and I was grateful.

I don't know how long it lasted; I stopped paying attention after my flesh tore. I tried to focus on something I could control. I thought about the blood that would stain the pretty yellow sheets with pale violets on them. What would remove it? *Is it hot or cold water that works best on bloodstains? How long should I let the sheets soak before washing?* I couldn't recall, but I knew I had a bottle of *Shout!* downstairs; that would be a good first step.

After some time passed—it might have been three minutes or thirty—I heard him snoring. He was dead weight, but I pushed up on his shoulders with all my strength and urged him to my left. He rolled off me and repositioned himself, snuggling up with his pillow like an innocent toddler.

I never hated anyone so much in my life.

I eased out of bed. As I stood, a searing heat radiated from the depths of my vagina and stretched out to inflict pain on the outer folds of my skin. Walking the fifteen feet to the bathroom brought new tears. I turned on the light, locked the door, and lifted my nightgown. At the first sight of blood smeared on my inner thigh, I started to shake and heave. I cupped my hand over my mouth, afraid to wake Eric with any noise. I forced myself not to throw up or cry out. I prayed the blood was only mine and had nothing to do with the baby.

I grabbed a towel off the rack and held it to my face. It softened the sound of my gasps for air and somehow calmed me down. My legs were wobbly. I wanted to sit, but I knew it would hurt too much. Leaning against the door for a few minutes, my head hung low enough that I could see where the polish had worn off on a few toenails. I was stalling, unable to bring myself to look in the mirror.

Taking the towel with me, I walked down the hall to the living room, one slow step at a time. As I reached for the cordless phone, I glanced upstairs to where my daughter slept. I listened carefully but didn't hear her stirring. After laying the towel on a cushion, I eased myself down onto the couch, sideways, taking pressure off my lower half.

I never hesitated, and I didn't stop to consider what I was about to do. There was no alternative. The line rang twice before a serious voice on the other end said, "9-1-1. What's your emergency?"

I didn't have time to soften what I said, and I didn't care how insane it sounded: "My husband just raped me."

•   •   •   •   •

A few days later, I stood in Emma's room, looking through the dresses hanging in her closet. I wondered aloud with resentment freezing my words, "What's the appropriate outfit a child wears to visit her daddy in jail?"

The answer stopped me short, as if someone were shouting right in my face: *Children ought never visit their daddies in jail!* Not today, not ever. Not Emma and not Evan.

The ER doctor had allayed my fears when he confirmed my baby boy was safe and sound, despite the unexpected commotion to his world. The blood I'd seen that horrific night had only been mine, nothing worse. I continued to feel him move as he should, a tough little guy already.

I knew what happened wasn't my fault. But the events of that night forced me to think about the previous months. Was there anything I did or didn't do that added to Eric's downward slide? Could I have changed this outcome? What would have made a difference along the way? I had no answers. But that particular path—and the knife wound it inflicted to my heart—was more than I could bear.

I took another look through Emma's clothes and found comfortable red overalls with blue piping. *Now, this is a perfect outfit to wear while Mommy calls a divorce lawyer.*

But what if the disease hadn't taken over?
What if Eric had been able to find himself again before it defeated him?

Biding Time
Winter 1994 – 1995

* Fork 6 *

Chapter One: Detaching

"Biding your time" is an interesting expression. I don't know where it comes from, and I don't know its historical context, but I know the connotation: It means waiting. Waiting out a terrible situation until you can make a change.

It seems harmless enough. It shouldn't hurt at all. There is no action to take and no action to avoid. It's a passive thing. An INaction, if you will. Doing nothing. Sitting on the sidelines. Watching the world go by. Kicking back. What other clichés can I toss out?

But waiting, biding your time, is an inhuman task when it's *your life* that's moving forward without you.

•   •   •   •   •

I never nagged or bitched or scolded him for his slips which came rhythmically every three or four days like emotional contractions. I kept to myself. He said he was trying, and I wanted to believe him, so I stepped back. I carried a mental image of my careful tip toe dance that illustrated the precarious spot I was in: If I stepped back much farther, I'd be out of the picture altogether. But it was better than fighting; I just wanted peace.

One of my favorite readings in *Courage to Change* during that time summarized the loneliness and emptiness I felt in our marriage:

"Turning to an alcoholic for affection and support can be like going to a hardware store for bread." You can't find what you need there.

I'd formed many expectations about life while growing up: If you do well in school, you get good grades. If you tell the truth, people will trust you. When you walk down the aisle, your spouse will be your partner: his ying to your yang. When you're down, he can help pull you up. When he's sick, you take care of him.

But my expectations fell apart when I accepted my husband had built a liquid wall around himself. And even though that shouldn't be solid enough to keep me out, it was stronger than any stone and metal gate.

During those days, I learned I couldn't go to him for anything: love, affection, reliable parenting, let alone stopping at the grocery store to pick up a loaf of bread. Turns out, he was in the hardware store, not the local Safeway.

But he wasn't absent all the time. He refrained from drinking on days when he had meetings, and he used that restraint to prove he had some control. If he had control, then he couldn't be a *real* alcoholic. I was stunned at how he could still rail against the label when he was a living testimony to the dysfunction that was alcoholism. How could he forget or blatantly ignore all he had learned during his month in the mountains and at all those meetings?

I withdrew into my own small world: tending to Emma, growing the baby inside me, and working my own Twelve-Step program. I clung to Al-Anon like a dieter holds a carrot stick: *This is my salvation. It will rescue me from temptation!* I held on to my healthy friends and the program literature with white knuckles, knowing it was the only chance for me to rise above the sea of hopelessness I was swimming in.

Months passed. We lived in a state of limbo. Our lives ran on parallel tracks, but we pulled into the same station at night. I stayed home with Emma, and he went to work. Some nights he came home drunk, and other times he was mostly a replica of my old Eric. I read my literature and went to meetings when I could, and he read magazines, cookbooks (though he rarely made any of those recipes), and the occasional Sci-Fi novel. He attended meetings only when a fellow member asked if he were going, as if an invitation were required.

Our conversations were predictable and shallow. If I'd worked in Hollywood, I could have written the scripts. Many of my Al-Anon friends relayed similar situations they were living or had experienced. That's what finally convinced me alcoholism is a disease. It wasn't all the science I'd learned. Instead, I couldn't ignore how the behaviors of alcoholics were so much alike, despite their backgrounds, jobs, marital status, or criminal pasts. The way the symptoms presented themselves, how conversations with loved ones were so alike. The commonalities addicts shared with each other made it seem like they'd all gone to the same prep school.

Oddly, it reminded me of children with Down's syndrome: They look more like others with that syndrome than their biological families. The physical and cognitive traits of the disease are more evident than the differences among those who embody them.

I shared this observation with Gwen one morning on the phone after Eric had gone to work. Emma was working on a puzzle at her toddler sized table in the living room. I sat with my swollen feet up on the coffee table.

"I've thought the same thing before. I'm not sure if there's any biological proof to back it up, but I know what you mean," she said.

"I keep trying to 'lead by example,' you know? Like, if I work my program and own my mistakes, maybe he'll do the same? If I eat a salad instead of a greasy burger and fries, maybe he'll join me? It sounds ridiculous, even as I'm saying it."

"Maybe, but there's no other healthy way to *be* in this situation as long as you're choosing to *be* in this situation," Gwen said with the wisdom of Yoda.

"You mean unless I'm willing to leave . . ."

"Yes. If you're going to be in the marriage, and if he continues to drink, you only have so many choices. You can yell and scream and beg him to stop. But you know where trying to change him gets you. Or you can remain focused on yourself, doing what's best for you and your babies, and hope he chooses to change on his own. He may or may not. There's nothing you can do about his choices."

I still believed in the possibilities that recovery could deliver: I saw families reunited and love rekindled; I heard stories of self-esteem reborn and crumbling futures reshaped. I'd never intended our marriage to be anything shy of forever, but I couldn't make it work alone.

Gwen reminded me of the Three C's: "We codependents think we can fix the ills of our loved ones—if we love them harder, or set enough boundaries, or stop enabling. We buy into the myth that our love can change them. Wrong. Remember, we didn't Cause it, we can't Cure it, and we can't Control it. We can only ever change ourselves."

Yes, the (Damn) Ray of Hope still lived in my house. And though I despised it for the redness it kept bringing to my face, I needed it. Like an abused child needs her parents, even though the same arms that hold her occasionally hurt her. I needed it.

•   •   •   •   •

Weeks went by, and I continued to focus on my own good health and happiness, despite Eric's dispassionate interest in either for himself.

I spent a lot of time with Leigh, helping her set up the nursery for the newest member of her family. They'd learned the baby's gender, and Leigh wanted to "girl it up" this time, having drowned in blues and beiges when Justin was born. The baby was expected in early February, so the soft pinks, butter yellows, and bursts of flowers added a special sense of joy during the middle of our frigid winter.

"She's been kicking me in the ribs all day," Leigh said, rubbing her abdomen as we walked down the aisle at Target together in early December. Emma and Justin were sitting inside the cart, crammed together like two turtles under one shell. In fact, that's what they looked like since Leigh had unpackaged the comforter she was buying for the baby's room and had placed it over the kids' heads like a tent cover. They were giggling and peeking out, one at a time—a silly game of peek-a-boo—as if we didn't know where they were. We laughed at their antics.

"Kicking you is her way of saying *I can't wait to meet you, Mommy. And by the way, I'm gonna be even more energetic than my brother, so be prepared.*"

"Oh, my God. I hope not. That boy . . ." She laughed to herself as she remembered Justin's babyhood squirminess. "I want an easy baby this time."

"I'm a little worried, then. Emma *was* an easy baby. Maybe I'll get a terror child this time?" I made a funny face at her. Emma and Justin peered up from the cart just in time to see my eyes wide open and my tongue out. They both pointed at me and laughed like I'd been standing on my head. I memorized the joyous sound to cheer me later.

•   •   •   •   •

On Christmas Eve, we joined Eric's family at Helen's house for their traditional crab leg dinner. Emma opened her gifts with excitement, but in every other way, the holiday was a nonevent. Eric and I gave each other presents we could have given to neighbors we only knew casually: He gave me a candle and body lotion, and I gave him aftershave and a gift card to the sandwich shop he liked to visit for lunch.

New Year's Eve was equally ordinary: We ordered in Chinese food and watched a movie. In normal times, that would have been a satisfying night, even on the last day of the year. We would've sat next to each other and maybe held hands. That evening, I sat on the love seat alone, contrary to its intended purpose of drawing two people close together. He sat on the La-Z- Boy recliner. We were just getting by.

In January, a new reality entered my life, twisting and turning everything I thought was important into a knot that would not be unbound: Leigh's baby died.

Although the pregnancy had progressed as expected, the nightmare of the baby's death began as soon as she was pushed into this life a month early. She wouldn't breathe. She was blue and limp.

As the doctor yelled for neonatal nurses, Leigh's sister, recording the happy event, turned off the camcorder in mid-sentence. The frenzy of specialists who ran into the room were not caught on film, and the cries of disbelief and despair would only be recalled from memory. Baby Hannah was resuscitated by the magic of modern medicine, but it would not cure her permanently.

The diagnosis took several days while Leigh and Keith spent every waking moment by Hannah's crib side. The fragile baby had been airlifted to the Children's Hospital in Denver, more than an hour away. Specialists pronounced the diagnosis as SLO/RSH, a rare genetic disorder. The biochemical defect is caused by the body's inability to produce adequate levels of cholesterol, which the brain and body need to function properly. There was little to be done, and the joy that had awaited Hannah's arrival grew into the grief of letting her go.

I helped in the small way I could: Emma and I spent a lot of time with Justin during those weeks. As my friend and her family coped (somehow) with the tragedy unfolding in their lives, I thought about my own. Certainly, I was not experiencing a tragedy. Nothing like theirs. Maybe mine was only misfortune or anguish, but Hannah's imminent death made me consider the choices I *did* have while Leigh's family had none. The Serenity Prayer teaches that there are things in life we have no control over and things we do. The key is knowing the difference. My thoughts focused on what control I had and where it landed on that scale.

After three weeks of splitting time in the ICU and quick visits at home with Justin, Leigh and Keith brought Hannah home, to die. They didn't want her to leave this world without having been welcomed home and knowing she was wanted and loved. I was the only nonrelative invited to the homecoming. It was an honor, and I didn't take for granted the gift of being allowed to hold the tiny child for a few minutes.

Even though she had been born near full-term, her disease hadn't allowed nutrients to absorb properly into her body. She'd been losing weight since her first day on Earth. Holding her was like cradling a whisper, an illusion caught between this world and the next. The experience was heartbreaking and life altering. I could not experience such senseless suffering and not allow it to affect the choices I made for my own children and my own happiness. Life was too fragile to waste a single moment on anything not entirely necessary.

Hannah died that very night, as if she'd only been waiting to leave the sterility of the hospital and be surrounded by the normalcy of a home she would never live in.

•　　•　　•　　•　　•

Appropriately, it rained on the day of her funeral, though the temperature hovered around thirty degrees. Snow would have seemed too festive in winter, so God sent melancholy drizzles instead.

I woke shortly after 2:00 a.m. that night and couldn't get back to sleep. I crept into the living room and sat on the couch, letting my eyes adjust to the dark. Physically exhausted and sluggish from the emotion of the day, in contrast, my mind raced and couldn't stop to focus on just one thing. I felt pressure to *make a decision*—to change my life, to take action—but I also felt paralyzed. Seven months pregnant, it seemed a bad time to make a new start when the start inside me hadn't even begun yet.

And then I wasn't alone.

Eric walked through the darkness of the living room and joined me on the couch. Although I'd held many middle-of-the-night, soul-searching vigils before, he had never been part of one.

He'd brought a blanket from our room. After pulling it over his legs, he extended his reach to include me under the fabric, as well. It was a gentle gesture, but after months of distance between us, it seemed out of character. I managed a "Thanks" and went back to staring at the recliner across from me.

We sat in silence for what became an uncomfortable amount of time. I was thinking about going back to bed when he finally spoke.

"This whole thing with the baby . . . Hannah . . . it, it really sucks." Well, Hallmark would never steal the phrase, but coming from this man who'd spent most of the last year self-absorbed and predominantly uncommunicative, it was profound.

I looked over at him and could only see his silhouette; the moon shone in from the back porch, and the soft glow hit the side of his face just so. I'd always loved his profile.

"Yeah, you could say that. It's been awful to watch," I said.

"You've been a good friend to Leigh and Keith, helping so much with Justin and all." I couldn't believe I was hearing this from him. Had he been paying attention? Maybe I'd given him too little credit. He went on, "Does this make you worried about our baby?"

Interesting question. Was he thinking about *my* concerns or expressing one of his own?

"Well, you can't see something like this, something so random, and not wonder. But it would be extremely unusual for us to be statistics right after our friends down the street were." I paused to think if I wanted to add anything else. "But yes, it does make me think about the ways things can go wrong." Another pause, then, "What about you?"

"I guess I've been doing some thinking, too, though not so much about the baby. More like about my life. Our lives."

I almost shook my head, denying he was able to think about such important matters. Instead of saying anything, I waited to see what would follow.

"I know I haven't done a good job of getting my priorities straight since coming home from Serenity House. I don't really know why except I felt pushed to do what everyone wanted me to do *right then*, you know? Like I didn't have a say in it. Kinda like when my dad pressed me into working at the shop. But anyway. I think I'm ready now."

"Ready now for what?" I asked, careful not to sound snotty. Curiosity grabbed me and held me captive as I waited for him to go on.

"I'm not going to drink anymore," he said. Confidence took charge of his voice, as if he'd been asked *What's the definition of prejudice?* and he was proud to know the answer.

The words floated like smoke swirls above our heads, ready to evaporate if I didn't reel them in.

"Eric—" I started, but he interrupted me.

"No, wait. I know you don't think I can stop. I haven't given you much reason to believe it." His tone changed from confident to quiet-but-steady. "Or maybe you don't think I mean it, but I do. I'm not stupid. I know what you're thinking, and I know how Hannah has affected you," he said, with a wisdom pulled from his long-ago past.

"What do you mean? How do you think I'm affected?"

"You're thinking life's too short. That you never know what's going to happen next." It sounded like he'd opened a box of clichés and was trying to see which one fit our situation best. "And you're thinking I don't care about you and our kids."

I shot him a guilty look that registered *I'm surprised and impressed.* I truly didn't think he knew how I felt. But did he know the depth of my concern?

"Well, your actions haven't shown you care about us, Eric, so I had to assume . . ." I trailed off. Without malice, but rather as a matter of fact, I added a softer observation: "I know you're not happy, and honestly, I'm not happy much these days either. Maybe we don't belong together anymore?" The words were out before I could choke them back.

"NO," he said more adamantly than I expected. He got up from the couch and paced the floor in front of me. "No, Kat. That's not the answer. I know I've disappointed you . . . *and* my family . . . hell, and *your* family. But I'm ready to do what I said I was going to do four months ago. I need to get a sponsor in AA. Going to the meetings is okay, but I need to do more. I know this one guy who talked to me about it once; he seemed cool."

There was something different about him in the moonlight. He stood before me with one hand in his robe pocket, and the other pulling through his dark blond hair. I missed the feel of it between my fingers. He looked determined, motivated, sure that whatever strategy he was concocting would work.

He looked like the man I thought I'd married a long, long time ago, but hadn't seen in as many years.

He came back to the couch and sat next to me. Taking my left hand between both of his, his eyes locked on my wedding ring. He fingered it for a minute and then turned to look at me directly. "I need you to believe in me."

"I've been believing in you since we met. That's never changed."

"And I've only given you reasons to doubt me; I know," he said. "But I promise you, Kat, I *will not* drink again. I've done it before. I know I can do it again. Can you believe me?"

"It hurts, Eric. Every time I trust what you say and it doesn't happen, I feel stupid for believing, and it hurts. I don't know how much longer I can do this." There. I'd never expected to tell him how fragile I thought our future was, but now it was there for him to hear and ponder.

He looked right into my eyes. "But I'm *promising* you. I've never promised like this before, have I? You have to try one more time," he whispered, then he looked back down at my hand in his. "I don't want to lose you."

No, he had never promised that before, right to my face, that he'd stop drinking. There had been other vows, similar proclamations, but technically, not this promise.

In typical weak-wife fashion, I started to cry. I knew he thought my tears fell because he was saying what I should want to hear, but that wasn't why. I cried because I knew I was getting sucked in. I could feel that (Damn) Ray of Hope wrapping its arms around me, pulling me into its grip. I suspected The Slap would come eventually, but I didn't care. Not that night.

I wanted to hear the words and to believe. There was so much at stake for our family. I had to give him one last chance to do the right thing—to prove me and my cynicism wrong. I felt compelled to try anything possible to help him succeed. The truth grabbed my heart: If the day ever came when I had to walk away, I needed to be able to look my children in the eyes and say, *I did everything I could.*

We sat still, side by side, for another minute, all the possible forks in the road ahead of us arranged neatly like a dinner table set for guests. I wiped my nose with my pajama sleeve and turned to look at him with watery eyes. I searched my internal thesaurus for the exact right words because I knew a significant moment was happening. Then I got brave.

"Eric, I will pull together my very last bit of trust. I will drudge it up from somewhere—though I don't know how—and I will support you and believe in you this one last time." I saw a glint of a smile forming under his mustache and a softening around his eyes.

Before he could get too comfortable with my words, I added, "*But*, I'm telling you this with no doubt in my mind: If you break my heart this time, there will be no putting it back together again. I know this."

"Okay," he said. Just okay, nothing more.

It was an audible agreement. I'd made my heartfelt ultimatum as clear as Waterford crystal. I told myself he got it. I convinced myself we'd finally turned a corner and were going to walk down the tree-lined boulevard of our future together this time, moving in the same direction. No more forks that ended with the stabbing pain of a knife to my heart.

He'd made a promise. I'd seized it. I had to focus on the positive and the possible, not worry about the plausible that might lurk in the shadows. If I didn't put all my faith into him this one last time, if I kept one foot out the door, ready to run if things went wrong, then I wouldn't really be "in it" fully. I had to be one hundred percent committed to supporting Eric to know I'd done my very best.

As we stood to go back to bed, the baby kicked me hard on the inside of my left hip bone. I wondered if he (or she) was trying to tell me I was being gullible and naïve, or if he was showing his support for my courage and conviction. My hand rubbed the spot where he'd let himself be known, and I sent him a mental message: *Go back to sleep, Baby T; I've got everything under control. I'm doing what's best for all of us, and we're going to be all right.*

Chapter Two: Recommitting

The next few weeks flashed like a traffic light: Some days I was GO—fully committed to Eric's new plan. Other days a glaring red light blinded me to a full STOP. I feared any difficulty or unexpected obstacle would cause Eric's resolve to slip. I didn't believe him one bit, and I berated myself every hour for it.

On top of that, I was certain that if he *did* drink, it would somehow be my fault for not having trusted in him as I said I would. I qualified my failings as an Al-Anon "relapse," but I couldn't bring myself to pick up my books or try to calm myself with the slogans that had comforted me before. Gwen called me every few days to check in; hers was the steady voice in my head, not my own.

I found it odd that I'd been able to work my program before his proclamation, but after, my determination faded. We'd been living parallel, separate lives, before Hannah died, and I was able to focus on what I needed to do for Emma, the baby, and myself. Once Eric held his promise up for the world (me) to see, I became obsessed with waiting for him to disappoint. After so many setbacks in the past, it seemed inevitable he would prove my trust in him was misplaced. I waited—not with hope that he would fail, but with the assumption of it.

But in contrast to my weakness, Eric maintained control of his life. We seemed to live on a scale, each of us on our separate sides, maintaining a careful juxtaposition where only one of us could be healthy at a time. The stronger of us somehow held the suffering one up, saving the fragile one from a deadly crash to the ground.

The physical changes in my body were obvious due to advancing pregnancy, but the psychological fluctuations were less noticeable to others. By the last days of February, I decided, intentionally, to let Eric be the sturdy one for a change. I'd been the sole support of our dysfunctional dyad for so long. I was damn tired.

Lying in the dark at night when I couldn't sleep—when the baby rolled mercilessly in my womb—I thought about how good it felt to be needy for once. I didn't want to take care of my husband anymore, and since he was living out his promise to me, I was able to let go. I had two real dependents who needed me. It was the most selfish I'd ever been, and yet, once I accepted my right to it—reminding myself it was normal for spouses to share that luxury—I started breathing easier.

For Eric, recommitting to our marriage was a *purpose*, and he tackled it with a fervor reserved for missionaries. He developed a recipe that worked for him: A bit of "Fake It 'til Ya Make It" mixed in with a pinch of daily meditation and readings. Stir in a handful of Twelve-Step meetings and bake in an oven of spending time together as a family. He told me he was focusing on The Prize at the end of all the effort: proving that my faith in him was well-placed. I hoped the goal also included pride in himself and the reward of living a sober life, but I didn't ask.

He also talked a lot about life in The Future: taking pictures of Emma in her prom dress as she descended the stairs; celebrating our twentieth anniversary (*Where should we go? Paris?*); Baby T sledding down a hillside or starring in the high school play; helping our parents as they age.

The pictures he drew of our happily-ever-after were similar to the fantasies I'd once held onto with the grip of a star quarterback; it was reassuring to hear some from Eric. They pulled me into the partnership of recommitment that I needed to be a player in.

When I first joined his team, I went through the motions like a stoic soldier, sensing doom around the corner, but heading into battle anyway. My commitment strengthened every day that things went well. I trusted him a little more.

After conditioning ourselves in full tactical maneuvers, our platoon of two moved as one. A new camaraderie blossomed between us, and we practiced patience, humility, and grace—for ourselves and each other. This was necessary because we both tripped up. This time, our missteps were acceptable because we were in the trenches together. He was present.

Instead of blaming and pulling away, he acknowledged when things were uncomfortable and talked to me: *I'm worried. What if I can't do this?*

When I slipped and hovered, trying to direct him, he held up his hand in a kind, not accusing way, to stop me: *I got this. I hear you.*

We were aware of each other's weaknesses, and we joined forces to help each other be the best versions of ourselves. I'd always hoped marriage would work that way; we'd just taken a long, sick road to get there.

Every day he was sober solidified his middle-of-the-night promise not to drink again. His words and actions aligned. When he said he was working his program, and I saw him reading and doing homework assignments from his sponsor, my belief in him grew. When he said he wanted to be closer to me, then rubbed my aching feet as we watched TV at night, my trust solidified. When he told me he wanted me to feel appreciated, so he and Emma let me sleep in on the weekends while they played in her room, that added up. And when he went to work every day and relayed positive stories when he got home, I felt hope blossoming.

Another gem from *Courage to Change* reminded me to focus on the process. It's never just one thing making the difference, it's many small motions repeated over time.

A stonecutter may strike a rock ninety-nine times with no apparent effect, not even a crack on the surface. Yet, with the hundredth blow, the rock splits in two. It was not the final blow that did the trick, but all that had gone before.

Many weeks of Eric's consistent effort and hard work were positively affecting my faith in him and reinforcing his resolve. Many small efforts, over time, laid the groundwork for rebuilding trust.

•   •   •   •   •

One moment that helped me commit to The Plan, as Eric had outlined it, was the day we went for our second ultrasound. I barely remembered the first one, right in the middle of baby Hannah's hospital stay. My blood sugar levels were ticking upward by the beginning of March, so my doctor wanted to check the amount of amniotic fluid around the baby. Watching out for gestational diabetes.

We were at my obstetrician's office—me lying on a table and Eric standing next to me. In the dark room, the only light emanated from the ultrasound monitor. Dr. Blake chatted at us, pointing out our baby's body parts that looked like nothing more than shadows and wavy lines: heart, spine, foot, kidneys. Really? She could have told me I was pregnant with a pineapple, and I'd have believed her from all I could tell.

"The baby looks very healthy, guys." Her eyes twinkled as she shared the good news. "The amniotic fluid is at a reasonable level for now, but we'll monitor your glucose closely over the next few weeks. If you need insulin, we'll go down that road later." I cringed thinking about injecting myself with a needle, but whatever it took.

I let out a cleansing breath, and Eric squeezed my hand. "The baby's been pretty active lately," I said, "but it's good to hear you confirm things are okay."

"Are you interested in learning the baby's gender?" she asked. "You're farther along now; I'm pretty sure I can get a good look if you want to know."

I looked up at Eric. We hadn't wanted to know when we were pregnant with Emma, but we hadn't discussed it yet during this pregnancy. There'd been more pressing issues in our lives over the past few months.

"I think it might be fun to know this time," Eric ventured, with a hopeful arching of his eyebrows. "What do you think?"

"Well . . . I guess it would make shopping and getting the nursery ready easier?" My voice was a question, even though I wasn't asking anything. "I'd be okay knowing if it's something you want this time."

Eric looked at Dr. Blake with a smile and nodded at her. I thought about what it would feel like to identify this baby with a specific name. Would I feel even closer to him or her than I already did?

"Here we go," said the doctor. "Sometimes these kiddos aren't in the right position or their hands are hiding what we need to see." She chuckled and repositioned the ultrasound wand. She pressed it gently to the curve of my abdomen and let it glide over the warm gel she'd placed on my skin.

"How many babies have you delivered, Dr. Blake?" I asked.

"I've been delivering babies for twenty-three years now. At last count, that was 2,173, including Miss Emma." She knew the exact number! Her face was a sea of tranquility, as if she were gazing at a mural where all those babies' faces were grinning at her. "Being part of so much joy has been a blessing to me."

Eric was practically buzzing beside me. "What can you see?"

"Hmmm . . . okay. There we are. You sure you want to know?"

I thought Eric would reach across the table and grab her shoulders. "Yes!"

"It's a boy."

I looked at Eric and saw how he glowed while looking at the indiscernible image on the screen. As he pondered the shape of his unborn son, I pictured a smaller version of Eric running around our house. And I felt myself falling in love all over again.

•   •   •   •   •

On Thursday nights, we each had meetings that met at the same church at the same time. The AA folks met in one room, and the Al-Anons in another. It was a strange "date night" for many couples, but we fit right in. We often went to get coffee after, and we listened as Emma babbled while she ate ice cream. She selected different flavors each time, so we still didn't know her favorite. I was suspecting she was a daddy's girl, though—more fruit than chocolate.

Even though the members remain anonymous, Eric and I talked about what had come up in our respective meetings. The material and concepts were the same, but the perspectives were different. We always learned from each other.

One night in mid-March, we sat at a booth in the corner at our favorite post-meeting haunt. Eric shared how a group member had been homeless for two years before finally getting sober. Somehow that alone hadn't been his "bottom," though. He had to go to jail for theft first, *then* he got sober. Eric said, "I can't imagine sleeping on a park bench or under a bridge. I'd like to think that alone would wake me up to better choices sooner than two years."

"But everyone's hitting-bottom moment is so different. It's a matter of tolerance, right? A lady in my group said her sister only stopped drinking when her three-year-old son was taken away from her, *and* she had so many health problems that she couldn't walk anymore—at thirty-five. Her sister said 'just' losing her son wasn't enough for her; both things had to happen."

"I can't imagine losing Emma. I'd do anything . . ." Eric's eyes watered. I felt his fear across the table.

"But you're doing everything possible to be the best father you can be—to her and to this little bundle," I said, rubbing my midsection. It had expanded to where it touched the table in front of me even as I leaned far back in the squishy bench seat. The baby demonstrated an offsides kick within my abdomen to let me know he was listening.

"I can't wait to meet that little one," Eric said, sipping from his coffee cup. "Where are we with boys' names? You were pretty sure it was another girl, so we didn't talk much about the what-if-it's-a-boy possibility." It had been two weeks since the gender-revealing ultrasound. Time to name this baby.

"That's true. Not sure what those girl feelings were all about. Maybe I just couldn't picture a child of mine that wasn't like Emma, you know?" He nodded his agreement, and I continued. "What about Westley? That feels Colorado to me. You know, *Go West, young man*, and all that?"

"Maybe. Or . . . Brady?" He'd been giving this some thought.

I laughed. "As in Brady Bunch?" I made a face.

"Okay. Not that." He paused, trying to remember other names he'd liked before. "Since Emma starts with an -E, should we stick with that letter?"

"That's a sweet idea. Ethan? Eliot? Not Edward, too English."

"What about Evan?"

"Oooh! I like that!" It felt right. I looked over at Emma and said, "Do you like the name Evan for your baby brother?"

Of course, we weren't going to count *entirely* on our twenty-one-month-old to help us name our child, but her opinion could factor in.

Emma nodded with her eyes wide open. Tootie Fruity ice cream dripped off her chin. I wiped it off—for the third time—and gave her a kiss on the forehead. "Then Evan it is! Emma and Evan. Evan and Emma. They go together nicely." Okay, maybe Emma *was* the decider, but I wasn't going to ask her if she liked Cecil or Vladimir. It was safe to give her a vote.

I smiled over at Eric. He looked happier than a puppy with a new bone.

PART IV

A memory: "Would you please put that thing down? You're following me around like a creepy stalker," Kat said. Her lips twisted into a smirk that betrayed her leave-me-alone directive.

"But I'm trying to capture you. You look particularly beautiful today," Eric said, laying on the charm thick as a Southerner's drawl.

"Oh, please. That's so blatantly manipulative. You think flattery is gonna win me over?"

"Yeah, I do. That, and the fact that I'm filming you for your parents. You can't deny them."

He was right about that. Ever since Eric had bought the handheld camcorder, he'd been talking about making a "day in the life of" video for Jack and Jillian. Not only was he trying to win his new in-laws over, but he also knew the two thousand miles between them and Kat were hard. He wanted to help them picture how she spent her time.

"You really think they want to watch us grocery shopping?" Kat asked.

"Why not? They'll be happy just seeing you, period. Doesn't matter what you're doing. Remember the last time they were here, your mom said something about how you're a grown-up woman now, but she couldn't imagine you taking care of the house or paying bills. I think this glimpse into our daily lives will be interesting to them." It was a sweet gesture on Eric's part, so Kat caved.

"Okay, okay. I give up, but it feels funny."

"Just pretend you're talking to me regular and ignore the camera. Embody your inner Katharine Hepburn; she's your namesake, right?"

They turned the corner into the produce aisle at the Safeway. Eric walked quickly ahead of Kat, then turned around. Walking backwards, he pointed the camcorder at Kat and asked, "What are you looking for here?"

Her theater background kicked in. Kat responded, in her best attempt at a Julia Child impression, "Well, Mr. Torrington, thank you so much for your interest in my shopping expedition. Your viewers will be intrigued to know I intend to purchase several vegetables in this section of the store. I believe in providing a healthy array of food items as part of every dinner I prepare. Today's collection includes shallots, mushrooms, and green beans. Of special note: If the asparagus is on sale, I may indulge." She could see Eric's big smile behind the camera.

Once she was "in character," Kat lost herself in the filming without busting up laughing. She and Eric continued through the butcher department and the bakery this way, Eric embodying the persona of a Universal Studios director and Kat trying out various accents as the whim struck her.

When he turned the camcorder off, an older woman sporting a helmet of hardened gray hair and contrasting bright pink fake nails approached them. "Are you filming a TV show?"

Without missing a beat, Eric said with a straight face, "Why yes, ma'am. We're hoping to interest a local producer in our idea for a show. It's designed to help newlyweds save money while learning to cook healthy meals."

"Oh, my," she said, clearly impressed. "What a wonderful idea! I wish you both much luck." She turned to push her cart to the checkout line, and the young couple smiled at each other.

Eric held the camera in one hand and cupped Kat's chin with the other. He balanced the two tasks, then kissed her softly on the lips, right in the middle of the store.

"I think we can do anything together if we set our minds to it, don't you?" he whispered. Then, "I've got it! Next week, I'll film you at the dentist. Do you think Dr. Willard will let me?"

Kat shook her head and giggled. "You're insufferable, you know that?"

Clarity
Approaching April 1995

* The Final Fork *

On Wednesday nights leading up to D-Day (delivery day), Eric and I attended a birth preparation class at the hospital. After Emma's arrival by C-section, we were hoping for a natural delivery this time around.

Bill stayed with Emma on those nights, and Eric and I considered it a pseudo-date night. The class ran from 5:30–7:00 p.m. We'd have a late supper out after: My craving for Chinese food was a never-ending yearning those days. Crab Rangoon, vegetable lo mein, Szechuan shrimp! I couldn't get enough.

One night, sitting across from each other in a shiny red booth at the Golden Dragon, Eric said, "You know, I was talking with James after our meeting last night; we're working on my Eighth Step. I don't know how it was for you with Gwen, but as a sponsor, James is pretty by the book."

He dipped a Rangoon into sweet and sour sauce and popped it in his mouth. I waited to hear what came next. "But I like his approach. I need the discipline," he said. The smile he threw my way let me know *he* knew I knew that about him.

"But it's still hard," I said, showing my support and empathy. I'd been through all Twelve Steps with Gwen, and some were harder than others. I appreciated how Eric was working his and open to discussing some of his "ah-has" with me. Some. I listened with attention when he did.

He nodded his agreement and wiped his mouth. His pause unnerved me. *Where's this going?*

He recited the Eighth Step from memory: *"Made a list of all persons we had harmed and became willing to make amends to them all."* I nodded for him to continue.

"It's daunting, but I'm making progress. Obviously, you're on that list of people I've harmed. When I get to the Ninth Step, I'll *make* those amends, but since I may not get there for a while, I want to tell you something." His nerves showed themselves as he ran his finger up the condensation on his glass of Diet Coke, but he pushed through. "I see what an amazing mother you are. I don't think I've ever told you that, and I'm ashamed it's taken me this long to say it." He looked at me like he'd never seen me before. I felt vulnerable, but also acknowledged in a way I hadn't felt with him since long before Emma arrived.

I had no response, so he went on. "Our lives have been so much about me for a long time. I see that now."

"I really appreciate you saying those things, Eric. I know it's hard."

"When I did my Fourth Step, I worked through my shortcomings. I think the most harmful one to you has been my self-centeredness." He paused to take a sip of soda. I played with my wedding ring, now hanging from a gold chain around my neck. My swollen hands hadn't allowed me to wear it on my finger since February.

Humility and self-awareness looked good on him, but I was still unaccustomed to seeing them. He was on a roll. "I never thought of myself as self-centered before, but it's true. The alcohol never helped. It kept me from supporting you—heck, from really *seeing* you—during those hard times. Hard times I created." He blinked back a tear but made himself hold my gaze. "I'm sorry for all of that."

I sat in silence and took in the weight of his words. The look on his face was sweet and genuine. I'd given up hope he'd ever say any of that to me, even convinced myself I didn't need to hear it, that watching him work his program was enough. But it mattered, and it felt good.

"I . . . I don't know what to say," I managed.

"Well, *that's* a first." His tease matched the twinkle in his eyes. I rolled mine.

"I know that wasn't your Ninth Step, but it was pretty darned close to an amends." I smiled over the table at him. "I've seen how hard you're working your program, and every day that you go to a meeting or call James, I'm relieved. You're putting your promise to me in action. But I wasn't sure how much it affected you."

"I'm meeting so many people who've changed their lives. They share their journeys, and holy cow, some of them have been harsh. I always learn something from them, even if their stories are far from mine. But I see myself differently after looking through their lenses." His face looked flush, almost like he was blushing. "I wish I'd been ready to face these things before, but I've also learned it happens in its own time."

"I'm just glad it's happening, period." I reached across the table for his hand and squeezed his fingers. "It's not really my place to say this, but I'm proud of you."

He changed the subject by adding some levity to the moment: "So . . . wanna make out in the car before we go home?" He wiggled his eyebrows up and down.

"Have you noticed I'm almost nine months pregnant?" I said with a teenage giggle.

"More of you to love, baby."

We paid the check and revisited our youth for an hour before pulling into our garage.

•   •   •   •   •

The time of nesting was in full swing. A month before our due date, Eric and I fluttered around the house like robins filled with purpose, preparing our home. I pulled baby paraphernalia from storage boxes that hadn't seen daylight since Emma started walking. I organized them into piles: bath time, sleepwear, toys, clothes. Oh, how I loved infant clothes! What's more precious than a three-month-sized onesie with images of sleeping sheep or dancing Snoopies?

I set up a diaper changing station in our living room and bought sheets for the cradle that would live in our bedroom the first few months of Evan's life. There were other last-minute things to do, but I was big and round and tired most days, so I got lax after my initial week of busyness. There was still time.

As for Eric, he finished putting together Emma's big-girl bed. She was still sleeping in a crib, but we introduced her to the toddler bed before her baby brother came home. This was a special present little girls got when they became big sisters, we told her. She was thrilled!

She loved "helping" Daddy put the bed together, though the extent of her assistance was chattering at him while he screwed in the bed rails and such. She also "tested" the bed in various stages of completion. When Eric was finally done, Emma snuggled in and pulled up the Ariel-covered comforter, humming "Part of Your World" as she pretended to fall asleep.

I didn't have the energy to make dinner most nights, so Eric stepped in as full-time chef. Emma loved his breakfast-for-dinner: scrambled eggs, featuring pancakes with smiley faces made of sliced bananas and strawberries on top. He also dazzled us with his famous hot dog casserole—a concoction of baked beans, mac-and-cheese, and hot dog pieces. He barked through the whole meal, and teased Emma, "Ouch! Don't eat me. I'm a small dog."

"No, Daddy. Hot dog!"

Bonus points for Eric: not only keeping us alive, but also making us giggle during suppertime.

My mom scheduled her flight to arrive five days before our due date. Her extra pair of hands would be invaluable to me, and Emma was counting down the days until her Bubbie arrived. I finished tidying up the guest room for her just in time.

• • • • •

The temperature was a lovely forty-eight degrees on that early April morning. The drizzling rain foreshadowed spring flowers. Nineteen days before my due date, but my son started his life with the determination and self-confidence that would later become synonymous with his personality: He decided to arrive early, on his own timetable.

While Emma and I played the piano (well, I played and she tapped keys on the upper register for added effect), I felt a pull deep inside me. I wasn't convinced that the slow cramping was "the real deal," since false contractions can mimic real ones. To be fair, I wasn't sure what real ones felt like since my last labor had been induced. But I'd done my reading, always a good student.

We continued to play and sing and be silly together for another half hour. I paid close attention to the big clock hanging in our living room. The cramps came at regular intervals, fifteen minutes apart. I was not prepared! I hadn't laundered the bassinet sheets yet; my bag for the hospital wasn't packed; and I was sure I didn't have infant-sized diapers in the house. I'd been nesting, but the nest wasn't ready.

I made a plate of cheese and crackers for Emma and settled her in the booster seat to snack for a few minutes while I figured out what to do. I called Eric at work, but his co-worker said he was out on a sales call, due back in an hour.

"Please tell him to call me the minute he gets back, Lenny. I know we don't know each other well, and I hate to give you this very personal message, but I think I'm in labor. It's early, so I'm not totally sure, but I'm going to assume."

"Gosh, Mrs. Torrington, that's great." He hesitated, then added his concern, "Are you all right? Are you alone?"

"Well, my daughter's with me, but she's not even two years old yet, so kinda," I chuckled. "I think I'm okay for now."

"Can I do anything?" he asked sweetly. I tried to picture his face, but his features were made of clay, forming and reforming into different visages I'd met at Eric's workplace over the years.

"Just give him the message to call, please. But . . . I guess if I'm not here, that means I went to the hospital, so he should go there, okay?"

"Sure. Got it. I'll see if I can find out where he is and get the message to him sooner."

Poor guy, I thought. He sounded like *he* was the nervous father, not quite knowing what to do with himself but feeling he should do *some*thing.

I hung up and realized I'd sounded a lot braver than I felt.

I hesitated to call her, but I picked up the receiver again and dialed Leigh. I had no way of knowing how she would handle being with me in labor when her own recent delivery had ended in tragedy. But I needed her, and I knew she'd be furious if she found out I hadn't called her out of respect for the open wound that was her heart.

"I'll be right there," was all she said. When she hung up, I started to cry. Is there a more amazing feeling than when someone who loves you drops everything to be at your side?

•　　•　　•　　•　　•

I lay on the couch, timing my contractions and listening to Emma and Justin sing songs between bites of their snacks. Leigh had made Justin a duplicate plate of cheese and crackers when she'd arrived.

Thirteen minutes apart. I listened from the living room as Leigh went through my dresser and packed up essentials for my hospital stay.

Feeling useless, though preoccupied, I saw Leigh heading upstairs to pack an overnight bag for Emma. I hadn't thought of that! The soon-to-be new big sister would stay with Keith and Justin while Leigh coached me through my breathing until Eric arrived. The plan was that Emma would spend the night there. My mom was supposed to be my labor partner backup if Eric was delayed, and she'd been assigned overnight duties with Emma while Eric and I were at the hospital. But this baby had other ideas about his entrance, and we were already onto Plan B.

Lying on my left side, I reached for the cordless phone and called Helen between contractions. "By chance, have you seen Eric today?"

"No, I haven't. Isn't he at work?" I could hear the familiar frost of worry penetrating her voice like an arctic wind blowing across an ice field.

I hesitated to explain. I didn't want to tell her what was happening; it felt like a betrayal. Eric should know first. But he wasn't there. I'd hedged a bit too long. A contraction assaulted me, and I couldn't talk. While I expelled quick puffs of air and brief *uhs*, Helen sounded more concerned with every question she tossed out at me:

"Are you all right, Kat? Is something the matter with you or Emma? Why aren't you talking to me?"

As the squeeze subsided, I said, "Sorry, Helen. I couldn't talk; I was in the middle of a contraction."

"Dear God," she said with panic. "You're still a month away, aren't you?"

"About three weeks, but it seems this baby wants to greet the world today. He has a mind of his own already," I said, musing that such a child would emerge from my body in what I hoped would be just a few hours.

"Where's Eric?" she asked, forgetting that I had called her to ask the same thing.

"I called his work, but his co-worker said he's out on a customer call. Lenny's trying to track him down so Eric can meet me at the hospital. My friend Leigh is going to bring me there now, and her husband is coming home from work to watch Emma and their son."

"Are you sure I can't help?" she asked. I imagined her feeling left out—

"Actually, would you call my mom and tell her what's happening? She isn't supposed to arrive for two weeks. Maybe she can change her flight?"

"Absolutely. I'll do that right now."

"Thank you. You can come over to Memorial after. Eric and I would love for you to be with us at the hospital." I thought of my own mom missing the event—a jab in my heart, then . . . another tightening above my cervix.

"Hold on, Helen, another contraction . . ."

Not even ten minutes between. *Shit, we'd better get going,* I thought.

I could hear Helen breathing on the other end of the phone, mimicking my rhythm, waiting for me to communicate with her.

"Helen, I've got to go now. I'm okay, but I need to get to the hospital soon or this future CEO is going to arrive in the passenger seat of Leigh's minivan!"

"Of course, dear. I'll see you soon."

When my breathing evened out, I watched as my friend wiped our kids' faces with a washcloth. "Leigh?" The word soft as a prayer. "I'm so unprepared. I don't even have clean sheets for the cradle."

She walked over and took my hands in hers. "I have plenty, and I want you to use them. Please."

Not even three months since she'd lost her baby, this was her blessing. She was talking about so much more than the bedding. "Now, let's GO!" She smiled as she helped me up.

Emma and Justin skipped out the door in front of us and headed for the van. Leigh had already told them about the last-minute sleepover. They were giddy at the prospect.

The eight years I had on Leigh had shrunk since Hannah died. The grayness of grief—the ugly reality of Nature's betrayal—had grown upward and outward from the pit of her soul. It distorted the very softness of her face, the clarity in her eyes, the youthful energy of her step—just enough. Just enough for those of us who knew her well to see how she'd changed. The void had found a permanent place inside her. She was learning, somehow, to make peace with its constant, uninvited companionship. But the price she paid was never being the same again.

Keith pulled into their driveway a minute after we arrived. I offered him an awkward hug through the car window, saying,

"Thank you for taking off from work to watch Emma. I'm sorry the timing is so bad."

"Hey, like I don't love a good reason to take a half-day?" he said with a wink. "It's not a big deal. I'm glad to help." Keith walked around to the driver's side and opened the sliding door. The children clambered out of the van and ran up the front steps of the house. They wiggled an impatient ballet as they waited for Keith to let them inside. But first, Keith leaned into the open window and kissed his wife with a tenderness that made me embarrassed to watch. Then, over his shoulder, he smiled and said to both of us, "Now, off you go."

I knew Emma would have a great time with her friend, but I was sad to leave her. In some way, I felt she should be with her daddy and me as her little brother made his entrance into our lives. But then again, the reality of seeing her mother beg for an epidural might not be her idea of a fun afternoon.

•   •   •   •   •

We arrived at the hospital and navigated the sea of required paperwork quickly. My contractions were coming closer together, but I felt less worried about having them there. I knew qualified medical people were lurking nearby, behind closed doors. The baby could start crowning right there and we'd be okay. Still, I was eager to get to a room and take my clothes off.

No sooner had I envisioned the privacy of a labor room when I felt a stab of pain so unbelievable that I screamed. The voice seemed to come from somewhere else; it couldn't have been mine. Immediately, several of those lurking medical people jumped out from behind closed doors. Within seconds, I was on a gurney, being wheeled down the smooth hallway.

An incongruent thought filtered through my pain: *Emma would have a blast being whisked around on such a cool contraption, her dark curls bouncing in the air.* I focused on her precious, smiling face—a face I knew better than my own—as I slipped into unconsciousness . . .

•   •   •   •   •

Placenta previa. When the placenta tries to come out before the baby. By not waiting its proper turn to be born, the life-sustaining mass often rips from the womb prematurely, causing significant bleeding. It also blocks the birth canal and denies vital nutrients to the soon-to-be-born child. The cure? A Cesarean section, to deliver the baby quickly and prevent permanent damage to the uterus, if possible.

My hopes for a natural delivery were dashed again, but I didn't care about that as I held my perfect son in my arms a few hours later. Evan looked up at me with the wisdom of an old soul, having already encountered a hardship some don't survive. He'd been through a life-threatening crisis even before his creamy white skin touched the air, but he was okay. And I was okay.

In truth, I was more than okay. A sense of gratitude and good fortune overwhelmed me. Nevertheless, I was intensely aware that my friend sitting beside me had been denied those very things. Leigh stood and reached out her arms. No words needed. I lifted my newborn baby and placed him in her arms. She smiled from a faraway place I couldn't see and walked around the room with my baby. As she cradled him, I imagined she soothed a sorrow inside her that had been rudely, but necessarily, ignored. The daily demands of tending her living child had undermined her need to grieve properly for the child who had moved on from this world before ever having known it.

As I watched my friend, the urge to cry gripped me like a choke hold, but I forbade myself. It was not my pain; I had no right. This was a joyful day for me, and I would not impose my useless sympathy on Leigh's moment of making some peace with pain. Carefully, and with some difficulty, I rolled over in my bed, clutching a pillow close to my incision, to face the door. I let Leigh and Evan look out the window together as she introduced him to the majestic Rocky Mountains. The fact that my son was serving as the conduit for such mediation filled me with pride. Only hours old, he was already helping others.

I must have drifted off, but I woke to the sound of my daughter meeting her baby brother for the first time. "Tiny, tiny BAY-beeeee," she cooed at Evan, in a very high, singsong voice, her little face ridiculously close to his. A nurse had wrapped him like a burrito in a green and yellow striped hospital blanket, his wispy blond hair peeking out from under a tight beanie. Leigh held him while sitting in the rocking chair so Emma could get a close look. With the careful approach of a grown-up, Emma examined every detail of Evan's six-pound, eight-ounce body she could see: She touched his soft eyebrows, his pursed lips, his puffy cheeks. It was love at first sight.

Helen had arrived at the hospital while I was in surgery, and once she knew Evan and I were okay, she drove to Leigh and Keith's house to pick up Emma. After a quick celebration dinner at Wendy's, they arrived to meet the newest member of our family.

After her lovefest with her new baby (I could already envision little conspiracies launched between them as they hid under the dining room table, giggling in a make-believe fort), Emma hopped up into my bed. The jostle it gave my tummy was a physical bump; her "Where's Daddy?" gave me a mental one. Once again, time to name the elephant in the room.

I had no idea where Eric was. If Lenny had called back, I wasn't home to get the message. Helen shook her head slightly as I looked over Emma's head in her direction. I hugged her from an awkward angle, from my propped-up-with-many-pillows position, and said, "I'm not sure, honey. Daddy doesn't even know yet that we came to the hospital today. I'm sure he'll come here as soon as he knows Evan's here."

She accepted my explanation with no concern, but I added, "Your little brother must have really, really wanted to meet you, huh? He just couldn't wait another day." She smiled at the thought that she was so important to him already, then she hopped down to go visit Evan again. Leigh had placed him in the clear-sided baby cart near my bed. It was warm inside, helping him transition from the womb to Colorado's climate. Despite arriving three weeks early, his lungs were very strong, and he didn't need any special attention beyond lots of love, sleep, milk, and a clean diaper.

While Leigh and Helen chatted, Emma sang and danced to "entertain" Evan. I took the opportunity to call my parents. Since a C-section requires a three-night hospital stay, I estimated I'd be going home on Friday. Mom had already changed her flight.

She made proclamations in my ear: "I will get the house in order before you even get home. Don't worry about anything." Then, "I will cook, grocery shop, do laundry, and take care of Emma for those first two weeks. You need to get your strength back from the surgery." Her final dictate: "Your sole purpose will be to breastfeed my new grandson and rest. Period."

There was no arguing with that woman, not that I would, because such indulgence sounded wonderful to me! I couldn't wait to see her and to have her meet Evan. She'd only had baby girls in her life—me and then Emma—so I was curious to see her with a baby boy. With our Jewish family roots, Evan was facing a circumcision. There was no way I was going to be there for that! Sounded like a perfect job for a Bubbie.

By 6:30 the sun was starting to set, and Emma was getting tired. Leigh smiled at me from the foot of the bed and squeezed my big toe. "I'm so glad you and Evan are both okay."

"I can't thank you enough for everything you did for me today. I'm so grateful . . ." She knew the rest; we both knew how the day *could* have ended. "And thanks again for keeping Emma tonight."

"Are you kidding? *She'll* be helping *me* by keeping Justin busy. I don't know about you, but I'm pooped!" She winked at me as Emma skipped over to say good-bye to me.

I hugged my daughter tight and kissed her beloved, soft cheek. "I'll see you tomorrow, baby girl. Have fun tonight."

"Bye, Gamma. Bye-bye, Evan," she tossed over her shoulder as she held Leigh's hand and walked into the hallway.

When the room had settled into calm, Helen broached the subject of Eric. I'd wondered how long we would sit together before she said something. I could have brought it up, too, but I knew the topic would dampen my mood. I wanted to hold on to my joy without that downer, but Reality stood at attention in the corner, waiting to be acknowledged.

"Where do you think he is?" Helen asked, the hitch in her voice conveying her concern.

"I don't know. He usually gets home from work by 5:30. I know Leigh left a note taped to the front door telling him where we were. I can't imagine he's at home and just ignored the note. He wouldn't do that," I said, confident I wasn't deceiving her or myself.

"I called his work around 4:00," Helen said, confessing like she'd done something wrong. "It was embarrassing, because I spoke to the same young man you did, Lenny? He told me Eric hadn't checked in all day, and that was unusual since he had several appointments out in the field. They were either expecting him back in the office by 3:00 or he should have called in."

We sat in silence for a minute. I assumed she was imagining plausible scenarios as I was. None of them good.

"What should we do?" she asked. Although thirty-one years older than I, she sounded like a child seeking advice from an elder. "Do you think he's in trouble?"

"You know, I've been going to Al-Anon for a few years now. You may find it helpful, too, if you ever want to go to a meeting with me. I'm trying to think about what the program would suggest." I looked up at the ceiling tiles and blew out a long breath before continuing.

"We don't know for sure Eric's fallen off the wagon, but this behavior does fit his past actions when he *was* drinking, so we should be prepared for that. If he did, in fact, drink today, we'll have to accept that. It's out of our control."

"But he was doing so well lately." She looked out the window, as if she could find him out there in the sunset.

"Yes, he was. But the truth is, no matter what he's doing, he's not here. Without a damn good reason, I'll tell you, I'm not only angry as hell, I'm also more hurt than I have words for. So instead of focusing on him and his behavior for once, I'm going to think about how *I* feel and what that means to me." I paused, allowing her time to consider the same. "How do *you* feel?"

"I'm tired." Her answer surprised me, but I didn't say anything. I waited for her to continue. "I'm tired of feeling let down by him. I'm tired of believing in him and then being disappointed. I'm tired of feeling embarrassed by him. I'm tired of defending him, and I'm tired of his selfishness and apathy toward his responsibilities."

She fiddled with her watchband for a minute as she gathered her courage to say what came next: "This is not how I raised him. Most of all, I'm tired of feeling guilty. But I must have done something wrong to . . ." She reached inside her purse for a tissue.

I'd never seen this woman cry before. She'd never allowed herself to be that vulnerable with me. I was proud of her and yet at a loss for what to say to help. I'd certainly felt all those things myself, but we'd never been close enough to talk about any of it before.

"Helen, you haven't done anything wrong," I said. "Not now. Not ever. And neither have I, by the way. Whatever mistakes you and I have made, we haven't caused this, and we can't cure it." She lifted her head and faced me directly. Our eyes met and I continued.

"It's easier to look for someone or something to blame, but the fact is, Eric's an alcoholic. It's often referred to as a 'cunning and baffling disease.' That's not to say he has no control, though. I think of it like diabetes. People who live with that know to check their blood sugar levels, eat appropriately, exercise. All those things help, but the disease itself doesn't go away. Eric needs to learn how to live responsibly with his disease. To respect it. He hasn't mastered how to do that yet, but I know it can be done. I've seen it."

"What if he can't or won't?" she asked with the weight of desperation heavy in her eyes. "How do I stand by and watch him make bad choices—especially when they're hurting him and all of us? You're a mother now; you understand how hard that is," she said. Her eyes pleading for me to give her answers.

"I know. It's impossibly hard, but there are tools that help—and understanding about the disease is useful. Eric's been in AA long enough to know how to help himself if he wants to. I've seen real growth in him these past several months, but slips can happen, as we know. In the end, he's the only one responsible for his decisions. But we have choices, too."

I sounded like an Al-Anon textbook. "Just because we love him doesn't mean we have to watch him self-destruct. 'Detaching with love' and 'setting boundaries' are helpful tools. They allow you to put distance between yourself and your alcoholic, so you preserve your own good health, no matter what they're doing."

"I don't know how to do that," she said through a ragged breath as she wiped her eyes.

"It's difficult, I admit. I didn't know how to at the beginning, and believe me, I'm still not perfect at it. But, when I'm able to do it, to maintain a healthy distance, I usually feel better. It may not change him, but I don't expect it to anymore. I can't change anyone but me."

And with that, right on cue, the star of our show entered. He walked into the room as if he were being directed on the set of a Hollywood movie. A few steps in, and I knew. His gait was off, his eyes were slow to blink, and he had a "caught-in-the-act" guilty look about him. Helen knew, too.

I couldn't have predicted what happened next if I'd had a crystal ball.

Helen stood and approached her son, placing her body between him and me—and Evan, who slept soundly in the baby cart on the side of my bed furthest from the door.

Eric had been intent on walking over to the bed where I lay. I imagined him leaning down to kiss me. I expected him to babble about being sorry for missing the birth—blah, blah, blah. I already knew what he was going to say. But Helen interceded. She didn't show any anger toward him, but she was unyielding.

"No, Eric," she said, reaching up and placing both of her hands on his shoulders to thwart his forward movement. His 6'2" frame towered over her, but she didn't move. "You can't be here right now."

"What? Whaddya mean I can't be here?" His volume was too loud and his words were sloppy coming off his tongue. He looked around her to meet my eyes, beseeching me, but I said nothing. I was immobilized by Helen's assertiveness.

"I'm sorry, son, but you've been drinking; that much is obvious. We didn't know where you were all day, and it was a very important day. You missed it all. Now Kat and the baby need their rest. I'll drive you home."

"I don't need'ya to drive me home, Ma," Eric said with a twinge of distain for the implication that he shouldn't be driving. "I drove *over* here, din'int I?"

"That's unfortunate, but what's done is done. You were lucky, as you've been before. But either you let me drive you home right now or I will call hospital security. This will be out of my hands then."

He looked as if she'd slapped him. I must have looked dazed, as well, because when Eric looked at me, he spit a litany of accusations: "What kinda bullshit'ave you been feedin' my mother? You're sucha bitch, sometimes, Kat. Why can'tchu keep private stuff between us? Ya hav'ta drag the whole'worl into our lives." Every word was an attempt to turn our attention away from him and onto someone easier to blame, me.

"I'm not the whole world, Eric. I'm your mother, and I won't tolerate you talking to your wife that way," Helen said, her tone calm, but the implication authoritarian.

Eric rolled his eyes and snorted a series of insincere chuckles, as if he were the offended party. And with the speed of a camera click, he shoved his mother backward, pushing her away from him. Although she managed to catch the side of my bed with her left arm, her legs slipped out from underneath her. One foot caught the self-standing hospital tray parked by my bed, sending everything scattering to the ground in a loud crash. My dinner plates, various utensils, a big water bottle, and a tissue box all went flying, and in the middle of the mess sat Helen, grabbing her left knee and rubbing it briskly. More than any physical pain she'd endured, my newly brave mother-in-law donned her rage like a suit of armor.

"How DARE you?" she yelled at him from an awkward, seated position on the floor. "How *dare* you push me? Don't you see what you're doing, Eric? Do you see what you've become? You need to get out of here *right now!*" She turned herself over onto her good knee and pulled herself up using the metal frame of my bed for support.

Finally ripping my eyes away from the action unfolding in front of me, I looked over at the baby cart next to my bed. Evan hadn't woken from all the noise; he continued his newborn slumber, peaceful as, well, a baby.

Three nurses rushed into the room. "We heard some commotion. Is everything all right?" one nurse asked, surveying the disarray in the room. She assessed the situation quickly and spoke only to Eric. Her voice was calm, but practiced: "Sir, I must ask you to come with me. Please. Let's not have any more disruption." She wasn't a large woman, but I could see from her demeanor that she knew a thing or two about handling disorderly patients—and visitors. She was not a wallflower.

The other two nurses stayed by the door but showed their intent to assist their colleague if the need should arise. One woman had her hand on a phone mounted on the wall. She looked ready to call for help if things didn't go well.

The vocal nurse stepped toward my husband with caution, as if he were a cornered animal. Her eyes darted to the baby cart to make sure Evan was okay.

"Let's walk out of here, okay? We can talk in the hall." She used a voice that schoolteachers adopt with bullies on recess playgrounds.

Eric stood paralyzed. Although he'd been verbally abusive and had physically overpowered his own mother moments ago, he turned docile. Whatever anger had built within him in his defensiveness was dissipating. His outward aggression was turning inward, and he would eventually feel sorry for himself. Sad as that was, I was grateful he was no longer pushing his self-loathing onto others. With his head hung forward, he stood like a thug awaiting handcuffs.

Eric locked eyes with me and then his mother. All he said was, "I'm sorry," and walked out with a nurse on either side of him. Not once had he looked at our baby.

I don't know how—or if—he got home that night, but Helen decided she would stay at the hospital with Evan and me. The chair in my room folded out into a single sleeper. I asked the nurse to give Helen a once-over to make sure she was okay after her tumble. After, my mother-in-law sat near my bed, sipping hot tea.

We sat for a long, long time without words. What should have been a happy milestone moment in her son's life was now an ugly memory. I wondered what Helen thought of her newfound courage. She'd been forced to acknowledge the extent of her son's illness, and she'd expressed her disappointment to him in no uncertain terms. This was a lot of change for her in one fell swoop.

"For a woman who said she didn't know how to 'detach with love' or 'set a healthy boundary,' you sure learned quickly," I said, with a slight chuckle, hoping to show my respect and gratitude.

"Yeah, well . . ." She shook her head. "I've been sitting here replaying the whole thing in my mind, and I swear, I don't know where it came from. It all happened so quickly; the words just came out, an unplanned response. Is that strange?"

"I don't think there are any right or wrong ways to get through difficult moments. We do the best we can—and tonight your best was awesome!" I smiled at her. It was the warmest moment we'd ever shared. "I can only imagine how hard this has been on you. Thank you. I'm grateful you were here when Eric came in. I don't think I could have handled his twisted anger tonight."

"You shouldn't have to. Certainly not tonight, after giving birth, alone, and enduring surgery! But you should never have to deal with it." She paused and gathered her thoughts. "I'm so sorry, Kat. All this time, I've been consumed by my own shame about Eric. I didn't think about what living with him every day must be like for you. And Emma! Oh, God, I'm so angry at myself for ignoring what this must have been like for her, my sweet baby girl!"

Helen's eyes watered again, and she reached for the tissues between us. I jumped in to help alleviate her guilt. "I believe things happen for a reason, and they happen in their own time. We can't rush our emotions; we make peace with them when our minds can accept them, but not a moment sooner. For whatever reason, you weren't ready to face some of this until now."

My turn to be vulnerable. "I was in denial about it all for a long time, too. I was so determined to hold our family together that I couldn't see what was in front of me. And even after I knew the demon we were fighting, I clung to whatever straws of hope I could. I desperately wanted us to be the family I dreamed of, and I saw glimpses of it when he sober, so I held on. But it never lasts." I played with a corner of my comforter, looking away from her for a moment before I said more.

"As far as Emma is concerned, I assure you she's fine. I've always tried to keep her far removed from the chaos. Plus, she's focused on her own world—which is a good thing at her age. As long as she has her favorite movies to watch, a grilled cheese sandwich when she's hungry, and enough sleep, she's happy. She accepts life as it happens."

"I wish my needs were so simple," Helen said with a thoughtful smile.

"Me, too. Maybe we can take a lesson from her? I think we make our lives more complicated than they need to be sometimes. Why can't we choose to focus only on things that make us happy? Things that keep us healthy?"

"I like the sound of that. I'll have to spend some time thinking about what those things would be for me. The architects of our own lives? How empowering," Helen said. "So often, I feel like things are happening *to* me. That I'm just along for the ride."

After a long, healthy snooze, Evan made his presence known with a quick intake of air and a long, slow whimper. It wasn't a cry yet, just a mini proclamation: "Hey, I'm waking up now, and I think I'll want some milk soon."

Helen stood and walked to the cart, speaking sweetly to her grandson as she scooped him into her arms. "Yeeeesssss, my sweetheart. Don't you worry. Grandma and Mommy are right here. Did you have a nice little nappy-nap? Yeeeeesss, you're such a handsome boy. You're hungry, aren't you?" She kissed the top of his head before placing him in my arms.

I opened my hospital gown to accommodate his searching mouth. Helen looked away. I imagined her thinking back to long-ago moments from her own earlier life. Perhaps she was remembering a similar mother-child moment when her own son suckled at her breast. A time when she provided everything he needed. Easier days when she could comfort him, and he didn't seek unhealthy solutions elsewhere?

Helen and I sat in comfortable silence while Evan nursed. I presumed each of us was lost in our own thoughts on love, parenthood, expectations, and acceptance.

We bring our children into the world and prepare them for life. Our hope is that they will embrace that gift—smart decisions, healthy choices, striving toward happiness. We cast our vision far into the future and imagine them parenting their own babies, passing on the love and lessons we instilled in them. It's our legacy; it's how we live on.

But we can only do so much. Our love is not a guarantee that our kids will never feel anguish or have to figure out some hard things on their own. We love them. We do the best we can. The rest, at some point, is up to them.

On the day my second child was born, I felt the joy. Of course I did. But I also felt the emergence of an upcoming fork in the road of my life. What did Evan's arrival mean to my future? Would Eric ever find real, long-lasting Sobriety, capital -S? Could our family stumble through the façade of normalcy and fool others for another few years? Could we fool ourselves anymore? And most important, should we?

I'd given Eric an ultimatum a few short months before. I'd mustered my last ounce of trust and faith in him. He knew my heart was a fragile bundle he held in his hands, and yet . . . whatever his reasons or however the disease was controlling him, he had unequivocally tossed it by the wayside. I had a choice to make, too: either follow through on my promise to move on or stay with him and be the embodiment of a sellout. But there was no choice to make. Not really.

My cells spoke to me. In a rare, united front, my head and heart stood side by side and told me: *You'll never look yourself in the eye with respect again if you stay with him now.* Emma and Evan would grow to see me as pathetic. So would I.

In that moment, there wasn't a decision to be made. I just had to affirm what I already knew. Eric would have to define his role in his children's lives. The time had come for him to take charge of his own life, too. Alone.

The dream life I'd imagined and strived for faded like a rainbow vanishing after a storm. My instinct was to worry that my kids wouldn't adjust, but they would. Millions of children navigate their parents loving them from different households. Emma and Evan would survive the upheaval, too.

I looked down at the newborn in my arms and tried to picture his future. Impossible. But my job hadn't changed. My role was to love my kids, no matter what path we were on, despite obstacles placed in front of us. Nothing would ever change that. I feared what lay ahead, but I also felt at peace. Something better awaited me; I just couldn't see what yet.

I'd taken many paths along the way. Some had been confusing, and sometimes I'd picked the wrong one. A few roads caused pain, sharp as a knife's edge. But no path is inevitable or unending. The power to choose is mine. I'd always have the option to change direction, to take a different fork in the road.

Author's Notes—2022

In the aftermath of my divorce, life revolved around homemaking. Not in the 1950s definition, but rather the spirit of that term: *Making a Home* for my children to ensure their stability, security, and safety. My cooking and cleaning skills never rivaled Betty Crocker's or June Cleaver's (do readers under forty know who those women are?), but my kids had food on the table and clean sheets.

Parenting and maintaining the house (such as it was) took my mind off the emotional welts that calloused my heart. I pushed those scars from my contemplation and got on with the business of living, forging a future for my new family of three. I didn't have time to dwell on the wounds I'd earned during the battles I'd lost with my ex and his disease. I couldn't consider the lessons I should have learned from the war itself. Not then.

But time doesn't slow for anyone. My life—and therefore my children's lives—shifted direction when I met Stephen. Love doesn't always offer a second chance, but I was blessed that Stephen not only loved me, but also opened his arms, time, and heart to my kids. He was a father to them in ways their biological dad was unable to be.

Stephen and I created a "mini-Brady Bunch" when we got married. I was happy to open my arms, time, and heart to his two children, as well. The kids all lived with us full-time. A blended family has its challenges, but what family doesn't? We navigated the bumps, and over the decades, we grew closer.

My children continued to see their father for visitations over the years—sometimes supervised when the court was in charge. He enjoyed a few periods of sobriety, but never stopped drinking for good.

A few years after my kids and I moved (an hour away) to start our life as part of a family of six, my ex lost his driver's license permanently. His ability to visit the kids became more difficult and less frequent. As a result, his in-person influence in their lives dwindled, especially as they got busy with their own activities.

From the security and happiness of my second marriage, I penned the first, very rough draft of *Forks & Knives*. One of the weird benefits of insomnia is that it provides quiet time in the middle of the night with nothing to do but think. The unresolved nature of my first union gnawed at me; I had to get those thoughts and feelings out. What I discovered was that some of the things that pulled at my brain were not just events that had happened between my ex and me, but also the things I *feared might* have happened during that time. Additionally, I wanted to consider the options I'd had that I didn't pursue. What poured out of me was a compilation of the "what ifs." The forks showed themselves, and I needed to peek at them. I wanted to explore the ways I'd grown—or hadn't—during the years of navigating the disease that lived in our house. I also had to acknowledge the unhealthy conditions that lived *inside me* during that time. Two people make up a marriage.

After I wrote the draft, it sat inside my computer for over seventeen years; I never thought of it again. A truly cathartic process, writing that long journal entry allowed me to put a symbolic red bow on the box that held my early, naïve adulthood. I moved on, as healed as anyone can be after a divorce that breaks your heart.

In 2021, I retired from my professional work life. I'd always known I wanted to try my hand at writing, but about what? Then I remembered: *I wrote that thing a long time ago.* What should I call it? It wasn't a memoir, but it wasn't fiction either. More important: Was it any good? Would anyone care to read it? I had no idea.

Enter again, Stephen. A retired journalist and high school English teacher, I asked him to look at it. In a selfless, supportive gesture, he put aside any awkwardness he might endure and began reading about my tortured first marriage with his objective, literary eye. As a writer/reader, he said, "Yes, this is worth revisiting." I'm grateful for his love and encouragement. Without it, *Forks & Knives* would still be sitting in the forgotten shadows of my hard drive.

By the time I began re-writing the draft, my ex had died. I don't think I could have pursued this book if he were still alive. The narrative of this journey is just as much mine to tell as it would have been his. However, I wouldn't have put him (even a fictionalized version of him) in the public eye while his eyes might've been watching. I've tried in earnest to tell the authentic parts of our story in an honest and compassionate light. My oft-spoken words of comfort to my children hold: *He loved you to the best of his ability and more than any other people in this world.* Their challenge as his progeny is to accept the full range of his humanity—to see past his flaws into the sweet, lost man he was. We are all more than our lowest moments. And just to be clear, the scene that unfolds in the chapter titled "Descent into Hell" *did not* happen. It is a fictional representation of what can happen when fear, desperation, and alcohol meet up. It didn't happen to me, but it does happen to other women living in similar situations around the world; my heart aches for them.

Although my ex-husband maintained employment throughout his life, he never lived independently again after leaving our marital home. The decades of his alcohol (and cigarette) abuse finally took their toll on his body. Still living with his mother, he succumbed to a heart attack at the young age of 57. His body was found in his bedroom two days after he'd passed.

•   •   •   •   •

In early 2022, Stephen encouraged me to join a writer's group. The members of Penpointers gently guided me through the Do's and Don'ts of writing, novel structure, and storytelling. The years between writing the original draft and reworking this final version of *Forks & Knives* allowed me emotional space to develop Kat and Eric as (somewhat) separate people from my ex and me. I tell people this is a work of "autobiographical fiction" or it's a "fictional autobiography." None of the individual forks tells the truth linearly as it unfolded, but real pieces of our journey—the anguish and the growth—are entwined throughout the various paths, those we took and those we might have taken.

Acknowledgements & Gratitude

I have loved two men, for very different reasons. They both live in the pages of this book, and I am grateful for each of them.

The person Eric is based on, my first husband, helped me grow into the person I am now—a woman I respect and like. Not because he was able to give me the love I needed, but because he couldn't. I mean no disrespect to him in telling—and fictionalizing—this story. It is, after all, my perception alone. His was a painful journey, filled with self-doubt and missteps. I hope he's finally at peace.

Stephen: You have supported me as your equal and embraced my strengths and flaws in equal measure. I thank you and I love you more than I can say here. You are my best friend, my partner, and my sounding board. (Listening to me "process out loud" is not an easy task!) The love you offer *is* the kind I need, and it is the kind I now know I deserve. I had to take a long road—and travel down a few forks—before I got to you. You were so worth the wait.

My parents, Rachel and Joe Cassidy, did not live to see the day that I completed this book, but are with me at all times. They were my roots and my wings. They taught me the beauty and importance of writing; the benefits of reading, curiosity, and education; the courage to strive for self-improvement; and the joy of sharing life in its full authenticity with those you love. I miss them every day.

Elaina and Adam: It's impossible to put into words how loving you has shaped me. I am a flawed mother, but I have always done for you what I thought best at every given moment. You know my wishes for you—I have bored you to tears through your lives, telling and retelling you my hopes—but they are real and strong; they will survive me. I adore you both, and I know you are my greatest contributions to the world.

Laura Mahal, editor extraordinaire: If I could have dreamed up the perfect professional to guide me through the task of preparing my manuscript for public consumption, I couldn't have conjured a better fit. From your first passionate and welcoming email, I knew we were a perfect match! Thank you for your encouragement, honesty, and grammar wisdom. You're a gem.

Penpointers: Thank you for inviting me into your writer's group and teaching me so much. Your common goal of "helping to make the writing the best it can be" is invaluable, and your encouragement to keep going, well . . . kept me going. A very special thank you to Brian Kaufman who has become a mentor, even though he never officially offered. I'm grateful for your unique support throughout this entire journey.

Julie Rich and Jeff Bibbey: Thank you for being my Beta Readers. What a favor! I asked you to read my manuscript and provide feedback on whether it was "good enough" for the public. You both accepted the challenge with commitment, candor, and compassion. Thank you! You helped make the book—and me—better.

Reagan Rothe and the publishing gurus at Black Rose Writing: I'm grateful for the opportunity you gave me when you accepted my manuscript. I continue to learn so much from you and the process. Thank you for helping me share my book with people outside my immediate circle.

Finally, to all the souls I met along the way in the rooms of Al-Anon and AA: The program "works if ya work it." I'm grateful for all the honesty, vulnerability, and wisdom shared there. The unique camaraderie sustained me, the principles enlightened me, and the real-life Gwen held my hand as I worked through the actual forks I faced on that road. Thank you all, and I hope that anyone who is or loves an addict finds the support and strength the Twelve Steps can provide. There can be peace in the middle of the tornado.

•   •   •   •   •

None of the characters in *Forks & Knives* exist in real life as they do in the pages of this novel. They are mostly compilations of traits from several people who aid in the telling of the story—with the exception of Hannah. Her name is real and used with her mother's permission. Her story, brief as it was, is told without fictionalization. Julie and Mark: I held your precious baby for only a few minutes, and yet she changed my life.

About the Author

Mimi Wahlfeldt wrote the first draft of *Forks & Knives* as a cathartic exercise following her divorce. After retiring from "real work," she revisited the pseudo-memoir—unread on her hard drive for seventeen years—with the goal of fictionalizing it for an audience broader than herself.

Prior to this, her primary writing experience was work-related, centering around marketing: newsletters, press releases, brochures, and promotional articles for local newspapers or company websites.

Wahlfeldt is happily remarried to her best friend Stephen and lives in Colorado. The couple successfully raised four children together. She is a member of the Northern Colorado writer's group Penpointers and is currently working on her second novel.

Note from Mimi Wahlfeldt

Word-of-mouth is crucial for any author to succeed. If you enjoyed *Forks & Knives*, please leave a review online—anywhere you are able. Even if it's just a sentence or two. It would make all the difference and would be very much appreciated.

Thanks!
Mimi Wahlfeldt

We hope you enjoyed reading this title from:

www.blackrosewriting.com

Subscribe to our mailing list – *The Rosevine* – and receive **FREE** books, daily deals, and stay current with news about upcoming
releases and our hottest authors.
Scan the QR code below to sign up.

Already a subscriber? Please accept a sincere thank you for being a fan of Black Rose Writing authors.

View other Black Rose Writing titles at
www.blackrosewriting.com/books and use promo code
PRINT to receive a **20% discount** when purchasing.